Read what reviewers are saying about
LYNNE KAUFMAN

"Lynne Kaufman has the wisdom to understand that the spiritual
and sexual needs of women are really inseparable, and the
narrative skills to make this forbidden truth a fascinating novel."
—*New York Times* bestselling author
Tom Robbins

"*Slow Hands* is a smart, intricately woven story
that dares to challenge the norms of society.
Filled with courage and uncharacteristic approaches...
Slow Hands will stop and make you think."
—*The Word on Romance*

"Lynne Kaufman has brought psyche and
sensuality together in this absorbing
and imaginative women's novel."
—Jean Shinoda Bolen, M.D., author of
Goddesses in Everywoman

"In her first novel, Lynne Kaufman has succeeded
in drawing readers in."
—*Romantic Times*

"A delightful story with many layers...
Highly entertaining with a provocative plot,
Slow Hands kept me amused with its
effortless writing. A perfect summer read—
give this novel a try."
—*Romance Reviews Today*

"Riotous... *Slow Hands* is about every woman's longing
to be adored...."
—*Woman's Own* magazine

Also by LYNNE KAUFMAN

SLOW HANDS

LYNNE KAUFMAN

WILD WOMEN'S WEEKEND

MIRA®

ISBN 0-7783-2054-5

WILD WOMEN'S WEEKEND

www.MIRABooks.com

Printed in U.S.A.

For my wild women friends, and especially for MaryAnn, without whom this tale would never have been told.

Dionysus: I have driven these women mad
                Turned them all frantic out of doors
                Their home now is the mountain
                I have made them bear the emblem of my mysteries.
                                                —Euripides
                                                 The Bacchae

The ancient Greeks tell of Dionysus, the god of wine and music,
and his retinue of women, the maenads—mature women who
followed him into the wild, intoxicated, ecstatic. If they encountered
a young animal or young male, they would tear it apart and drink
its blood. They were feared and revered. There are two sides of
human nature, the Apollonian and Dionysian—the civilized and
the wild. We eliminate either at our peril.

PROLOGUE

"I can't go through with this," Sabrina cried as she struggled to lift the dead man's leg from the back of the silver Jeep Cherokee. Her normally rosy face was ashen as she glanced fearfully about the fog-shrouded redwood forest that flanked both sides of the road. The immense trees stood dark and dripping like silent witnesses.

"Then don't look. But for God's sake, don't drop that leg. We need you," Ann commanded as she crouched in the back of the Jeep holding the man's head.

The other two women, Deb and Maria, stood at the ready. At Ann's signal and with great effort, the four women hoisted the body out of the Jeep. Each held an extremity as they inched their way along the wet gravel. But Maria was not strong enough. Surrendering to her fatigue, she let the man's arm and shoulder drop. The fingers of the man's right hand trailed through the crushed leaves and underbrush as they dragged the body, by fits and starts, into the woods. Deb held on to the corpse's left arm and shoulder as if it were a stray calf attempting to wrestle free from her shaking hands.

The man's face was bloated, moon-size, a sickly blue coloring the chalk-white skin. His eyes were closed; his features flattened by swelling, looking more like a beach ball than a face. Only the brown, shaggy hair hanging limply from the head looked human. The man's trunk, wrapped in a pink wool blanket like a shroud, was completely rigid, resisting their efforts to move it.

"All right, this is it. We can't go any farther," Ann said, her voice taut with effort.

In their relief to release their burden, the women hurriedly dropped the body. It landed with a sickening thud. The blanket partly unwound, revealing the corpse's gleaming white chest and thigh. Deb winced; one hand flew to her mouth, the other to her stomach.

The silver Cherokee was now barely visible between the looming trunks of the redwoods. In the forest it was far darker than it had been on the road. The silhouettes of the four women shone ghostlike in the dim mist.

Ann stood erect, her gleaming cap of hair damp with sweat. "We'll bury him right there next to that big redwood stump that looks like a bear." She gestured with her shoulder to the looming brown trunk in the distance.

"I'll get the shovel," Maria offered and trudged back to the Jeep, her steps slow, her broad shoulders hunched forward.

"The rest of you help me wrap him up again in this blanket," Ann commanded.

"Why do we have to wrap him up again if we're just going to dump him in the ground? No coffin. No nothing," Sabrina protested. "I can't bear to touch him again."

Deb turned away from the corpse, her hand still covering her mouth.

"Forget it. I'll do it myself," Ann snapped. She grabbed the straggling ends of the pink blanket and attempted to pull them over the exposed parts of the naked body. The man's feet still stuck out under the lower edge of the blanket. She tugged it downward, but as she did so it slid off the chest and one side fell onto the ground again.

"Damn!" She kicked in fury at the wet gravel and turned away from the body to compose herself. She watched as Maria walked back toward them carrying the shovel against her chest with both hands. The weight of it seemed too much for her. Her steps were slow and short; her head bowed.

They all took turns digging. Even though the ground was moist and clammy, it seemed to take forever. Each turn of the shovel spat out but a scant mouthful of shiny black dirt to add to the slowly growing mound. Between their turns each of them wandered away from the body except for Ann, who remained at the grave site with the corpse.

"Let's do it now," she cried at the end of her third turn at the shovel.

Sabrina peered with dismay into the raw gash in the earth. "Shouldn't it be at least six feet so the animals won't get him?" They had scooped out barely two feet of earth. The hole was irregular, more circular than square. It did not appear as long as the man's body.

No one responded. Deb averted her eyes and folded her arms tightly across her stomach. She had not uttered a word since they had parked the Jeep. Maria remained sitting on the boulder she had chosen as her resting place between her turns at the shovel. She did not lift her head.

"Just pick up the part you held before," Ann said.

All four took their positions around the corpse. They struggled to lift the body off the ground, but somehow it had grown heavier. Ann raised the man's head off the ground and Sabrina lifted the left leg, but the other two, struggling with the left and right shoulders, could manage to walk no more than a few feet without dropping them again.

"Let's just roll him," Ann said wearily.

They had to cover about twenty feet. Each time they turned the corpse over, more and more leaves, twigs and forest debris stuck to the body and to the pink blanket. The limp brown hair was now matted and filthy, but the moon-white face was still clean as a new plate. On the last turn the body rolled over the edge and propelled itself downward into the hole. It struck bottom and that face glared up at them from the shallow grave.

"I can't stand this. We've got to turn him over," Sabrina cried.

She climbed into the shallow trench and Ann joined her. They tugged and pushed the body until it heaved over and the white face was pressed into the earth. Ann tried once again to pull the pink blanket over the top part of the body. It was stuck underneath the heavy middle section. She succeeded in covering only half the back of the head and part of the right shoulder. The right arm was caught under the body, but the left lay crooked, its swollen hand gleamed white in the dark hole.

Refilling the hole went quickly. The damp clods of earth slid easily back, slowly covering the pink blanket and white patches of skin. Finally, only the puffy left hand remained exposed and soon it was hidden under damp earth. The extra soil was a problem. There was not much room for the removed dirt in the shallow grave, now that the corpse nearly filled it. They took turns carrying shovelfuls into the surrounding woods. At the grave site Maria carefully arranged handfuls of leaves and twigs to blend with the surrounding forest floor.

The women gathered around the grave site, now barely noticeable.

"Shouldn't we say a prayer, or something?" Deb asked. "It doesn't seem right to just leave him like this."

Sabrina picked up a clod of earth and crumbled it over the grave. *"Baruch atoi adonoi elohayne, schmah Israel,"* she intoned.

"From dust to dust," Deb sobbed, tears streaming down her muddy cheeks.

"Mother of Jesus, pray for us," Maria whispered, her head bowed low.

"Amen," Ann barked. "Let's get out of here."

The women piled into the Jeep. The last thing they saw as they pulled away was the highway marker 13. Unlucky 13.

CHAPTER ONE

The appointed meeting place of The Coven, as the four women jokingly call themselves, is as always Lake Street, as close as they can park to the entrance of the Golden Gate Bridge. They will leave the cars there and drive up together in Ann's new silver Cherokee. "High noon. Be there or be square," said Ann's e-mail, which Sabrina read just yesterday. It was a final reminder, following up on her voice mail and snail-mail messages. Ann is the convener of these annual retreats. She is also the most organized and it is at Nirvana, her sumptuous vacation house, that the women will spend the weekend.

Sabrina is usually late and today will be no exception. Indeed it is almost noon, and she is still in her spacious Sea Cliff living room when she feels her stomach rumble. She leaps up from her tapestry-covered couch and darts through the doorway, a wave of movement from her mass of black and silver curls to her billowing red caftan, to check the kitchen clock. No wonder she's starving; it's lunchtime. She's been at this meeting since nine this morning. "Hey, guys, let's wrap this up," she calls. "I've got to hit the road."

"Listen up, girlfriend," Tony, her lighting designer, says, throwing up his bejeweled hands. "Rehearsals for *Macbeth* start in one week and we have no agreement here. Nada...zilch...bupkus."

Esme, the set designer, laughs in derision, her wide-open mouth displaying the stainless-steel ball embedded in her tongue that Sabrina is still trying to get used to. Esme has pierced virtually every visible body part and has made not-so-veiled allusions to what lies under wraps. "Tony," Esme drawls, "I have submitted my designs. All you have to do is light them."

"Oh, I get it," Tony sniffs. "You're the artist. I'm just a technician."

"Tony, dahling, you are a genius," Esme coos. "We all know that. But the set has to come first. Then you have something to light."

"And what about the costumes?" Fanny Mae, the costume designer, snaps. "Are they chopped liver?"

"Please, people," Sabrina sighs. "You are each wonderful. You are each essential. You are each my favorite child. So...to recap, we're setting it in a bordello, right?"

"But what period?" Tony asks.

"Contemporary," Sabrina says.

"That's why I've done an S and M dungeon. Chains. Whips." Esme pauses. "I'd really like a flying harness."

"If we can swing it." Sabrina's attempt at levity brings

a good-hearted groan from the others. Encouraged, she continues, "This is supposed to be fun, remember. That's why we work around the clock for peanuts." That and the knowledge that they are keeping a ritual alive that began in the cave, Sabrina thinks. Her theater company, The Edge, is committed to reviving the classics and giving them a modern, relevant spin. The company is in its fifth year and is almost in the black. This season though, the National Endowment for the Arts has radically reduced its grants and The Edge hasn't gotten one. She hasn't told the rest of the company yet; time enough after *Macbeth* opens. With that major funding gone, they will have to scramble for money, depending even more on the generosity of their board.

That's showbiz, she reasons. If you want security, go into law like Ann, her dear and driven friend. When faced with divorce and supporting her baby daughter, Ann got a law degree at night while holding down her day job as a paralegal, and still finished number one in her class. But that's Ann, Sabrina thinks. Ann has the adrenaline of a charging bull and the metabolism of a hummingbird. She shouldn't even think of comparing herself to Ann. Ann is probably consulting on a Supreme Court case with one hand while dialing Gourmet on Wheels with the other and will still be on time.

Sabrina reflects that she is already late and still has to return four phone calls, pack, stop by Moise Pipick for her contribution of pastrami and Jewish corn rye and drive to the bridge. This little mental walkabout has also caused her to miss the last few minutes of the discussion.

Her tech staff is tolerant, though. They've been together since The Edge was conceived. They're tight, a family. And they're all good. Consummate professionals.

"So, Sabrina," Tony summarizes, "the lighting will be red and white. The red will suggest blood and the white... semen."

"Terrific," says Fanny Mae. "Then I'll use nude silk for a subliminal condom motif."

"And I'll add some sex toys," Esme contributes.

"Way cool," Sabrina laughs. "Thank you all. Now I'm out of here."

Everyone embraces everyone else and they are gone.

The living room is strewn with coffee cups, cookie crumbs and crumpled papers. "Charlie," Sabrina calls. "Sweetie?"

Charlie comes padding down the stairs, a burly man with the sweet smile of a boy. He glances at his wife and at the living room and in the shorthand of twenty years of a working marriage says, "Sure, go ahead."

"Thanks, hon, and by the way, can you pick up Tamar?"

"Where is she?"

"Swim meet in Novato."

He nods. "Okay, just leave the directions."

An hour there and an hour back. What would she do without Charlie? Awash with sudden appreciation, Sabrina hugs her husband hard and plants a big lipstick-smeared kiss on his bald spot. Charlie is short, several inches shorter than Sabrina, even in her stocking feet. But that has never mattered to her. Charlie may not be glamorous, but he is something far more important: he is her anchor, her support, her biggest fan. It was Charlie who had encouraged Sabrina to leave her high-school teaching job and follow her dream. And it was Charlie who helped found The Edge by doing everything from hammering scenery to manning the box office.

As Charlie sets to straightening the living room, Sabrina dashes upstairs to pack. She finds her best jeans, very flattering although she can't sit in them when they're buttoned, a fringed Annie Oakley jacket in butternut suede, a black sombrero and every piece of Native American jewelry she owns, silver and turquoise concho belts, squash-blossom necklaces, an armload of bracelets. What she doesn't wear she'll lend to the others. For her last production, *Our Town...on the Rez,* she had hired a Hopi woman shaman as a consultant. When Sabrina had asked her about her philosophy of life, the woman had answered, "I have only one rule, little sister—a woman can never have too much Indian jewelry."

Across town from Sabrina's airy Sea Cliff home, Maria sits in her tiny Mission District office jotting down notes from her last counseling session. She glances out the window at the bright sunlight and busy traffic of Guerrero Street. With its colorful *mercados,* corner burrito stands and boom boxes blaring Spanish hip-hop, she could be back in Tijuana where she spent her girlhood.

The last couple she saw, Emilia and Juan Gonzalez, were referred by Catholic Charities. Maria works these cases for free. The Gonzalezes have been ordered by the court to seek therapy after Juan beat Emilia, who was pregnant with their second child. Juan had lost his job in the Bay Area economic downturn and his frustration turned to violence. Through five long months of counseling in Spanish, Maria has tried to help Juan control his drinking and curb his abusive outbursts but to no avail.

This morning she insisted that Emilia seek shelter in a battered women's facility, at least until the baby was born. But Emilia is either too much in love or too afraid to leave her husband. Maria uncharacteristically lost control, exploding in anger at both of them, the victim and the aggressor. Their situation brought up so many painful memories. Today the cycle of poverty and despair seems endless. She needs a break.

She needs some kindness. Some laughter. Some hope. And in a few moments she will be getting exactly that from her girlfriends. From the Coven.

Of course they hadn't called themselves the Coven when they all first met at the Blue House, the nursery school Maria ran. The name had slowly evolved to reflect the playful chemistry and sly mischief that emerged when the four were together.

Maria rises, stretches her tall broad body and pulls out a small duffel from her closet. She feels a rush of anticipatory pleasure as if she is already on the redwood deck gazing at the Pacific. She checks the bag's contents; she packed it hastily this morning before going to church. She knew she was going to miss Sunday Mass so she made a quick novena instead. For Maria, it is important to offer a prayer in its proper place. The candles, the incense, the stained-glass windows and polished wooden pews help to quiet her mind. Monday is her checkup; her last mammogram was equivocal. The doctors are watching for any changes. Nothing to be alarmed about yet, so she decides not to mention it to the Coven. As Tia Teresa said, "The world is bad enough; don't send trouble ahead." She takes a deep breath and dismisses the troublesome thought. At least until Monday. Instead she thinks fondly of Tia Teresa, the counselor in the California Youth Authority, a dead ringer for Mama Cass, who helped her through her dark adolescent years.

Time to get going. Maria zips the duffel closed. She hasn't packed much. She'll wear what she has on for the ride up, chinos, a turtleneck and a loose cardigan, her working clothes. For tonight she's brought a pair of well-worn jeans, a red velour T-shirt and, at the last minute, has thrown in a pair of shoulder-length red feather earrings. Although the red will highlight her dark eyes and tawny skin, she has spent far more thought on her share of the provisions than on her outfit.

The Coven loves Mexican food and Maria knows where to find the best. This time she has discovered a new Oaxacan restaurant and the women will be feasting on four different kinds of mole. To wash them down she has made a gallon jug of her special sangria. It should be perfectly blended by now. She reaches for her favorite United Farm Workers cup, pours an inch and takes a sip of the fragrant, potent brew. Deb is coming by in a few minutes and they will drive together to Lake Street. When Deb smells the wine on Maria's breath, she'll insist on driving. Let her, Maria thinks, smiling. Sweet, puritanical Deb.

Maria lifts the mug high and in benediction recites what the Coven has dubbed Maria's Mantra. It was the way she used to say goodbye to her little charges at the Blue House and what the women have now adopted as the rallying call for their reunions.

"Have you sung today? Have you danced today? Have you let your wild child play?"

Maria downs the remainder of her cup in one thirsty swallow.

Deb calculates that, barring a tie-up on the Bay Bridge, she will be precisely on time to pick up Maria. She had hoped to be early so that she could arrive relaxed and cheerful, not frazzled and needy. She is so looking forward to this weekend and wants to hold her own. She does not want to be seen as poor Deb, just a housewife, while everyone else has a major career. Of course, she knows the others don't really feel that way; it's her own low self-esteem talking. She has good reasons to be at home, but still it troubles her.

Deb is deeply into physical fitness even though each year it takes more effort. Exercise makes her feel good. Her body is the one thing that she can control. For the past year since her youngest, Danny, began regular school, she has gone faithfully to the gym three mornings a week for a grueling class in step aerobics and extreme yoga. She also works with a personal trainer and is ten pounds below her college weight. Her pale skin is glowing, her auburn curls shine and her petite frame is trim and fit. Then what's wrong with me? she thinks, fighting tears. What does that other woman have that I don't?

She decides to put her question to the Coven and they, in their collective female wisdom, will search for answers with her. But meanwhile, she's got to get out of here. She pulls her to-do list out of the pocket of her new black leather jacket. Ellen, the baby-sitter, will pick Danny up at the Berkeley School for the Deaf and take him to the playground and then home. Kevin has basketball practice, Brian has soccer and then they'll be home for dinner. Deb checks to make sure the amplifier is on the phone and TV for Danny's use. He's come so far and is now a happy, active eight-year-old. She's proud of him and proud also of the way she and Donald weathered the news of their baby's disability. Some marriages break up; theirs got stronger. So why this trouble between them now, she wonders. She dismisses the thought by consulting her list.

Food. She can always take refuge in food. She has made the boys' favorite dinner: macaroni and cheese, three-bean salad and chocolate cake. Heavy on carbs and fat but it was a special occasion. All of it is neatly packaged in the fridge. Ellen will serve dinner and Donald has promised to be home before the boys' bedtime. She and Donald had harsh words about that last night. For the past week, he has come home after she's been in bed, mumbling excuses about having to work late, although when she called his office, there was no one there. Last night she screamed her ultimatum. "You be home at nine tonight or don't come home at all!" He called her a shrew and slept on the couch. She fell asleep crying. What would she do if Donald ever left?

He couldn't leave. Wouldn't leave. They were a family; they were just going through a bad patch. She wrote down the phone number of Nirvana, Ann's Mendocino showplace, for the boys, and then added a note to her husband:

Dear Donny Duck, sorry I squawked at you. Didn't mean to ruffle your feathers. See you on Sunday. Love, your Daisy.

She wouldn't want the Coven to see that silly duck talk, a talisman from a happier time. She folds the note, seals it in an envelope and looks around her tidy, shining house. Everything is in order. She has even watered the plants. She loves the house. When Donald got his assistant professorship at Berkeley, they moved from the flat lands to the Oakland Hills to this wonderful old house with a real basement and attic, so rare in California. The living room has wide window seats where she can sit and dream while she watches the sun set over San Francisco Bay. She has laboriously scouted auctions and estate sales to find vintage furniture and then tenderly restored the finish to the good sturdy wood. Deb has created a nest and that bastard is trying to fly out. Who mates for life? Swans...and they have such nasty dispositions. That's a line worthy of Sabrina, Deb thinks, smiling. Oh, how she longs for the tonic of a little healthy cynicism. She can't wait to see her friends.

Deb lifts her flowered canvas suitcase. It is one of five graduated sizes. She has chosen the next to largest. Might as well bring anything she might need. Last night, before the fight with Donald, she stood before the full-length bedroom mirror trying on all her possible outfits. She now decides on moss-green warm-ups for the drive, and for the evening, to top the requisite jeans, a new black cashmere sweater with a sweetheart neckline. It is decorous yet festive. She knows the others will be wearing their flashiest duds, but she isn't comfortable in that kind of display. She wants to be noticed but not too much. She adds a robe, nightgown, slippers, two changes of underwear and a bathing suit for the hot tub, although she knows the others will not wear one. Then she throws in a raincoat and umbrella. No rain predicted but you never know. To read, she adds the latest issue of the *Mother Earth* newsletter. Deb is an ardent environmentalist with a soft spot for old-growth forests and endangered species. Sabrina will probably be reading Shakespeare, Ann the *Law Journal* and Maria...Maria will order them all to get their noses out of those books and into her home-brewed sangria.

Deb opens the refrigerator and takes out her contribution to the weekend, an exact duplicate of the meal she has left for the boys. Simple, homespun and rib-sticking. She hopes the Coven will find it amusingly "retro," not stultifyingly suburban, and hurries out the door.

Ann takes off her heavy gold earrings and places them carefully on her massive cherry-wood desk. Next she removes the solid gold cuff links that adorn her cream silk blouse. She scoops them into one hand and with the other spins the dial of the office safe. Laying them in a felt box inside the safe, she reflects that these pieces are her medals. She wears the gold cuffs, earrings and necklace just as she wears her Armani suit, as a uniform. She opens her Vuitton bag, stowed under the desk, and pulls out a pair of jeans. Suit off, jeans, T-shirt and running shoes on, she catches a glimpse of herself in the mirror. Her carefully cut helmet of blond hair catches the light of the panoramic office window. Ann moves closer to the mirror, parts her hair with her fingers and inspects the dark roots. Time for a touch-up. Maintenance...maintenance. It seems to require more effort each year. Yet she still does her own hair and nails. The old habits of economy and independence remain. Anything she can do for herself, she does.

Hanging her tailored work clothes in the small office closet, she realizes how much she has looked forward to this annual weekend, this "Calling of the Coven," as they have come to speak of it. Ann sees it as a safety valve, a chance for four overextended forty-something women who have little time for themselves to let off steam: to eat too much, drink too much and laugh too loud. Most likely on Monday she'll feel tired, maybe even a little hungover, but she knows she will also feel happier and more relaxed.

Should she call Richard? When she left at seven this morning he was already gone. If she does call him, she can imagine the disapproval in his carefully modulated voice. "Have a good time, Ann. I'll send your regrets to the governor."

Richard has pressured her for weeks to attend the political fund-raiser tonight. But, dammit, she has already
spent too many dreary evenings at his rubber-chicken
dinners. His political fund-raising activities have accelerated in this election year; he claims he needs the governor's favor for his real estate business. Ann feels she is just
being dragged along as an appendage. She isn't exactly a
trophy wife, but she is a good deal younger than Richard and his cohorts.

What about Kim? Should she try to reach her at her
father's house? Kim was probably still asleep. And then she
would have to talk to her ex, Steve, about their problem-
atic sixteen-year-old daughter. Her failing grades. Her
troublesome friends. When she was thirteen, Kim had her
shoulder tattooed, her eyebrow pierced and donned the
protective oversize clothing of the punk culture. Ann
would like to think of Kim's adornments as just another
uniform, like her own signature jewelry and designer
suits. But it is more than that for Kim; it is a shield behind which she hides from Ann. Maybe Steve has better
luck reaching Kim, Ann thinks. She doubts it, but knows
that if she speaks to him, he will once again make her feel
guilty about her inadequacies as a mother. It isn't what he
says directly, it's the comments about her busy life and society parties that sting.

No, she will just go to the French charcuterie and
then to Lake Street to meet her friends. Her mood
lightens as she climbs into her Cherokee; she thinks
about the three women who have become dear to her,
whom she depends on. Ann remembers when she was

introduced to the Coven. Maria was the head teacher at the preschool on Clay Street, and Sabrina and Deb each had children there about Kim's age. Sabrina's daughter, Tamar, was Kim's closest friend then and for many years after. Deb had two boys there; Kevin was the girls' age and Brian was only two. Her Danny wasn't born yet.

It was Maria who brought them together, Maria with her warm generous spirit. Everyone, both children and adults, wanted to be as close as possible to this large dark woman, a source of tranquillity combined with a joyful presence. In those days Maria always had a kettle boiling in the small kitchen when they arrived to pick up the kids. After a short time, it became a habit for the three women to linger with Maria over their tea whenever they could, their children usually the last to leave the playground.

When the children began kindergarten, Ann lost touch with Maria and Deb, but she continued to see Sabrina, as their girls begged to play together on the weekends. And even after the girls drifted apart, she and Sabrina continued their friendship. They were vastly different personalities yet together they felt more complete, more alive. It was Ann who supported Sabrina through the deaths of both her parents within six months of each other. And it was Sabrina who Ann called upon for help when Ann's estranged father came to town demanding money from his "rich daughter," threatening to expose her to all her fancy friends. And now Richard was the chairman of the board of Sabrina's small theater company, The Edge, so the two friends frequently mingled in the same crowds at openings and benefits.

Ann remembers when five years ago, long after the Blue House time, she got a call from Maria inviting her to lunch. Maria said she was also inviting Sabrina and Deb and that she had some big news. Ann was surprised at how eager she felt to see them all again. The four women embraced each other with evident emotion. They all started talking at once as though no time had passed and they were back having tea at the preschool. Then Maria, after serving a bountiful paella lunch, made her announcement. She had just gotten her license as a marriage and family therapist and was going to open a counseling practice.

When the women congratulated her, Maria made light of the praise in her typical fashion. "It's just like nursery school," she said. "When they fall down, you pick them up, dust them off and send them back to play."

Lunch lasted until Deb realized it was almost five and she had to pick up Danny. The four women found it hard to break away, just as they had at the Blue House, and before they left they had planned their first weekend getaway for a time several months in the future. Ann wasn't sure how serious they all were, but as it turned out, they all managed to make it. After that first weekend, they hadn't missed a year, not even the time Maria was recovering from cancer surgery. The weekend after Labor Day had become the Calling of the Coven.

This year she had almost reneged on this important ritual. She had felt exhausted by Richard's endless political dinners and dispirited by the continuing crises with Kim. She had tried to offer her excuses to Sabrina last week.

"Cut the crap," her friend had countered. "You don't want to get so high-flying that you drop your old buddies like middle-aged embarrassments. Besides, girl, you need some serious fun.

Thank the Lord for Sabrina, Ann thinks as she approaches Lake Street on this crisp September morning.

CHAPTER TWO

Ann folds her cell phone as Deb and Maria pull up in Deb's aging SUV. "Sabrina just called," she announces. "She's going to be late."

"So what else is new?" Maria says as the women warmly embrace.

Together they load the two duffels, large plastic cooler and four paper bags overflowing with food into the trunk of Ann's Cherokee. Then the three women lean against the Jeep and wait for Sabrina and the sun. The San Francisco sky is leaden, but a few lighter, brighter streaks are creeping into the gray canopy.

"Radio says the fog is supposed to burn off by early afternoon," Deb offers.

"Just in time for Sabrina's entrance," Ann says.

"I heard that," Sabrina cries, zooming up in her red convertible. She rushes to the Jeep, laden with food and gear, and flashes them a wide smile. "Ladies, are we going to be bad?"

Despite the fact that her best friend is late as usual, Ann cannot resist returning the grin. Neither can Maria or Deb. "Get your saggy ass in here," Ann says, slapping her friend's behind. "Fast."

Sabrina climbs into the front seat next to Ann. Maria and Deb pile into the back. And they are off. Dense fog covers the Golden Gate Bridge; Ann slows her speed and flicks on the headlights while Sabrina regales them with tales of her morning rehearsal. "My lighting and costume designers are like three-year-olds fighting over a crayon." She pauses to turn and gaze fondly at Maria. "Just like in the Blue House, remember?"

"Everything I learned, I learned in kindergarten," Maria says.

"A moratorium on problems," Ann pronounces. "At least until we've had a glass of wine." As the sun starts to break through the clouds, she fishes inside her CD box and finds the Mamas and the Papas. "Just right for four old babes," she proclaims. In a few minutes they're all singing, in attempted harmony.

Spirits continue to rise with the persevering sun. They are off to have a much needed break, a chance for laughter and friendship and cutting loose. By two, when they arrive at Willets, the closest town to the cottage, they have sung or hummed their way through the Beatles' *White Album,* Smokey Robinson's *Greatest Hits* and the whole of *Oklahoma!*

The Willets General Store, the only grocery within

miles of Ann's beach cottage, is about the size of a 7-Eleven and specializes in beer and fishing bait. They have learned this from hard experience and buy only milk and butter for the morning breakfast. Everything else they have brought with them. On impulse, Maria adds a bottle of tequila.

"You cain't never tell how much moonshine it's gonna take to get four old broads plastered," she says.

The women burst into girlish giggles. They are ready to laugh at anything now, and the remark and hillbilly accent are completely at odds with Maria's own liquid Latina rhythms. The four friends tumble into the Jeep in high humor and drive on.

Nirvana looms on the left hand side of the road, almost obscured by several tall Monterey cypresses. The twisted branches create the illusion that a fierce wind is blowing even though the day is still. It is not until they have navigated the long curving driveway that they catch a full view of the cottage.

Even after all these years this first sight is thrilling and a little frightening to Ann. This "cottage" of ten rooms won the *Architectural Digest* award for best sea retreat when it was built in the 1980s. Angled to take advantage of the jutting cliff upon which it's perched, its grayed redwood exterior winds around the rock in serpentine fashion. A gray flagstone walk borders the house, echoing the stark boulders lining the edge.

Nirvana originally belonged to Richard's first wife, Anna-Lisa. Ann thinks of her as Ann Number One. Conveniently, Richard didn't have to change the monogrammed towels nor worry about saying the wrong name in bed. He said he got the cottage as one of the chips in the divorce negotiations. Ann didn't ask what Ann Number One got in exchange.

When Ann first saw this striking retreat she couldn't help wondering if Richard had indeed married Ann Number One, an heiress to a major meatpacking fortune, for her money. That had been the gossip. Richard hasn't wanted to talk about it, and Ann hasn't pried. His first marriage is one of several topics on which he has taken a "don't ask, don't tell" policy. She has come to live with Richard's "zones of privacy," as she thinks of them, but not without some disquiet. It makes her feel like an outsider, not trusted enough to be fully confided in. Richard often comes to this cottage on his own for days at a time. He has told her he has business dealings in this north coast region, these dealings also forbidden topics.

As they pull up to Nirvana, Deb voices a related thought. "Fess up, Ann, did you fall in love with Richard or with his beach house?" She says this in a light, teasing voice, but a note of envy adds a sharp undertone. Ann knows that Deb, with her academic husband and three children, has to struggle to maintain their determinedly middle-class lifestyle. A showplace like Nirvana would be forever out of reach.

"Never mind," Sabrina quips. "They're both well built."

Saved again by Sabrina's able wit, Ann thinks, although she's sure Sabrina's take on Ann's life is not that much different than Deb's. Sabrina had been quick to note that Ann's success as a top-level high-tech lawyer has been earned almost as much in the marital bedroom as in the corporate conference room. Although, Ann thinks, that high-mindedness has not kept Sabrina from making Richard president of the board of her theater.

The view from the cottage is strikingly clear that Saturday. Not a wisp of cloud or fog shrouds the long blue horizon. The four friends unload their groceries and their gear quickly. They know the routine and they each know which bedroom is theirs. Ann heads toward the master bedroom, a huge high-ceilinged room furnished with a handcrafted ebony-and-redwood bed and dresser, compliments of Ann Number One. When she returns to the kitchen the food is already shelved, the sangria and white wine chilling in the giant refrigerator. All she has to do is unstack the deck chairs. Maria cracks open their first bottle of wine and the women take their glasses out onto the deck. They settle into their chairs and silently gaze at the sea for several long, slow minutes.

Deb is the first to interrupt their sea-induced trance. "Is it okay to talk about problems now?" she whispers.

"In a minute," Sabrina says. The women hold up their glasses in their ritual toast. "*L'chaim*...to life," Sabrina pronounces. They each take a long swallow.

"My life may be over," Deb says, twisting uneasily in her chair, "I have something awful to tell you." She takes a deep shuddering breath. "I think Donald is having an affair."

The women are stunned as they silently take in the news.

Maria pulls her chair closer to Deb and places an arm

around her friend's shoulders. "Oh, Deb," she says with great feeling. "I'm so sorry."

"The hell with sorry," pronounces Sabrina, her reaction characteristically extreme. "I say take a knife to bed and Bobbit him."

"Now, just a minute. I don't doubt that Donald is capable of an affair. What man isn't?" Ann says in her careful legal fashion. "But even husbands deserve their day in court. Sometimes suspicions are unfounded. Do you have any hard evidence, like a letter or a hotel bill?"

"Yeah, is he suddenly too nice to you?" Sabrina adds. "Does he bring you flowers and sexy underwear for no reason?"

Deb's details are disappointingly few. "There are the occasional telephone calls, a young woman's voice and a few classic hang-ups. And he goes to a lot of evening meetings now, he says he's helping the dean with fund-raising. Donald used to be in public relations, so it could be true. But every night?" She pauses thoughtfully. "And he doesn't complain anymore when I go to my Save the Spotted Owl meetings."

Ann has pledged Deb to silence about her passion when visiting Nirvana. The lumberjacks could do crazy things if they learned she was a "spotted owl nut." They blame this hated group for nearly shutting down lumbering in Northern California.

Deb's head is lowered, and her eyes are starting to glisten with tears. "He's probably gotten tired of me. You know I never finished college and Donald's an assistant professor."

"That's got nothing to do with it. You're every inch as good as Donald," Sabrina says. "You don't want to whine, you want to get even. The best way to stop worrying about Donald's dick is to find yourself a new one. Get a lover. Best cure for marriage blues known to woman."

Deb flushes at Sabrina's remark. Is she considering the advice, or is she simply embarrassed? Ann wonders. Deb is still a striking woman, with glossy auburn hair, warm dark eyes, and the kind of small shapely body that instinctively prompts men's glances. And is Sabrina really so cavalier about extramarital affairs? What sort of an arrangement does she have with Charlie? She's never spoken about it.

As for herself, Ann has followed her own strict set of rules about fidelity, based not on love or morality, but strictly on survival. Growing up in her bone-poor family she has seen how a woman's momentary sexual passion can disrupt a marginally functioning family, initiate bloodshed, scatter children. Only the rich can afford such indulgence, she has always thought. And even though she can now be considered rich herself, she hasn't forgotten.

"How about some food?" Maria suggests, shifting the focus from Deb's growing discomfort. "The gray cells work better on protein."

The women rise to help set the table. Sabrina spreads the moss-green Belgian-linen tablecloth as Ann raids the china cabinet, bringing out the delicate Sevres bone china and Rosenthal crystal wineglasses that, like almost everything else in this house, had belonged to Ann Number One. She knows it is foolish to leave all these elegant things in this weekend retreat, but she doesn't really consider them hers; they belong here in Ann Number One's home.

Maria lays out her sangria and her exotic chicken with four moles. Sabrina breaks into an appreciative chorus of "The Mexican Hat Dance."

Deb shyly adds her macaroni casserole, bean salad and chocolate cake, disparaging it as ordinary. "It's gorgeous," Ann says. "Just like my mother would have made...if she were ever sober." Ann unwraps her own contribution of pâté, Brie and fresh baguettes to Maria's murmured strains of "The Last Time I Saw Paris."

Sabrina adds a heaping platter of pastrami and Jewish rye, with a little Tevye finger snap. "Of course I *can* cook," Sabrina sniffs. "But thank God I don't have to. He gave me a sign from the mountain. 'Sabrina, take off the apron, already.'"

"And where is rest of the vino?" Maria asks.

Each of the women presents her contribution. Sabrina a New Zealand sauvignon blanc, Ann a French burgundy, and Deb a local zinfandel.

On the elegantly set picnic table, there are nearly as many bottles of wine as there are dishes of food. *"In vino veritas,"* Maria says, playfully blessing the feast as the women raise their refilled glasses.

The afternoon drifts along. Lounging in their deck chairs, the women happily graze at the lavish picnic. It is a normal Coven Calling, Ann thinks, four tipsy, very relaxed women of a certain age, getting a lot more sun than is good for them.

As the wind picks up they move themselves and the remains of their feast into the shelter of the living room, resuming their sea watch behind huge windows. The conversation, which has lulled in the afternoon sun, picks up again and the talk turns to children. Their hostage to the future.

"How's Danny doing?" Ann asks Deb.

"Just fine," Deb says with enthusiasm. "Those new digital hearing aids make such a difference. He's in school full days now, so I thought I might look for a job."

"Now, why would you want to do that?" Ann asks. "You'll be working nine to five and still packing lunch for everyone."

"Charlie makes lunch for Tamar and me," Sabrina comments. "He says I don't cut the bread right."

"Sabrina, you spoiled brat!" Ann says. "No man has ever made lunch for me."

"The trouble with you, darling, is you are just *too* independent," Sabrina teases.

"Just what does that mean?" Ann counters.

"A little learned helplessness. It passes for artistic temperament."

"Don't talk to me about artistic temperament," Ann sighs. "Kim's 'hair du jour' is purple. And the only class she tolerates is ceramics."

The others look at her with quiet sympathy. Kim has been the subject of many past meetings.

"She's been living with her dad in Antioch since June," Ann continues. "He says she's going to school. But of course it just started last week. We'll see if she lasts this time."

Maria puts her hand on Ann's arm. "It'll work out...at sixteen she needs to separate."

"Separate!" Ann's voice is sharper than she intends. Although she's extremely fond of Maria, she finds her occasional lapses into what Ann considers psychobabble irritating. "Kim has been separating from me from the day she was born, or at least from the time Steve and I divorced. And that runaway episode two years ago. This time though she specifically left to hurt Richard." She imitates Kim's Valley Girl outrage, "'I can no longer live a life of lies. I must live with my real father, not an impostor.'"

"The little shit," said Sabrina, raising her chin and arching her carefully formed eyebrows. "But at that age, they're all a pain in the ass. Tamar looks at me as if I were an alien life-form—my mother, the flake."

Ann knows this is meant to make her feel better, but it doesn't. Somehow, Sabrina's gripes with her sixteen-year-old honor student do not seem in the same league with Ann's worries. While Tamar's main concern will be whether to choose Berkeley or Stanford, Ann is not sure whether Kim will stay in high school long enough to graduate. And then what? She tries to imagine the possible lives in store for her daughter. In the Willetts grocery she sometimes sees young girls, not much older than Kim, in long hippie-style skirts, often with babies balanced on their slim hips. She knows these girls live in "weed communes" as they are called, growing Northern California's largest cash crop. The woods are full of them, she is told. She can visualize Kim following this route; it is one of the better scenarios she tries not to think about.

"Well, at least your daughters talk," Deb says. "My sons have the inner lives of snails. They'd only know I was gone if they ran out of food."

Never having had a son, Ann is not sure that Deb's three boys, now eight, twelve and fifteen, are any worse than others, but they certainly make no effort to charm adults. In the rare event that Ann sees them anymore, they are like a pack of hunting dogs hot on the scent, pushing their way into the car for a ride to their soccer or basketball practice. Rarely do they raise their heads to make eye contact with her. Danny, the deaf child, has limited language ability, but in that busy pack he doesn't need it.

Sabrina helps herself to the last slice of pastrami, peels off the edge of fat, then, thinking better of it, pops it into her mouth. "That's where all the flavor is," she says.

"And all the calories," Ann admonishes. "Okay, ladies, enough about kids, let's get down to us. Body time. Has anyone found a diet that works? And why does it get harder each year?" The talk then turns naturally to matters of health and maintenance: the merits and hazards of hormone replacement therapy, the antiwrinkle diet, pilates and yoga, glucosomine and Botox. The women present symptoms and experiences and under-the-dryer reading for group discussion.

Only Maria does not participate. The others respect her wish not to talk about her own health, but privately Ann knows they can't help wondering what's going on. Ann is certain that Maria has lost weight and noticed that Maria dozed off on the deck during lunch. When Ann inquired about it, Maria's response was deliberately up-beat. "Love those little catnaps," she said, smiling.

Maria rarely speaks about her own worries. Maybe without a husband or children she doesn't have any, Ann thinks, or maybe the Coven doesn't allow her to have them. They count on her to soothe away their problems, not to offer new ones. Only last year after her lumpec-tomy for breast cancer did they concentrate on her. Even then Maria would not let them fuss. "I can afford to lose some," she had assured them. "I've got the large economy size."

The women have always found comfort in Maria's sim-ple homespun wisdom. In the many years she taught nursery school before becoming a psychologist, she saw all kinds of children and has watched those children grow up. She tells stories about girls more troubled than Kim who found their calling and peace of mind in their twen-ties. She knows about handicapped boys and philander-ing husbands. They want to believe her happy endings, and the more wine they drink, the more they do.

The meeting is running its usual course, Ann thinks. They have shed a few tears and teased each other into some good laughs. But by the time the blazing ball of sun strikes the edge of the ocean, she notices they have fin-ished two bottles of wine and the entire pitcher of san-gria. This is far more than usual. The women are quiet, each wrapped in her own thoughts.

Deb breaks the silence as she rises to clear the leftover food. "My mother used to say when the conversation stops like this, an angel is passing overhead," she muses.

"Angels are boring," Sabrina scoffs. "All the great literature isn't about heaven. It's about hell." She spears the last of the pâté, eating it directly from her knife. "Sin is much more interesting. So...ladies, what kind of guy would you like to screw? What's your bottom line, the most important thing in a lover?"

The women smile, redirecting their thoughts to this provocative new direction. None of the three would have introduced the topic, but since Sabrina has, they're game.

"Okay. He's got to own a tuxedo," Maria says. They look at her in surprise. It's hard enough to imagine Maria with a guy; they've never seen her with one, but a guy in a tuxedo? In the Mission district?

Maria breaks the stunned silence with a belly laugh. "Gotcha! My real bottom line is that he doesn't tote a gun."

"For me," Sabrina says thoughtfully, "he's got to be smart."

"Bullshit with smart!" responds Ann. "I've had smart, give me rich."

Ann's ex, Steve, is a talented but unpublished writer and hence depressed and broke.

"Give me warm and affectionate," Deb says, closing her eyes. "Give me someone who thinks I'm the center of the universe."

"What about sexy?" Sabrina cries. "That's the only bottom line. Do we remember lust, ladies? Remember being so crazy about a guy that you'd kill for him?"

"You mean like in *Fatal Attraction*?" Deb asks.

"Sort of, but not 'boiling bunny' crazy," Sabrina says.

"I felt like that once," Ann said after a moment. "I was so crazy for Steve when I first met him that I actually thought about killing his girlfriend." She pauses reflectively. "Of course, a year later, I wanted to kill *him*," she laughs.

"I think I would die if Donald ever left me," Deb says, tightly gripping the arms of her chair.

"No man is worth dying for," Maria says.

"Divorce isn't the end of the world," Ann adds. "It just seems that way."

"Hey, enough gloom and doom," Sabrina says quickly. "There are plenty of fish in the sea. And I say we go trawling."

"Trawling?" Deb asks. "For what?"

"Let's go find us some cowboys." Sabrina licks her lips lasciviously. "And..."

"*And* what...?" Ann asks with alarm.

"And...go dancing," Sabrina says.

"But you know we always go out to dinner," Ann insists.

"Don't tell me you're hungry?" Sabrina asks.

"Well, no, but we always go to the Captain's Palace and—"

"All the more reason to break the mold. How about it? A real girls' night out?"

Each of us plays her role, Ann thinks. Sabrina, the outrageous. Maria, the nurturer. Deb, the insecure. And she, the practical. Break the mold, not likely. But perhaps she can crack it a little. Have some fun and show her friend she isn't that straitlaced, after all.

She surprises Sabrina by reaching for the local paper, the *Mendocino Times*. "There are two possibilities," Ann says. "The Long Horn is a down-home establishment that specializes in Nashville Noise. The Last Roundup is about a mile farther down the coast. They advertise 'square dancing with caller.'" This sounds safer to Ann, so she talks it up. "I've heard the Last Roundup has the best-looking cowboys in Northern California. That's where they find the Marlboro men."

"Come on, baby, light my fire," croons Sabrina. "Let's get ready."

The women head for their respective bedrooms. They do not have to make a decision about jeans, the required uniform for that neck of the woods, but each has brought at least one silk blouse or fancy sweater for evening wear, which has to be put up for group approval. Ann is first. She struts about the living room in her new gold blouse, hands on hips. The others applaud, then follow suit, with even higher steps and fancier shuffles. Like drum majorettes at a high-school tryout, Ann thinks, hoping the football team will notice.

And then there is the makeup. Sabrina is the expert. The women look forward to these transformations almost as much as the talk. Sabrina always brings a huge duffel bag filled with powders and pencils and paints. What doesn't come from her own heavily laden dressing table is augmented from the makeup room at her theater. Ann smiles as Sabrina reverentially lays out her dazzling wares. For Ann, Sabrina is smoke and mirrors, over the top. Always vivid, always changing. Ann loves that about her. She never wants to see her friend as ordinary, unimaginative, bone-faced real.

Sabrina tries, with her makeup, to share her magic with the other women. With a flash of pencils and tubes Deb is changed from a prim suburban housewife into a sensuous beauty whose well-defined red lips literally pout. Sabrina tucks Deb's black sweater tightly into her jeans, emphasizing the curve between Deb's narrow waist and rounded hips.

Maria experiences an even greater transformation. Her dusky skin metamorphoses into a creamy caramel, setting off the dark flashes of her velvet-brown eyes. Sabrina pulls down strands of Maria's pinned-back hair to soften the geometric severity of her face into a regal grace. The women gaze with appreciation at their friend, her familiar inner beauty now strongly visible.

They watch as Sabrina does Ann. Lots of blush, layers of mascara. She uses a curling iron to produce soft waves. "You look beautiful," Deb pronounces.

Sabrina agrees. "Softer...more Marilyn Monroe, less Meryl Streep."

Ann is not sure she likes the look, but somehow it affects the way she moves. Her body feels looser, more liquid. Maybe it's the gold blouse, but she is definitely arching her back and pushing her breasts forward.

The friends agree that it's time to go dancing.

CHAPTER THREE

"Okay, ladies, who's going to drive?" Ann dangles her car keys.

"I always drive," Deb protests.

"I hate that curvy road," Maria says. "Especially after a couple of margaritas."

"I'll do it," Sabrina offers. "I can't even get drunk when I try. I love that tipsy feeling of two martinis. But the third one makes me throw up." She seizes the car keys and races for the car. "We're outta here." The rest pile in gleefully; Ann in front, Maria and Deb in back. They pull out, CD player roaring *Born to Run* and Sabrina bellowing, "Bruce."

Since the Long Horn is closer, they stop there first. As Sabrina pulls into the parking lot, she flashes her brights.

"Looks awfully quiet," Maria says as she gets out to investigate. "Sign says it's closed," she calls a minute later. "Sheriff's orders."

"I remember now," Ann says. "They were busted for selling pot."

"Before we scored any," Sabrina complains.

"Marijuana is illegal," Deb adds.

"Thank you, Mother Teresa," Sabrina says.

"Never mind, if that's what you want, all you have to do is ask," Ann volunteers. "Richard always has a few joints at the house."

This is a side of Richard even Sabrina didn't know about. She glances at Ann to see if she is kidding. "Great, it'll be my reward for not getting sloshed with the rest of you." She grins.

"I don't get sloshed," Deb protests.

"Sloshed," Sabrina scoffs, "you don't even get damp. I don't know why we put up with you, Miss Manners."

"Well, you don't have to," Deb says, coloring, easily offended.

"We put up with her because we love her." Maria throws an arm around Deb's shoulders, and punches up Deb's favorite James Taylor album on the CD player.

They drive to Taylor's gentle admonition to "Shower the people you love with love," and as they park at the Roundup, Sabrina notes that Deb is smiling again. Thank goodness for Maria, the peacemaker. Actually, all the women are smiling as they pass through the swinging door of the bar; they know they are making an entrance. There is power in four grown women, each attractive in her own way. Ann is the showstopper, a cool elegant blonde. Sabrina is quick and animated with an extravagant mane of black and silver curls. Maria is the earth mother, solid and generous. And Deb, with her auburn hair and freckles, combines the innocence of a farm girl with the toned silhouette of an aerobics instructor.

The women glance around the room. The bar is dimly lit, sawdust on the floor, a lineup of stuffed deer heads upon the wall with "mine's bigger than yours" antlers.

"First round is on me," Maria says and, without asking, orders their usual: single-malt scotch for Ann, vodka martini straight up for Sabrina, bourbon for herself and for Deb a Coke. "Diet or regular?" she asks.

Deb hesitates for a moment, then, "I'll have a margarita. On the rocks."

"Alllll right," Sabrina says, giving Deb a high five. "Good for you. Why should Donald have all the fun?"

The women pool their quarters, and Sabrina makes the pilgrimage to the jukebox. The choice is country-western; take it or leave it. Sabrina finds her favorite, Patsy Cline's "Crazy." She pushes that button twice. Then "Girls' Night Out" for Ann, and for Deb she chooses Garth Brooks's "Standing Outside the Fire."

Maria hates country-western. "All those victims of love," she complains. "Isn't there anything else?"

"Lost love, old dogs and pickup trucks," Sabrina retorts. "What more do you need?" The women take seats at the bar and survey the action. There are a few couples scattered at gray Formica tables with pitchers of wilting beer and baskets of stale popcorn. One couple is looking into each other's eyes, the others looking everywhere but. "They're the married ones," Sabrina sighs. "What happens to lust after it's legal?"

Maria sips her bourbon and provides a capsule analysis. "Marriage is about peace and security. Love affairs are about excitement and novelty. Don't confuse the two. Men have known that since the cave."

"No one's confusing them," Sabrina protests. "But don't we need a bit of both once in a while? Just to see if we're still attractive, to see if the old pheromones are still working. Isn't that why we're here tonight? To rev up the old engine and get the rust out?" She gestures behind her. "So what are we waiting for?"

The women turn their attention to the end of the bar. There are the cowboys, as advertised, half a dozen of them, leaning on the bar, drinking their beer straight out of the bottle, smoking, laughing. They look pretty good, she thinks, thirty-something, tight jeans, broad shoulders in freshly ironed denim shirts, gleaming hair, the clean smell of oatmeal soap and Old Spice. Nice boys. Not cowboys really, but blue-collar guys; carpenters, plumbers, lumberjacks...guys with tools.

"I love men who work with their hands," Sabrina confides. "Unlike the *artistes* I deal with most of the time, big phonies who pretend they don't care about money but hold you hostage for every dime. And the egos, industrial strength. Now these are nice, simple, good old boys who talk about sports and the weather and the latest Sly Stallone movie. And they are so polite. Old-fashioned and sweet and a little shy. We'll probably have to make the first move."

"'We' meaning you," Ann says. "With all that acting training, you can start a conversation with a cantaloupe, and that young blond hunk sitting on the nearest bar stool seems to be ripe for the picking."

"What are you going to do?" Deb whispers nervously.

"Just watch," Sabrina says. She turns to the young man, smiling broadly, "Hi, there."

He freezes, not sure she means him.

She leans closer, taps his sleeve. "Great place," she says. "How long has it been here?"

He wrinkles his forehead and scratches his chin. "Don't rightly know, ma'am, but I reckon it was before I moved here."

"And when was that?"

"Round about six years ago," he says, turning to face her, and the conversation is off and running.

In a few minutes he is smiling at her with the most astonishing sky-blue eyes and offering, "Excuse me, ma'am, I can't help noticing your glass is empty. I'd be honored if you'd let me buy you another."

Bingo! The evening is taking off and not just for Sabrina. She catches Ann's eye as Ann's glass is being replenished by a dark-haired Montgomery Clift look-alike. Not that he'd know his namesake. He's much too young. Ann winks at her and tosses back her blond hair. Already she looks ten years younger, Sabrina thinks. The strain of always being smart and in control is a hell of a burden. It must be a relief to drop the facade once in a while and be a good old girl.

The jukebox switches to the fast-paced "Standing Outside the Fire" and Sabrina's guy asks her if she would like to dance.

"Damn right, honey." Sabrina jumps to her feet. She loves to dance. Charlie hates it. Always has. He obliges her by doing one turn around the dance floor at bar mitzvahs and weddings. "I can play six sets of tennis in the boiling sun," he tells her. "But get me on the dance floor and I'm exhausted after five minutes." "If you bent your knees, Charlie, it would help." Never mind, Sabrina thinks, what's the point of nagging; people don't change. Better to change partners. At least for the occasional dance.

The other women are on the floor, too, Sabrina notes; Ann with her Monty, Maria with a big guy wearing a ten-gallon hat. Only Deb is still at the bar, licking the salt off the rim of her second margarita, looking flushed and re-laxed. Sabrina starts to wave, but Deb is turning the other way, talking to the bartender. He is introducing her to someone, a new guy who must have just come in. Sa-brina looks him over: tall, dark, a bit scruffy with some sexy stubble. Somewhat older than the rest, yet just as attrac-tive from the rear. Oh, those tight butts and full glisten-ing heads of hair. No balding pate there, unlike Deb's dear Donald. Sabrina notices that the man is putting on a pair of square-rimmed glasses the better to see Deb. They give him a rather scholarly air. Maybe he's smart, too. Sabrina's bottom line. Good going, Deb.

Sabrina tries to get a better look, but Blue Eyes pulls her closer for a fast two-step. She is flat up against his hard muscular thighs and chest, and it feels just fine. She re-laxes in his arms and lets herself be led. Two bodies mov-ing smoothly to the music. He is a natural dancer, nothing fancy but a sure sense of rhythm, easy to follow.

They dance two more numbers, and he leads her to a table. Sabrina feels the wetness under her arms and breasts, between her legs. She smiles up at Blue Eyes. "Sure beats the treadmill."

"Now, why would you want to be using something like that?" he drawls.

"To stay in shape, of course."

"You don't have to worry about that, little lady," he answers, giving her hip a gentle squeeze.

"Why, thank you, kind sir," she says. "And isn't it lucky that dancing is such good exercise."

The Coven gathers at the table, each with a man in tow. Ann's guy and Maria's are friends; they work together on a logging crew. Lots of testosterone there, like firemen and policemen. Sabrina loves men who do dangerous work, who lift heavy things. The only thing Charlie lifts is a Water Pik. She sighs; there are husbands and there are lovers and not much overlap. Women are different, she thinks, we can do both, the maternal and the erotic. As if to test her thesis, Sabrina sips the last of her second martini, glances down at the denim bulge in Blue Eyes's lap and giggles.

"Now, what's so funny, pretty lady?" Blue Eyes asks.

"Just wondering," she says boldly. "Briefs or boxers?"

He tilts her chin up, holds her gaze, "How about... nothing."

That launches a conversation about lingerie and X-rated movies and sex scandals and "let's have another round," and there's lots of easy laughter and grazing touches. It's sweet, Sabrina thinks, this dancing and drinking and bit of a cuddle. She leans across Blue Eyes to reach the popcorn, and he places his large hand around her waist, making her feel delicate and desirable. Charlie's fingers are small and bony, which make him an excellent orthodontist, but Blue Eyes is something else entirely. His fingers are strong and sturdy, and the curly blond hair that escapes from his open-necked shirt promises a thick animal coat on his chest. A young, healthy male. She watches the easy way he kneels at her chair. No creaking knees, no awkward stiffness as he rises. He has the natural ease of a cat. Sabrina feels a liquid rush of desire.

"Last call, boys and girls," the bartender says, hitting a gong. A chorus of moans from the table meets his directive. Ann looks up, scans the room. "We're the only ones left."

"Dios mio," Maria says, yawning broadly.

Sabrina checks her watch: 2:00 a.m., it's been a long day, and she is the one driving them back. "Sad to say, ladies, but it's time to move."

They gather up their coats and say their goodbyes. Ann gives her cowboy a quick hug, shoulders only touching. Maria pulls off her partner's ten-gallon hat and whirls it into the air. Deb lingers in whispered conversation with her dark man until he kisses her gallantly on both cheeks. Blue Eyes touches Sabrina's shoulder and asks to walk with her to her car. She mock-curtsies. "Why, I'd be charmed."

The fog has rolled in and the mist turned into a fine drizzle. Sabrina and Blue Eyes dawdle a bit behind the others, and in the shadow of the eaves he stops. They both stand motionless. She feels time spin out like cotton candy in that sweet tension that precedes a first kiss. He is waiting for a sign. She turns toward him ever so slightly, and he pulls her to him, eagerly pressing his mouth to hers. His lips are soft and springy; his breath fresh despite the beers. She feels his tongue make a slippery foray into her open mouth. She answers it with a flick of her own and then reluctantly pulls away.

"Sorry, darlin', got to call it a night."

"Why?" His voice breaks with boyish disappointment.

His tone is reminiscent of all the boys she'd refused in high school because she was a virgin. This time she says gently, "Because I'm married." Nevertheless, she feels the same rush of exhilaration; it feels good to be wanted.

"I see," he says softly. Then, "Well, can I still call you sometime?"

"Not a good idea."

He nods. "I'd sure like to see you again." He adds shyly, "I'm in the Roundup every Friday."

"I'll look for you," she promises. And if she ever goes back, she will.

The others are already in the car when Sabrina ambles over. She is greeted with hooting and catcalls just like in high school. She pretends to ignore them but is secretly pleased. Letting this part of herself out is fun. Tonight she is nobody's mother, nobody's wife and nobody's artistic director. Tonight she is just herself. And isn't that what every woman wants...to be appreciated just for herself? Not for what she does, but for who she is. Doesn't every woman want to be seen by fresh eyes, discovered anew?

Now, where are the car keys? She fumbles in her purse. She knows she put them in there. So where the hell are they? She opens the car door, feels around on the front seat, reaches behind her. "Did anyone see the keys?" The others start scrabbling around in the dark. Finally she remembers; she hung her purse on the back of her chair; they must have fallen out.

"Be right back, girls," she calls as she heads to the bar. It's empty except for the bartender and the dark man who had been with Deb. The two men are huddled together in close conversation. As she walks toward what had been their table, the dark man wheels around. He holds up his hand and the light catches the glint of metal. Her keys. He dangles them like wind chimes. "Great," she says. "Can't get far without them."

"No problem." He extends the keys.

"Thanks, I appreciate it."

Still holding his half of the keys, he says, "I'd appreciate a ride."

"Don't you have a car?"

"No, ma'am, I don't."

"How did you get here?"

He takes a hitchhiking stance. "The kindness of strangers."

"Well, where are you going?"

"Not far, just down the road a piece. I'd be much obliged."

Sabrina checks him over quickly; his clothes are a bit shabby but his hair is trimmed, and he smells okay. He doesn't appear to be drunk. Still...

"Enjoyed talking to your friend Deb tonight. Real nice lady. Said you were staying up on the ridge. That maybe you could fit one more in the car?"

Good old charitable Deb. Well, if he's already been invited, why not? "Okay," she says. "Let's go." He reaches for something under the table. It is large and bulky. He stands carrying a heavy backpack and thick blanket roll. She doesn't like the look of it.

"Where are you staying?"

"Camping at Van Damme. Real nice on the beach."

"Not tonight. It's raining. Do you have a tent?"

"Tents are for wimps. Real men travel light." He winks his farewell to the bartender and follows her out to the parking lot.

Sabrina dumps his gear into the trunk as he stands looking at the car. Deb, in the front passenger seat, grins shyly. Maria and Ann, in the rear, look back surprised. "We're giving him a lift," Sabrina explains.

"Where do you want me?" he asks. His tone is teasing.

The innuendo is not lost on Sabrina. "Next to a door," she says. "For a quick exit."

"There are four of them. Which one?"

"The front," she says. More control there.

Deb reluctantly moves to the rear. Sabrina can hear the Coven's whispered laughter as they huddle together in the back. There's a different feeling in the car now. The presence of a man. An attractive man. A stranger.

"Don't believe I got your name?" Sabrina says.

"Hughie," Deb calls, her voice high with excitement.

"So where's Louie and Dewey?" Ann's voice is slurred

with scotch. She does her Donald Duck imitation, squawking deep in her throat, flapping her arms wildly. Sabrina laughs at her best friend's mimicry. It's so unlike Ann's normal controlled demeanor. It was a survival skill, Ann had told her, that she developed as the lone scholarship student in her class at boarding school. She had lampooned all of her teachers and a good number of her fellow students; an adolescent satirist skewering the pretensions of her self-proclaimed superiors.

We all had that wildness once, Sabrina thinks. Ann used to jump horses, Deb climbed mountains, Maria was the leader of a street gang, Las Muletas, named after the sharp hidden sword with which the matador kills the bull. And for herself, it was men. Before Charlie, she had played the field. "Nibbling on men's hearts like a handful of raisins," one of her theatrical conquests had accused. Since her marriage, though, she'd limited herself to flirtation. To fantasy. And she hadn't even indulged in that for quite a while, she reflected, until tonight. Too busy or too staid? Had she lost her wildness, settled for being safe and contained? A wife. A mother. A good girl. There were other choices, more exciting, more dangerous. Every society knew it. Beware the outlaw, the crone, the witch...the wild woman.

There is a certain animal excitement with Hughie in the car: his smell, a slight musk; his bulk; the way he sits, legs spread wide apart. His voice is throaty and deep. He laughs as Ann imitates the cowboys in the bar. She is mimicking Blue Eyes. She captures his earnestness perfectly. "Excuse me, ma'am," she drawls, "but I couldn't help noticing that your vagina is empty."

The women roar, and Hughie laughs along with them, a bass note anchoring their sopranos. The shared laughter releases the last vestiges of tension, and soon the Coven is dishing sex and true confessions, as if they were alone. It must be the safe gender ratio, Sabrina thinks as she turns on the windshield wipers. The wet fog has turned into a drizzle. By the time they drive the few miles to Van Damme, the wind has come up and there is a driving rain.

Sabrina pulls into the state park parking lot. It is completely deserted. Not a car, not a soul. The Jeep's headlights pick up a few streaks of grease lying forlornly on the cracked concrete like a blurred distress signal.

"Not a fit night out for man nor beast," Deb intones.

"Is there any shelter? A cabin or something?" Maria asks.

"Nope, just campsites." Hughie closes the zipper of his thin jacket.

"Well, why don't we just drop you off at a motel," Sabrina suggests.

"That won't work," he says, turning up his jacket collar against the cold.

"I know one that stays open late," Ann assures.

"I haven't got the money." His tone is matter-of-fact. No shame, no entreaty.

"We can lend you some," Sabrina offers. "You can pay us back."

"Against my personal code." He raises his hand high. "'Neither a borrower nor a lender be.'"

"Hamlet," Sabrina acknowledges.

"Polonius's advice to Laertes. Act 1, scene 3," he says, grinning.

"So what happened?" Sabrina teases. "Lost your job as an English teacher?"

"Nope. Just like to read. I've done a lot of things." He pauses seductively. "But not that."

"Like what?" Ann probes.

"Little bit of this. Little bit of that."

"And...what are you doing now?" Maria asks.

"I'm in between," he says.

Intriguing or irritatingly evasive? Sabrina wonders. Meanwhile, the rain is drumming hard on the roof in a steady tattoo. The women are silent for a moment. The banter stops. None of them has the heart to put him out in this downpour. Ann's house is large, lots of bedrooms and the den. And after all, there are four of them. There is safety in numbers. What the hell, Sabrina thinks, I'm ready to take him in. But it isn't her place to invite him. It's Ann's house. Sabrina glances at her friend; she can almost read her thoughts. They have gotten especially close since that bad time after Ann's divorce and subsequent remarriage.

Sabrina remembers the many times she took care of Kim when Ann's sitter didn't show and how Ann had canceled all her appointments to drive Sabrina to the clinic and wait with her for the results of an equivocal Pap smear. They could depend on each other. Although they were very different, they understood each other.

Ann is weighing the risks right now, Sabrina thinks. She can hear the tap of her friend's fingers against the door as she totes up the factors on her mental legal pad. The upside is compassionate action; the downside possible trouble. What if someone found out? Especially her jealous and controlling husband. Richard Salant gives new meaning to the term *patriarchy*. He could be a mean bastard, Sabrina thinks; that's how he made his fortune in arbitrage, buying failing businesses and showing no mercy. He had courted Ann with the same single-mindedness that he pursued anything he desired. Granted, Ann had been willing, glad to be taken care of financially, to give up the burden of being a single mother. Although Sabrina sometimes wonders how happy Ann is. There is a shadow side to Richard, and Ann is probably discovering it. Still, he can be wonderfully generous and loyally enthusiastic. Sabrina could never have started her theater company without him. And she can't keep it going without him, either, especially not now.

It is Deb who breaks the silence. Her tone, like a kid who's just spotted a candy store. "Hey, why don't we let him stay with us just till the rain lets up?"

It's a good temporizing move, Sabrina thinks. It's reassuring to take things in steps and reevaluate at each juncture.

"That's okay with me," Ann says. "Wouldn't let a dog out on a night like this."

That launches a barrage of shaggy-dog stories that takes them the five-mile winding road to Ann's house, aptly named for the Buddhist paradise where one is forever released from pain and sorrow.

The women are damp and chilled as they enter the

house, and Ann lays a fire immediately. As the logs catch, Sabrina pours a vintage cabernet she has brought. Hughie, to his credit, doesn't bat an eyelash at the lordly manor or the largesse. He partakes as if it is his due and comments on only two things: the Deibenkorn over the fireplace and the Klee in the dining room.

He swirls the wine in his glass, noting its color, its bouquet, and takes a slow sip. He smiles his approval. "Eighty-five was a good year for French cab."

"Not bad," Sabrina says. "So you know wines?"

"I know what I like," he demurs.

Maria brings out the prosciutto and figs; Deb the jumbo pistachios; Ann the Belgian chocolates.

"Welcome to gustatory excess," Sabrina says. "To the land where too much of a good thing is divine."

Ann puts their cult classic on the stereo, the soundtrack from *The Big Chill,* their era. They sing along gyrating in their seats.

Hughie is on his feet, pulling Sabrina with him, and before she can say "Joy to you and me," they are bopping to the music in a classic jitterbug. He draws her close and then spins her out. The man has moves, she thinks, even better than Blue Eyes. Very smooth. He leads with his pelvis, and as they sway together she lets her belly rest smack against his. Nice. Sexy. He ends the dance with a long slow dip and she is reluctant to let him go.

Sabrina watches with a twinge of jealousy as Hughie moves from woman to woman distributing his attentions equally, waiting for the song to end before bringing each of them back to her seat, bestowing a courtly bow or a gentle caress before moving on to the next one. She lies back against the brocade pillows on Ann's enormous leather sofa, sipping her wine as she admires his technique. He dances differently with each of them, adjusting his style to their personalities, their predilections. With Maria, he dances companionably, his arms draped loosely around her shoulders. With Ann, he maintains a decorous cushion of air between their hips. With Deb he takes a strong lead, challenging her to keep up.

So who is this guy? Sabrina wonders, carrying a bedroll and dead broke but well versed in the wine and art departments. Some sixties dropout? A doper? Or just a Renaissance sort of guy? Whatever, in the flickering light of the fire and the beeswax tapers, he is starting to look pretty good. And there is something oddly exciting about his being the sole male energy in the room, circled by the women, contained by them. The Coven has its token male; its ritual phallus; priapic, mysterious. And the man can dance. Good thing there's safety in numbers. She could fall for this guy. So could any of them. Easy to lose your head.

Sabrina refills her glass and, already a little high, closes her eyes and gives her imagination free rein. An image floats into mind. A group of women wildly dancing in flowing white togas on a rocky hillside. A distant rumble of Greek Mythology 101. Then she remembers...the Maenads...women followers of Dionysus, running wild on the hills of Thrace in spring, high on something. What was the drug in the mystery cult? Soma? Some mind-altering hallucinogen that frees the animal spirit, that lets loose the part that wants to devour, needs to tear things apart. And women who normally heal, who nourish, who bind the wounds of the world have gone mad and are dancing, shouting, foaming at the mouth, and racing naked down the mountain. Woe to any living thing that crosses their path for they will tear it limb from limb and drink its blood. Whether it be a young deer or a young man. *The Bacchae.* Yes, Euripides's *The Bacchae.* That's it, she thinks, that's my next play at The Edge.

She turns to Ann to tell her but sees that her friend is in no mood to talk business. Ann lies sprawled on a bed of pillows, her cheeks flushed, her hair rumpled, her usually composed lawyer's face looking young, animated and expectant. Sabrina looks out the floor-to-ceiling window, out into the waving eucalyptus, the sea beyond. The stars are resplendent; there is a full moon. It has stopped raining. It's been a good night.

"Where's Hughie?" she asks, noticing that he is no longer dancing.

"In the john," Deb says.

"Isn't it about time we send Mr. Bojangles on his way?" Sabrina asks. "I'll get my car keys."

"I'll drop him off," Ann offers. "You did the last drive."

"That's okay. I'm not tired," Sabrina says.

Deb sidles up and whispers, "Not on your life. I saw him first."

They are tired enough, close enough, and have drunk enough, Sabrina thinks, to be absolutely honest. They each want the last moment with Hughie...what did he say his last name was? He didn't. What do they know about this guy anyway? They huddle together, pooling their information, which turns out to be scant and contradictory.

"He told me he's been on the road for a year. Downsized from a computer job," Deb says.

"Told me he ran a surf shop," Maria adds.

"Then where did he get all that Shakespeare from?" Sabrina asks.

"He taught high-school English," Ann says.

"But he was downsized first," Deb insists.

"Whatever." Sabrina yawns widely. "I'm going to bed. You three can battle it out for who's playing chauffeur."

Ann calls the game. Rock, paper, scissors. And to no one's surprise, she wins. Her intuition is witchy, Sabrina thinks, although Ann claims it's all reason and logic: figuring the odds based on each one's pattern of risk taking. Well, hell, they all do that. The point is that Ann does it faster and with less second-guessing.

When Hughie emerges from the bathroom, Ann is waiting. "Time to go. Got everything you came with?"

He grins slyly. "Unfortunately."

Although the women get the innuendo, no one rises to it. Instead, they walk out onto the large back deck to say goodbye.

Maria shakes Hughie's hand. Deb gives him a decorous hug, Sabrina kisses his cheek and adds, "Thanks for the dance, sailor."

He turns around to shoulder his bedroll, and that's when he notices it. "Is that a hot tub I see before me or an apparition of my teeming mind?"

Macbeth, Sabrina thinks, aptly paraphrased.

Hughie is admiring Ann's state-of-the-art hot tub, gleaming Jacuzzi jets, burnished redwood, broad and deep enough to soak six in steamy comfort. Sabrina looks at it longingly. The night is crisp and fresh, her legs ache from dancing, and her head is woozy from wine. All she wants is to get Hughie safely out of there and to get naked. The women tell their best stories in the hot tub. Removing their clothing removes the last layer of subterfuge, of discretion. They divest; they dish; they amuse and surprise each other.

Hughie plants his feet squarely on the deck. "Ladies, I have not yet revealed my main claim to fame."

"Cajun dancing?" Deb says.

"Cadging rides," Sabrina adds.

"I am," he says, "a certified Esalen masseur."

"What's an Esalen?" Deb asks.

Sabrina's been there half a dozen times, but she is the only one of them who has. "It's a conference center in Big Sur. It was where the New Age began."

"The Human Potential Movement," Maria adds. There is still no glint of recognition in Deb's eyes.

"Encounter groups," Sabrina explains.

"Oh, yeah," Deb says, nodding. "That nude-bathing place."

"So what kind of massage do you do?" Ann asks. "Swedish, polarity, Feldenkrais, cranio-sacral, acupressure?" Ann gets weekly massages at the Olympic Health Club along with regular waxings, facials, and cellulite pummelings. She's up on this stuff.

"I've developed my own style," he says. "Combination

of long slow body strokes and energy trigger points. Revs you up and smoothes you down. Keeps you looking young."

Another addition to the "Hey, lady, I can't help noticing" series pops into Sabrina's head. Normally she'd suppress it, mixed company and all, but the wine and dancing have loosened her tongue. "Hey, lady, can't help noticing your tits need re-touching." The women roar at their running joke. Hughie looks puzzled. Sabrina thinks how different they are with him as compared to the way they are around the men who count, their husbands, colleagues. Hughie is outnumbered big-time; they can be their true, wild, politically incorrect selves around him. He doesn't cramp their style. She wonders when they began to dissemble, to present a proper face. Men do that, too. But the sad thing about men is they intensify it around other men. At least women have the refuge of each other.

It doesn't take Hughie long to recover. "I'd like to repay your hospitality, ladies, and offer a little fair trade. Say, a massage for a place to spend the night." He looks toward Ann, holds her gaze in a bold challenge. It's her call.

Ann slowly finishes her wine, extending the silence, clearly enjoying the suspense. Then, "Make that four massages, and you can sleep in the guest house." They don't call her the Velvet Hammer for nothing, Sabrina thinks.

"Four it is. Let's get going." He throws down his bedroll like a gauntlet.

Sabrina surveys his muscular arms. She can already feel them ironing out the kinks in her neck and back. Feigning solicitude, she inquires, "Won't that take a long time?"

"It'll be my pleasure. Now, what can we use as a massage table?"

"How about a massage table?" Ann says. She goes into a back bedroom and emerges with a fold-up, leather-topped professional massage table.

Sabrina grins. Of course Ann and Richard always have top-flight equipment. They had taken a massage workshop once, during their courtship phase. She remembers Ann telling her that any time Richard began a new pursuit he would insist on buying all the best and latest paraphernalia. Outfitting is instant gratification, Ann had added ironically, so unlike the tedious process of actually learning the skills.

"Only been used once," Ann says as she sets up the table in the den, a cozy wood-paneled room that can be made toasty warm with space heaters. She covers the table with two of her pink Porthault sheets, one to lie on, one to hide under. A telltale sign of the moneyed class, Sabrina thinks, le monde *Français*...French lingerie, French wine, French linen. Ann's towels and blankets are of the finest fabrics and reside in tidy stacks in a cedar-lined, wall-length closet scented with, what else, French lavender.

They all belonged to Ann Number One, but clearly she has taken possession, made them hers. Ann likes elegance, luxury and beauty. But then again, thinks Sabrina, so does she. She loves sleeping at Nirvana under those pink cashmere blankets, bound in heavy tea-rose silk. Soft as a cloud, they never scratch, never pill. That's what it means to be rich. You never have to be tacky. You never have to be uncomfortable. You never have to finish all the food on your plate.

Ann, by *droit du seigneur*, is first. It's her house. Her body gets to lie on the table first. The three of them will soak while Ann is stroked and pummeled. Decorous before the stranger, they return to their respective bedrooms, close the doors and disrobe. Sabrina ties up her hair in a scarlet scrunchie and pads onto the deck in her white terry-cloth robe. It is her vacation-only robe, still pristine and fluffy.

The hot tub is steaming; bubbling like a witch's cauldron. Sabrina's thoughts drift back momentarily to *Macbeth* and this morning's meeting. If her staff could see her now. Deb and Maria are already there immersed up to their necks as she climbs in. She slowly sinks into the hot liquid, moaning low and deep. Maria gives her a naughty wink. "Sounds orgasmic."

"Next best thing." Sabrina smiles.

"And next to that..." Maria passes her a filled champagne flute. Sabrina sips the chilled effervescence. "Wow," she says, checking the label. "Richard's private stock."

"Ann broke it open to ease our waiting," Maria chortles. "Like this is hard to take." She flings her head back. "*Dios mio,* look at those stars. You can really see them out here." She points her index finger at the heavens. "Cassiopeia, Andromache. Castor and Pollux."

There are those Greeks again, Sabrina thinks; they've given us so many good words and so many good stories. Like Cupid and Psyche. Like Leda and the Swan. They understood the wild side. "More, please," Sabrina asks, holding out her glass.

Maria begins to sing, "The night they invented champagne." Deb hums along, correcting the melody. She has perfect pitch, but in typical Deb fashion denigrates her voice because she's not Barbra Streisand. Nevertheless, she anchors the three of them as they work their way through the score of *Gigi*. Strange that they never sing in the city, but out here they never stop, and it doesn't matter if they know the words.

It is half an hour later when Ann saunters out to the deck, her robe untied, her lovely long torso framed by the two panels of her cobalt-blue robe, shining like marble. She snakes her fingers through her tousled hair and throatily asks, "Next?"

Maria begins to stand, then falters and grips the side of the tub. "Just a little light-headed," she says, brushing off their concerns. She strides forward into Hughie's waiting towel, still a strong-willed, self-confident woman with great presence. Sabrina glances at Maria's heavy breasts, relieved to see that the lumpectomy scar barely shows. No need to talk about it.

Deb turns eagerly to Ann, shutting off the Jacuzzi jets the better to hear. "So how was he?" she asks.

Ann considers the question thoughtfully. "Professional."

"That's all?" Sabrina is disappointed. This guy is a mystery; a drifter, an independent scholar, a masseur cum Cajun dancer. The pieces are alluring but they don't fit. And the Coven has brought him home and let him stay. She feels a small chill of uncertainty. Is this wise? Judicious?

"Well, were you naked?" Deb asks.

"Completely," Ann says.

"Did you use the sheet?" Deb continues.

"No."

"Did he try anything?" Sabrina asks.

"Like what?"

"You know," Sabrina says. "Accidentally brushing against your breasts. Spending a long time on the inside of your thighs? Was it sensual?"

In answer, Ann sinks down into the tub until all that is visible is the very top of her head. Ann, who is always so careful to preserve her hairdo, her perfect cap of blond hair. She rises up from the tub, hair streaming, face shining. "He's the real thing, baby. He's got great hands."

Sabrina can hardly wait. Patience is not her long suit. To displace her restlessness, she heads for the kitchen and prepares a fruit plate to bring out onto the deck. Everything she touches, the glistening grapes, the slippery papaya, the fleshy pink watermelon is moist and juicy. You don't have to be Sigmund Freud to get the picture, she thinks. Halfway out the door, she decides to garnish the plate with a border of pecans, and then adds a sprinkling of salty cashews and a dusting of pine nuts. Nuts and seeds.

And then she spies the pomegranate on the counter, nestled in a group of ripening plums. She pulls it out, splits it open. Demeter's daughter, Persephone, was abducted by Hades, the god of the underworld. And Demeter, goddess of fertility, mourned her loss and nothing grew on the face of the earth until Persephone was restored. But the girl had eaten six seeds of the pomegranate and for six months each year she must return to dwell underground, and again nothing would grow. Yes, Sabrina thinks, this can be a scene in her new play. Life comes in cycles, birth and death and rebirth. She returns to the deck bearing her offering.

"I've never had a massage," Deb confesses, reaching for the pomegranate.

"Well, you've got a little miracle coming," Sabrina assures.

"Being naked with a strange man and letting him touch you all over?" Deb pauses. "What do you do while he's…?"

"You lie back and enjoy it," Sabrina says. "It's a blessing, like grace, and it just keeps coming. You don't do anything but receive. Surrender."

"I don't think I can do that," Deb says.

"Do what?"

"Surrender."

"Oh, just give her a little more champagne," Ann says.

Sabrina fills Deb's glass. "What's the worst thing that can happen?"

"That I'd like it," Deb laughs. Then surprised at her own answer, the laugh catches in her throat and becomes a sob.

"Hey," Sabrina says, taking Deb's hand. "Is it that bad?"

"Don doesn't touch me anymore. He sleeps on the opposite side of the bed, and if he accidentally brushes up against me, he apologizes."

"God," Ann says. "Get out of that marriage."

"And go where?" Deb retorts. "It's fine for you to talk. You've got a career, you've got savings. Me, I'm a lousy housewife. I never finished college. I've never had a real job in my life. I have no skills, no training. I'm nothing. The only reason you guys hang out with me is because of Maria and the Blue House."

"Not true," Ann says. "You're smart and funny, and you're the only one of us who can carry a tune."

That brings a small smile. "That's for sure," Deb agrees.

"Dammit, Deb, this sexual thing has sapped your self-confidence," Sabrina says. "It's coloring everything. Girl, you need to get laid."

With impeccable timing, Hughie makes his entrance trailed by a blissed-out Maria. Both have shed their clothing. Maria is stark naked, her ample body glistening with massage oil. Hughie has tied one of Ann's pink Porthault towels sarong style around his waist and rakishly perched a rose behind his ear. The flower and the plush pink towel provide a witty counterpart to his furry well-muscled torso and the bouncing bulge beneath.

"Your turn," Deb says, turning toward Sabrina.

"No, you go," Sabrina demurs. "I want to soak a bit more. I'm just starting to loosen up." When life gets simple enough, Sabrina thinks, pop lyrics provide all the wisdom you need. Sabrina waits until Deb is out of earshot before hatching her plan. "I bet he's great in the sack, and she can really use some," she whispers.

"And I can't?" Ann protests. "He was kneading my ass and I grabbed his hand."

"To stop him?" Sabrina asks.

"To make him go lower and faster," she laughs.

"You didn't," Sabrina scoffs.

"If it weren't for Richard, I would have," Ann says. "If he ever found out, he'd kill me. You could though," she says to Sabrina. "You're lucky, Charlie is so mellow."

"Well, maybe," Sabrina says, thinking that she wouldn't want to push her luck. Charlie was tolerant of her flirting, attributing it to the emotional excess of the theater, but she had never given him cause for real concern. "Tonight is Deb's night. She needs it the most because of that asshole Donald. I say we make the supreme sacrifice and give Hughie to Deb."

"How?" Maria asks as she sinks into the tub. "On a platter with an apple in his mouth?"

"The old disappearing act. We three will slip off to bed, and when they reemerge, they'll be alone. The rest is up to Mother Nature," Sabrina says.

"What makes you think Deb is going to want him?" Maria asks.

"That's up to her. But no matter what happens, it's got to be an adventure."

Ann fills their glasses with the last of the champagne. "Mae West got it right—too much of a good thing is...terrific."

"To Aphrodite," Sabrina toasts.

"To doing the dirty," Ann laughs.

The three women down their champagne and head for their respective bedrooms. What happens afterward is a blur. A nightmare. A descent into the underworld.

CHAPTER FOUR

It is one month later. By mutual agreement, the women have neither seen nor spoken to each other. But Maria has stayed in touch with all of them by e-mail. She knows that each one has used the time to practice her own most effective coping strategies.

Sabrina reports that she has doubled her rehearsal time, fueled by her favorite comfort food, butter pecan ice cream. The combination of sweet cream and salty crunch are particularly satisfying, she says, although the weight gain is not. Her conversations with Charlie have become strained as she is constantly guarding against an inadvertent disclosure.

Ann sends messages about working late into the night on new legal cases and avoiding Richard. Although she has increased her dose of sleeping pills, she still wakes up before dawn, nerves jangling. She has lost ten pounds and is using heavy rouge and foundation to hide the dark circles under her frequently bloodshot eyes. She has developed a nervous hand-washing mannerism that is getting increasingly more difficult to curb.

Deb states that she has devoted her days to her children. The house has never been cleaner, even the boys' underwear and socks are ironed. She has added three new classes of water aerobics to her gym schedule. But as her body has become more flexible, the lines of tension around her mouth and eyes have increased. She has been especially kind to Donald, not complaining about the hours he keeps. Somehow the importance of his affair, real or imagined, has faded before the enormity of the Coven's weekend.

Maria, herself, reveals that she has taken on extra counseling sessions, pro bono. She has asked for the worst cases the church can find. She attends services twice a day now pouring her heart out to God, asking forgiveness. In the evening she baby-sits her young nieces. It is a comfort to be useful, but after she puts them to bed, she lies upon the couch, short of breath, exhausted.

But tonight is the opening event of The Edge's season, Sabrina's much touted production of *Macbeth,* and they have all planned on attending. The date has been set months in advance.

Yet when Maria closes the door on her last client, she goes directly upstairs to her bedroom and phones her regrets to Sabrina's answering machine. "I am so sorry, my friend. I'm just not up to it. I wish you great success." Then she remembers the perverse theater terminology and adds, "Break a leg." The theater is rife with superstition; good wishes must take the form of a curse to ward off the evil eye. Sabrina has explained that backstage *Macbeth* must always be referred to as 'the Scottish play.' No one remembers why. So much trouble in the world, Maria thinks; accidents and misfortune lurk around every corner. We do whatever we can to protect ourselves.

Maria takes her pain pills then writes a few notes about Emilia Gonzalez, whom she has just counseled. Emilia has moved back in with her mother but she is lonely, depressed and planning to return to Juan. Discouraged, Maria closes her eyes against a rising headache.

Deb, too, has decided to forego the opening. To Donald's surprise, right after dinner, she calls to cancel the baby-sitter. When he queries her, she pleads fatigue. "I thought you loved hanging out with your friends," he says.

"I just saw them," she answers.

He considers that, then asks, "Didn't you have a good time?"

"It was fine," she says.

"You were awfully quiet about it. Usually you tell me every detail."

"There was nothing to tell," she says, quickly. Then, avoiding his eyes, she heads to the bedroom to call in her regrets to Sabrina.

Her newfound skill at deception frightens her. Who and what is she becoming?

For Ann, just home from the office, it is the longest period without contact since she and Sabrina first met at the

Blue House. Ann misses her friend, the laughter, the warmth, the sharing of confidences. Despite the recent traumatic memories, she is looking forward to seeing her tonight.

Ann kicks off her high-heeled pumps and picks up the *Mendocino Times* from the pile of afternoon mail. It is delivered to her San Francisco home weekly. She relishes it for its small-town gossipy news; it's like reading pulp fiction. Before pouring herself a glass of wine, she washes her hands twice at the kitchen sink, scrubbing her nails with a brush.

Carrying her glass of chardonnay, she sits down at the kitchen table for a quiet read. Richard is flying back from Los Angeles, and Kim, who has decided to be with them this week, is upstairs watching *Gilligan's Island* reruns. Tonight, the three of them will attend the premiere, but for the moment she is free.

She skims the front page of the newspaper; underneath a vivid story about a DEA drug bust in a commune north of Willets, she notes a small announcement about logging starting up again. Just hometown news. She almost doesn't read it. She is tired of the environmental wars and not sure who the good and bad guys are anymore. Then her eye catches the phrase "old logging road" and reads further.

A spokesman for the Zellerbach Paper Company announced yesterday it is preparing phase two of its northern Mendocino logging operation, delayed for over four years by bitter battles between the foresters and conservationists. Scheduled to be logged by Thanksgiving are the four land tracts north of marker thirteen on the Old Mendocino Log Road.

Ann's hands are shaking. The Old Mendocino Log Road. Marker thirteen. That's the tract where they've buried him.

Clear-cutting begins next week. Reforestation efforts begin next week....

Next week. She can't believe it. She has almost talked herself into thinking that their problem was buried forever. She has willed it into nonexistence. This new road doesn't necessarily mean trouble, she tells herself. The land tract is huge. But her legal mind can't let it go. What if the tractor digs up the body?

Ann retreats to her study and takes up her ever-ready yellow pad. At the top of the page she writes in large capital letters: DISPOSING OF THE BODY. Underneath she outlines various solutions. Ignore it. Incinerate it. Pay someone to remove it. She visualizes each option; each is unworkable. Ultimately it comes down to the same procedure they used to dispose of the body in the first place but in reverse; take the Jeep, dig up the corpse, dump it in a really safe place this time. But there are problems with that. Getting all the women together on short notice will be difficult. And she doesn't trust Deb. Deb was in bad shape when they parted. God knows what she has done or whom she has told. Deb is definitely their weak link emotionally; she is best left out of it. Maria is dependable, but she's not physically strong enough. She could barely carry out her part of the burial.

That leaves only Sabrina and herself, but they can't do it alone. Too much weight.

And then the idea comes to her. Equipment. That's what the loggers use. It can be done, she thinks. It only needs planning...and it needs Sabrina's help. Ann drinks her wine slowly, willing herself toward calm, toward compartmentalization.

An hour later, when Richard arrives from the airport, she is showered, dressed and waiting on the living-room sofa. Richard kisses her lightly, smiles approvingly at her new black silk pantsuit, then changes into his own navy pin-striped Armani. Expertly tailored, every well cut silver hair in place, he looks like the CEO he is. The clothes and the man are one, Ann thinks.

Ann calls up to Kim, "Are you ready? We're leaving."

"In a minute," the girl shouts back.

Ann steels herself for her daughter's appearance. Ann has decided to choose her battles, and Kim's clothing, despite an ever-deepening devotion to Goth, is not a war she's going to fight. She is relieved when Kim appears, minus the ghoulish white powder and with only a minimum of dark eyeliner. Kim's spiky tufts of dyed black hair have been brushed smooth and her body jewelry reduced to a single nose stud. In her black sweater and long black velvet skirt she looks young and coltish. And the torn-up army boots add a piquant touch.

The three climb into Richard's Mercedes and drive

South of Market to the fringe neighborhood of storefront theaters and tapas bars that houses The Edge. As they enter the theater, Kim studies the billboard setting the play in a bordello with Lady Macbeth as the leading role. "Cool," she pronounces.

In the crowded lobby, Ann catches a glimpse of Sabrina dressed in leather pants and bustier, and waves. Sabrina turns quickly away, appearing not to see her. But Ann knows her friend too well. Sabrina is afraid to look at her. This is not going to be easy.

Sabrina is surrounded by admirers. She is the queen of The Edge, the center of her own universe. Ann didn't know her in her actress days, but she suspects Sabrina lived for the attention then as well. Well, why not? Ann thinks. Sabrina has star quality. When Sabrina sweeps into a restaurant, people turn their heads. You can tell they think they recognize her, they just can't place her. Is it a TV sitcom or a Woody Allen film?

Tamar, Sabrina's daughter, is not in the theater lobby. Ann suspects Tamar is why Kim wanted to come, even though the two girls have not seen each other in years. Kim saunters over to the hors d'oeuvres table and studies the display intently. "Anything macrobiotic?" Ann hears her daughter ask Charlie, who is helping with the food. He could be one of the caterers, Ann thinks. Like them he is pleasantly anonymous, wearing the requisite tuxedo and focused entirely on moving small appetizers onto serving trays.

Ann looks at Charlie with sympathy. She likes Charlie. He is a decent, low-key man of few words. Clearly he is the ballast in the marriage. He adores his wife, indulging her, picking up after her, clearing away her little messes just as her friends do. Ann fears that Sabrina, in her usual style, will try to avoid responsibility for the aftermath of their horrific weekend. But this time, she cannot allow it.

Richard returns to Ann's side. He, too, is waiting for Sabrina to greet them. Finally she comes toward them, her massive, silver-streaked black curls swaying. Her smile is wide, but her eyes are wary.

She hugs Richard. "My dear guardian angel, if you hadn't flown back in time, we couldn't have opened."

Richard beams at her. He cannot resist Sabrina's charms any more than anyone else can.

She turns toward Ann and without meeting her eyes, hugs her lightly. "Ann-neee," she croons.

Ann hugs her back, holds on for a moment, and, placing her cheek next to Sabrina's, whispers, "There's trouble. We've got to talk."

Sabrina conceals her alarm beneath a radiant smile. "Later," she hisses, pulling back quickly. "I see our favorite critic. I've got to go 'make nice.'" And she is off.

Ann spends the next twenty minutes in idle chitchat with The Edge regulars. She notes, without surprise, that neither Maria nor Deb is there. Just as well, she reasons, it would only make the masquerade more difficult. She keeps glancing at Sabrina, hoping to attract her attention again, but Sabrina relentlessly works the room, not once turning in her direction.

Unable to stand the pointless chatter a moment longer, Ann heads for the ladies' room. En route she notices that

Kim is still standing by the hors d'oeuvres table, but now she is sampling the vegetable platter and talking animatedly to Charlie. Bless him, she thinks.

Ann enters the ladies' room. She looks around; it is empty. She stands by the sink, head bowed, and lifts her hands to her face. Since that weekend she has not been able to stop smelling her hands. Eating is her most difficult task. When she lifts her fork to her mouth she can't resist delaying its return, allowing her hand to remain for a moment under her nose. She thinks her hands smell of decay, much like the sharp, but not unpleasant, odor that clings to them when she picks wild mushrooms with Richard in the woods near Nirvana. Oddly, this decaying odor does not really upset her. The urge to smell her hands is a distraction, but it is something she can deal with, fight to control.

She wonders if some of her clients have noticed. Men can be unnerved by women with odd bodily habits. Now, every night, when she lays out her clothes for the next day on the chair in her dressing room, she chooses a skirt or pants with pockets. And unless a gesture is essential, she keeps her hands well hidden.

The lights dim. Ann rushes into the theater, scrambling over Richard and Kim, whispering her excuses. "Sorry, my stomach is not doing well." It is not altogether a lie.

She tries to concentrate on Sabrina's play. The lights go up on three women in black lace teddies and thigh-high leather boots. They sit on the edge of what appears to be a steaming hot tub, their garter-belted legs spread suggestively wide.

"When shall we three meet again?" they intone. "In thunder, lightning, or in rain?"

They light massive hand-rolled joints.

"Fair is foul, and foul is fair. Hover through the fog and filthy air," they chant.

The audience murmurs appreciatively. This is vintage Sabrina. Take a classic and turn it on its head. No one will admit to not loving Shakespeare. But whether they do or not, these novel witches force their audience to hear the lines with new meaning, a subtext that makes this bizarre setting plausible.

As advertised, the entire cast comprises women, some dressed as men, and the action all takes place in a brothel. Lady Macbeth, it turns out, is the madam of the whore-house and a drug lord. She has just wiped out Banquo, another drug lord, with whom she is vying for power. Richard and Kim watch attentively, but despite the lively staging, it is an excruciatingly long hour for Ann.

As soon as the lights come on for intermission, Ann rises, hoping to rush into the lobby to catch Sabrina before the crowd does. But if Sabrina is the queen of The Edge, Richard is its king or at least an important cere-monial figure. He is confronted in the aisle by a gaggle of well-wishing friends of the theater. All wear broad smiles, no matter what their real thoughts are about the play. Ann gets stuck behind him as he busily shakes hands. Looking over her shoulder she sees Kim bolt down the row to the far aisle. She is about to follow her when Richard takes her firmly by the elbow.

When she finally reaches the lobby, still walking behind

a glad-handing Richard, a waiter pushes a glass of champagne into her hand. She cannot see Sabrina.

Paul Terkel, a clothing designer and Edge Board member, comes up from behind. "Annie dear, what do you think of those patent-leather embarrassments?"

Ann is not sure if he is referring to the boots, the actresses, or perhaps the whole campy concept of the play.

"Viva Sabrina!" she responds vaguely.

"Our queen does get away with murder, doesn't she?" Paul says pointedly.

"What?" Ann shudders. "What did you say?"

"Nothing, darling." Paul gazes at her with concern. "Annie, my love, you're so jumpy. You must be working too hard. Your pretty eyes look positively raw. Don't let those corporate bullies drain away your good looks. After all, sweetheart, what else have we girls got?"

"Everything is fine," she says. "Really. Work is great."

Paul looks her up and down. "Stunning suit, darling, but you look worried. I bet it's man trouble. Men are such shits. Can I help?" He places a sympathetic hand on her shoulder.

To her astonishment, Ann feels tears well. She had not realized how tense she was. It would be such a relief to unload her worries on someone, even in carefully veiled allusions. And Paul is known for both his sympathetic ear and his discretion. But this secret is too fearsome. She pats his hand. "Paul, dear, can you give me a rain check? I'd love to have a long lunch...someday soon. I promise."

"You know my number, Ann," he says, walking off with a smile. "I'll bring the hankies."

Ann thinks wryly that she has man trouble, all right. But not the kind he can imagine. Not the kind any of them can imagine. Not in real life. The act of murder belongs on the screen or on the stage where it can be watched in voyeuristic safety, the culprit punished, and then everyone goes out for a drink afterward.

The warning lights flash, announcing the end of the intermission, but Ann still cannot spot Sabrina. Is she in hiding because she's afraid the play is going badly or is she just giving last-minute directions to the cast? Ann imagines the scene backstage as the prostitutes peel off their long boots and undo their garters in order to change into gangster outfits for the battle scene to come.

Ann catches a glimpse of Kim standing again by the hors d'oeuvres table, this time talking to Tamar, who must have arrived late. Tamar, like Kim, is dressed all in black; gauzy harem pants and a black silk T-shirt. Her long chestnut hair hangs across her cheek, hiding her face from Ann. The two girls slouch by the table, looking in profile like two sleek black herons.

As Ann approaches, she hears snippets of their conversation.

"So where are you going to school now?" Tamar is asking.

"Well, let's just say I'm figuring out my shit," Kim says. "I'm kind of living with my dad, but the kids at that school freak me out. They, like, live at the mall. I just can't deal."

"Yeah, I know what you mean," Tamar says. "Kids at my school think drinking a ton of beer and then puking it up is cool."

Tamar notices Ann and smiles shyly. Ann greets her with a hug. "Tamar, you look terrific. You get better looking every time I see you."

As Kim winces at the comment, Ann chastises herself. She should keep her mouth shut, as this is not the kind of compliment she gives Kim anymore. Yet Kim was so pretty once and could be again if she only stopped sabotaging herself.

She tries a safer tack. "How's school? Are you having a good year?"

Kim frowns. This is also dangerous territory.

"Oh, it sucks, you know," Tamar replies, delivering the standard teen line. She smiles her gentle smile. Tamar has her father's looks and her father's ways. They are both pale and softly defined compared with Sabrina's striking darkness. And instead of vivacity, they both offer a quiet kindness. Even as a small child at the Blue House, Tamar was the one who shared her toys and played with everyone. Ann tries not to envy Sabrina for having this lovely daughter who seems to sail through life with so much easy success.

She looks at own daughter, who is still frowning. In fairness, she thinks, Tamar has not had to endure her parents' bitter divorce before she reached kindergarten. And Tamar has not had to live with a stepfather she hates, although it has not always been that way for Kim. There were those few years when Kim admired and respected Richard.

Why does her worry about Kim so often turn her into

a harpy? Contrite, Ann reaches over to put her arm around her daughter, but Kim pulls away.

"We're going to be late," Kim says curtly.

No comfort there, Ann thinks. Not tonight. She takes her seat for the second half and desperately tries to focus her attention upon the stage as Lady Macbeth wanders about the haunted whorehouse entreating the prostitutes to kill the johns. The theme of planned violence, all the talk of ambush and murder is beginning to resonate in Ann's mind, blur with the events in her own life.

And when, after committing the bloody deed, Lady Macbeth wrings her hands and cries, "Out, damn spot, out...not all the waters of the sea will wash this hand clean," it hits Ann like an electric shock. She bolts out of her seat.

"Sorry," she says to Richard. "I've got to get out of here. I'll meet you in the lobby."

He stands up to let her by. "What's the matter?" he whispers with a half smile. "Can't stomach any more?" So he doesn't like the production either, she thinks. She rushes by him, her knees weak, hands shaking. She must find Sabrina.

Ann knows that Sabrina always watches the first night from a perch on the right side of the wings. She's not sure how to get there, but the theater is small, and after one false turn into a dressing room, she finds herself at the rear of the stage. The brothel residents, who are not onstage, are lounging on folding chairs behind the backdrop. They are not allowed to talk, but two of them are playing cards and another is knitting. The others appear to be dozing, or at least they have their eyes closed. In their garish whorehouse clothes and makeup, Ann imagines they look like their real-life counterparts, killing time between engagements.

She spots Sabrina seated on a canvas director's chair just off stage right. She approaches her from behind, grabs her by the shoulders. "I have to talk to you. Now!"

Sabrina wheels around angrily, brandishing her script. "I'm in the middle of a show."

"Don't give me that crap," Ann hisses. "Look at this."

Ann pulls the article from the *Mendocino Times* out of her pocket and thrusts it on top of Sabrina's script.

"So?" Sabrina demands.

"Marker thirteen," Ann says. "That's where we left him."

Sabrina's face blanches. Thrusting the script at her assistant, she walks rapidly down the long hallway where the dressing rooms are located, Ann following her. They enter the door marked Director, and Sabrina bolts it shut. She sinks into her desk chair and reads the newspaper article out loud, slowly, word for word.

Finally she looks up at Ann, her eyes wide with fright. "I told you it was crazy."

Ann nods.

"I told you we should have called the police right away."

Unwilling to rehash the experience further, Ann says, "Maybe we should have. But it's too late for that now."

Sabrina is breathing hard, staring at the newspaper article. "Oh my God," she keens. "What are we going to do?"

"Sabrina, get ahold of yourself. If we keep our heads we can still make this go away. I've got a plan."

"You and your goddamn plans!" Sabrina explodes. "I don't intend to spend the rest of my life in a concrete cell with a bull-dyke guard and a toilet that won't flush!"

Ann can't hold back a tight smile. This is the Sabrina she knows and counts on. Sabrina's histrionics she can handle; it's her terror that she can't.

"I've thought it through. They may not find the body, but we can't count on that. If they do, they could tie it to us. We've got to check the cabin again, too. Make sure we got rid of any evidence. We may have forgotten something. We'll go up on Monday."

"Do you think the others can get away that quickly?"

"It's just you and me. We dig up the body and get rid of it permanently this time. In the ocean."

Sabrina stares at her. "You're fucking crazy. The four of us could barely carry him. He was a goddamn beached whale. We'll have to get Deb and Maria."

"No way," Ann says firmly. "The more of us involved, the more chance things can go wrong. You and I are the strong ones. I've figured out how to do it. I can rent a block and tackle, like the kind they use to take out tree stumps, and there's a wheelbarrow at the cottage. I should have thought of it the first time."

Ann carefully lays out her plan, visualizing the steps neatly numbered on her yellow legal pad. They will dig down to the body, wrap a rope securely around it and with block and tackle hoist it into the wheelbarrow and then into a rented van. Ann will make sure to ask for a van with a ramp. She has picked out the perfect cliff, a couple of hours up the highway. It's a steep sheer drop; they won't have to worry about the body getting stuck halfway. It will be washed out to sea with the first tide.

Working out the details of a plan is something Ann is good at. She tries to conceive of the body as just another problem to solve, just another obstacle like a troublesome software deal. She doesn't let herself think about what the body might look like now, or even how it looked when they buried him. And she certainly cannot entertain any curiosity about the body as a person. That might lead to unnerving questions about who he really was and whether anyone has missed him.

"Why just us?" Sabrina cries. "It's not fair. If it hadn't been for Deb we—"

"I know it's not fair," Ann placates. "But face it, Deb is unreliable. I can't trust her not to squeal to Donald. He'll wonder where she's gone and twist it out of her."

Sabrina is silent. Neither of them is certain that Deb has kept her mouth shut even this long.

"And you know Maria's not well," Ann continues. Sabrina nods, leans heavily against the wall, staring straight ahead. Glancing at Sabrina's grim face, Ann guesses that her friend is allowing herself to wander into the unthinkable. For a moment she imagines it herself. She visualizes finding the grave, their shovels digging through the damp soil, the first flash of white flesh sticking out of the earth, like a turnip. Then using their hands to push away the dirt around the body so they can somehow pull it out of its cold dark grave. Maybe the cheesy white skin has mummified or worse. Ann shuts down this line of thinking.

"We have no choice," she says. "We're much more likely to be found out if we leave the body. There's just too much risk. We weren't careful about anything. There's fresh dirt on the grave and God knows what else we left behind. In the ocean there won't be anything left to identify us. And even if they find his body parts they won't be able to tie them to us."

The sound of muffled applause is a bizarre coda to her speech.

A moment later, there is a sharp knock at the door. "Sabrina? We need you. Curtain call!"

Both women jump as if struck by an electric prod.

Sabrina quickly splashes water on her face. "Hold on, I'm coming."

As she opens the door, Ann grabs her arm. "Meet me at the bridge Monday morning at nine. Our regular spot. I'll be in a van."

The look of fear returns to Sabrina's face.

"Don't even think about not coming," Ann says.

Sabrina nods and hurries into the hall.

Richard and Kim are waiting for Ann in the lobby. She forces a smile and tries to focus on her family rather than the planning that must be done by Monday. She notices that few of the audience members are talking. That isn't good news for Sabrina's play. If it's a hit everyone jabbers. This silence has the sound of failure. But for the moment, theater reviews are the least of her concerns.

As they make their way to the car Richard asks Ann how she is feeling.

"Better. It must have been something I had for dinner," she says.

Kim snickers and Ann remembers there's been no dinner. She was so busy worrying about "the problem" that she forgot about food. No wonder her daughter spent most of the evening at the hors d'oeuvres table.

"Kim, how did you like the play?" Richard asks. When there's no answer, he continues. "Was it a little weird for you?"

"It was okay," the girl says in a flat tone.

"No, really, I'd like to hear your opinion. As chairman of the board, I need to be in touch with the future generation of theatergoers. It's important."

Kim warms to this. "Well, at first it was cool, a real hot tub and all, and those black boots were nasty. But after a while, it just didn't work. Not that Shakespeare is ever user friendly...but this was over the top. And how can hos turn into gangstas without even changing their shoes?"

Ann smothers a laugh. The critics, if they're honest, couldn't nail it better. Ann suspects Richard agrees with Kim, but he can't help playing the wise sophisticate.

"Sometimes you have to stretch people's imaginations to make the old seem new," he says. "Like when 'Madam' Macbeth cries, 'Out, damned spot, out, I say,' it takes on a whole new meaning in this age of AIDS. And the whorehouse...a 'hotbed' for sexually transmitted diseases. And did you notice the dark purple spots on the johns? They're called Kaposi's sarcoma..."

Lay off, Ann thinks. Don't close this tiny window of communication that Kim has opened.

"Yeah, I guess." Kim fiddles with the car radio.

Another chance blown. This is the first time Kim has said more than two syllables to Richard in months, and he chooses to deliver a lecture. Ann doesn't know what went wrong between them. Kim worshiped him until she was about ten. Only Richard was allowed to read her a bedtime story. Only Richard could fix her morning cereal properly, bananas sliced paper thin, just the way she liked them. They had been a real family. But as Kim matured, and she matured early, she became shy with Richard, and in time that shyness turned to distance. It wasn't that they screamed and fought with each other, Kim saved that for her mother. It was just that they turned into strangers.

Ann doesn't know if Richard could have done anything to change it; adolescents have their own way of dealing with the world, but he has never really tried. Whenever she pleaded with him to talk to Kim, he would accuse her of overworrying and insist it was just a phase.

On some level Ann thinks he is wary of Kim. Of her sexuality? Her sharp and sometimes bitter tongue? Or maybe it's that she sees him too clearly? Sees the gaps between what he purports and what he really is.

"Well, dear, what did you think of it?" Richard turns to Ann.

She was hoping he wouldn't ask. Her mind was drifting during what she saw of the play and even now she is going over the list of tools she'll need to get at the U-Rent. She takes time to clear her throat.

"Well...I agree with Kim. The concept is intriguing. But then I'm afraid my stomach took over. I didn't see much of the rest. But I bet the critics like it."

This last remark is to soothe Richard. As long as the critics like it, the opinion of the audience is secondary. The foundation folks rarely see the plays, but they do read the reviews. Ann hopes the critics don't focus on the pot smoking or the simulated lesbian sex. The AIDS warning would be more politically correct.

"I wonder how Sabrina feels about the performance?" muses Richard aloud.

Ann doesn't respond. She doubts that Sabrina is thinking about the play. She's probably fixated on her own upcoming performance with an earth-covered corpse. For a moment, Ann flashes back on Sabrina's piece in tonight's theater program.

How did I conceive of my Macbeth? Sabrina wrote. *I took a wrong turn one night and drove through the red-light district, saw the hookers and their pimps and the johns and I thought of the enormously powerful emotions that must be playing out right there...lust, greed, secrecy, betrayal...and I realized, that's Shakespeare!*

And that was our weekend, Ann thinks, our wild woman's weekend.

Sabrina concluded her essay, *I picked Macbeth because of the powerful central woman. And then I thought, why not have all the women be powerful?*

Because they're not, Ann thinks, not in the same way.

She is right in not telling Deb and Maria. Maybe when it's all over. But will it ever be all over? What if they can't manage on Monday? What if there are people around? What if the hoist doesn't work? Tomorrow she will find a van to rent. Maybe a Toyota; they have good traction in case of mud.

"Are you okay, hon?" Richard asks.

Ann realizes the car is parked in the garage. Richard and Kim have gotten out and are staring at her still planted in her seat.

"I'll be fine after some antacid and a good night's sleep," she says.

Richard's face shows his disappointment. A tired wife with a stomachache is not what he'd hoped for. He has been gone all week, and the theater always revs him up, no matter how unsuccessful the performance. He will be gracious about her demurral, though, and infinitely solicitous. He will bring her a Pepto-Bismol, kiss her gently on the cheek and retire to his study so she can get some rest. No pressure, no cajoling. Richard is, above all, well mannered, so well mannered that Ann often doesn't have a clue about what he really feels.

Kim looks at her mother skeptically. Ann can tell she doesn't buy the bad-stomach story. "Is something wrong, Mom?" she asks. Ann is moved by her daughter's rare show of concern. Is she reaching out? Inviting a mother-daughter talk? Ann has so missed them. Would Kim want to share her true feelings with Ann once again? It would be a relief to talk about the girl's problems, a break from her own.

Richard goes to check the mail.

"Hey, honey," Ann asks her daughter. "How about a hot chocolate, or something?"

"No thanks. I'm going out."

Ann can't restrain herself. "At this hour? It's ten-thirty. Where are you going?"

"Just out," Kim says.

"And who with?" Ann persists, her voice rising.

"Friends."

Another part of Ann's brain kicks in. Cool it; don't make her run any farther. She changes gears swiftly. "Okay, sweetheart, just be back by twelve. Mothers worry." She opens her arms to her daughter.

Kim looks startled, but she advances slowly into Ann's embrace. Although the girl holds herself stiffly, maintaining a cushion of air between them, she allows herself to be hugged.

It's a start, Ann thinks as she hurries up to their bedroom. After Richard leaves for his study she will write down her lists and work out the details of her plan.

Richard appears in the doorway in his bathrobe, a glass of water and the antacid pill in hand, just as she anticipated.

Ann thanks him and swallows the medicine. He gives her a dutiful peck on the lips before retiring to the bed in his study.

Ann climbs into bed, pulls out her pad of paper and begins her list. Van. Block and tackle. Wheelbarrow. What else? Her mind is spinning. She is too nervous to do this tonight; sleep is what she needs. She closes her eyes, but after a moment they pop back open. Twenty minutes later she is still wide awake. Should she take a sleeping pill? No, she has to have a clear head tomorrow. There is only one other way to guarantee sleep.

She gets out of bed and pads in her bare feet down to Richard's study.

Richard's light is still on. She opens the door. "Hey, Big Daddy, want to play?" she says in a throaty whisper.

Richard looks up surprised. "Are you serious? Are you really feeling up to it?"

"Try me," Ann replies and returns to their bedroom. As Richard follows her, she pulls off her flannel sickbed nightgown and flings it on the floor.

Richard eagerly takes off his robe. He is naked beneath it. "Can I get the toys?" he asks.

She nods. It is a familiar part of their lovemaking, one that she has come to accept if not exactly welcome. Richard fumbles through his top dresser for the key and then unlocks the bottom drawer of the corner cabinet. Inside is a jumble of vibrators, and various silk, metal and leather sex apparatus.

"What's your pleasure, ma'am?" Richard asks in a low husky voice.

"Handcuffs and the whip," she says.

"At your service," Richard says.

Watching Richard return to the bed with the handcuffs and thin black riding crop, she wonders what the Coven would think about this side of Ann. She and Richard had been seeing each other for nearly a year when he introduced her to the world of role-playing. Ann had always enjoyed rough sex more than she thought she should. She feared it was one of the scars of an abused childhood. Richard, she learned, had previously only exercised these proclivities with prostitutes. Together they felt safe.

Tonight they take turns with the restraints and riding crop, the blows so light that the pink marks will disappear by dawn. The sex is intense, fierce and as always, impersonal. They do not open their eyes; they do not call out each other's names.

"Bitch," says Richard, "take that." He flicks the whip on her open thighs.

"You need to be punished," Ann says, in her turn, squeezing his hands into the handcuffs.

When they are spent, wet with exhaustion, they roll away from each other on the king-size bed. Richard buries his head in his pillow and begins to breathe deeply and slowly.

Ann returns to the present briefly. I must get up before dawn to make those lists, she thinks. Then she closes her eyes and gives herself gratefully to sleep.

CHAPTER FIVE

The trip to the cabin is very different this time. Sabrina fiddles with the radio dials in the rented van seeking something to distract her. But nothing holds her attention, neither the country-western songs, nor the celebrity interviews, nor the world news. The scenery is an undistinguished blur. She sits far forward gripping the edge of her seat. It feels as if the earth is giving way beneath her feet. She wonders if Ann feels that way, too, but decides not to ask. Instead, she flips to a golden-oldies station and tries to get lost in the uncomplicated past.

It is not until they pull into the familiar road leading to Nirvana that Ann finally speaks. "I've brought a block and tackle, two shovels and two miners' lamps."

"Miners' lamps? What for?" Sabrina asks. "Where did you get them?"

"You can rent anything. We have to wait until dark. We can't be seen, but it's a new moon, so we're in luck."

"God, I hope so," Sabrina says. "But I still don't see why we can't just leave him where he is."

"The grave is too close to the cabin," Ann explains. "If they find the body, they'll start investigating and eventually it'll come down to me. To us. We were seen. People know we were here. The bartender. The clerk at the grocery store. It's a small town, you fart and someone on the next block fans the air. We've got to dispose of the body much farther away."

"Like Tahiti?" Sabrina suggests.

Ann is not amused. "Albion," she says. "There's a steep cliff and a clean drop. There won't be a trace."

"Albion," Sabrina protests. "That's a hundred miles from here."

"Barely far enough," Ann says.

They climb out of the car, stretch the stiffness out of their legs and backs. The air is cold and damp, but neither of them is eager to enter the cabin. It now looks to Sabrina like something out of a Stephen King novel, haunted and repellent. This once alluring vacation house is forever tainted. Sabrina feels a sudden wave of compassion for Ann. After all, it must be even worse for Ann; Nirvana belongs to her, her beautiful refuge. Sabrina slips her arm around her friend's shoulders. With a shudder, Ann moves into the embrace. Sabrina is surprised; her supercool friend is as badly shaken as she is.

As soon as they enter the house, though, Ann quickly resumes her drill sergeant mode. First they will remove Hughie's clothes from the basement closet where they'd hidden them. On the way to the grave they will bury them at the city dump. Then she will clean the inside of the house and Sabrina the outside, both alert to any tell-tale signs of Hughie's presence.

Ann immediately retrieves the plastic bag of Hughie's clothing from the basement and places it in the van. She then gets out the vacuum, the furniture polish and sets to work with her usual vigor and meticulous attention.

Sabrina heads outside, finds a broom and sweeps the deck. She checks under the picnic table and chairs, pulls up the heavy cover on the hot tub and forces herself to look inside. Thankfully, no trace of blood. She peers back through the living-room window; Ann is still cleaning feverishly.

Sabrina sits down, stares unseeing at the splendid view. The idea of exhuming Hughie's body turns her stomach. It's been more than three weeks. It must be decomposed by now. What happens to a body left in the ground with nothing to protect or preserve it? Wasn't it a sin, just throwing a body into a hole in the ground, unmarked, unmourned...like the carcass of an animal? After all, he must have been dear to someone, a lover, a friend? A child? Oh, God. Sabrina thinks of Tamar, her own beautiful daughter. What has she done? She enters the house, trembling.

Sabrina walks into the kitchen, stands behind Ann, who is scrubbing the sink. "What if some animal has gotten to him? Eaten his face? What if it's disgusting? What if we get sick? If we can't do it?"

"You do what you have to," Ann says, carefully rinsing and wringing out the dishcloth and hanging it to dry.

"Remember giving birth? Remember dirty diapers? We did it. Now stop thinking about it. Look around, see how nice this place looks."

It does look lovely, Sabrina thinks, the late-afternoon sun streaming through the newly washed windows, everything polished and in place. Can one placate the gods with an orderly house?

Ann retires to the couch with a thick stack of old *New Yorker* magazines. "Weekly magazines...who can keep up? Just one more thing to feel guilty about," she says as she thumbs through them, scanning the movie reviews, the cartoons. Sabrina reaches for her copy of *Plays in Print,* but she is dry as a bone. She can't concentrate and, even worse, she doesn't care.

Ann takes pity on her, "Put that book away, in moments like this you don't want to think." She reaches for the remote and zaps on *Days of Our Lives.* Today's episode is on teenage pregnancy. They watch for a few moments as the blond ingenue dissolves into tears as she delivers the unwelcome news to her bad-boy lover.

"That's going to be Kim, any day now." Ann sighs. "You've got it so easy with Tamar."

"Easy!" Sabrina protests. "She criticizes everything I do. Said my *Macbeth* was embarrassing."

"At least she talks to you. For Kim, I don't exist."

"The thing is you exist too much. She's got to find her own way."

"What about Tamar? Doesn't she have to rebel?"

"She does, but not against both of us. She's got Charlie. She's always nice to Charlie."

"So you're telling me I ruined my daughter's life by getting a divorce." Ann rises in anger and walks away.

"Hey, Annie," Sabrina says, going after her. "Come on, I didn't mean anything of the kind. You know that. We're both edgy." She pauses, offers a smile. "Low blood sugar."

"You're right," Ann relents, grateful for the excuse. "We haven't had lunch." She rummages through the nearly empty cabinets and emerges with a bag of tortilla chips, a can of guacamole and half a box of chocolate truffles. "Salt, fat and sugar. The three basic food groups. Only one thing missing." She opens the freezer. "Tequila…ninety percent proof." They limit themselves to one margarita each, albeit a large one. It cushions the wait until dark.

It is a testament to the power of fear that despite the tequila, they are stone-cold sober when several hours later they don the black hooded sweatshirts that Ann has provided and head for the back road. Ann drives, stopping first at the city dump to quickly unload Hughie's clothes, then on to marker 13. Sabrina navigates, but once they leave the highway, it's confusing in the dark; she's disoriented. They take a few wrong turns, a few dead ends but then Sabrina sees it. "That's the one. The stump over there. It looks exactly like a mother bear standing on her hind legs, getting ready to attack. Remember?"

"Don't project. It's just the biggest stump around. Let's get started."

Ann hands Sabrina a shovel and they both begin to dig. The weather has been unseasonably dry and the earth is hard as a brick. Sabrina breaks into a sweat and peels off her hood.

"Leave it on," Ann hisses.

"Who the hell is going to see us here?" Sabrina protests.

"Just put it back on and keep digging."

Sabrina is annoyed but complies. This is not the time for power struggles; they need each other. They dig silently, piling up an impressive mound of earth. "We must be getting close," Sabrina offers.

"It was a very shallow grave," Ann says. "We've been digging for thirty minutes. Something's wrong."

"This was the tree," Sabrina insists. "We just haven't hit the right spot."

"We've dug around the entire perimeter. It's not here."

"It's got to be here. Where could it have gone?" She pauses thoughtfully. "Maybe it sunk through."

"Yeah, to China," Ann scoffs.

"Maybe it disintegrated."

"It couldn't. Not that fast. This just isn't the right place."

"Well, I can't dig any more ditches. My back is killing me."

"It'll hurt a hell of a lot more in a jail cell," Ann snaps.

"Unless..."

"Unless what?"

"No...it's too improbable."

"What? Tell me."

"What if it never happened?" Sabrina says. "What if the whole thing is just a bad dream? A collective hallucination?"

"No," Ann insists. "It happened."

"Then where's the body? Where's the material evidence? There is none. Maybe we just got drunk and crazed and made up the story?"

"Made up Hughie?" Ann shakes her head in disbelief.

"Made up the really bad part. One of us started it and influenced the others, like those experiments in psychology class where you convince people they've seen something they haven't. We're just suggestible, that's all."

For a moment, Ann looks hopeful. "Maybe he's not really dead. Maybe he crawled away. Maybe he woke up with this enormous hard-over…" Ann sputters with laugher. "I mean hangover."

Ann's laughter is contagious, inciting Sabrina's own peals. They howl with it, maniacal with relief. Just a bogeyman, a shadow on the stairs, not a real threat at all. They made up the whole thing. Like a bad dream. Wake up and everything is just the way it always was. They are respectable wives and mothers, successful career women, upstanding members of the community. They are safe, restored, whole. Redeemed. Sabrina looks over at Ann. Ann's hands are clasped, her head bowed. She is back to her Catholic girlhood, praying for salvation, for a miracle. Her lips are mouthing the Jesus prayer; all she needs is a rosary.

Sabrina reflects how much further Ann has departed from her own upbringing than she herself has. Sabrina grew up in the comfort of Westchester County with a psychiatrist father and an English-teacher mother, both liberal and loving. Ann grew up in poverty with abusive alcoholic parents and six younger siblings. She has created herself out of whole cloth, established a new and better life through her own fierce determination. She has gone from a railroad flat to a Pacific Heights mansion, from Sears and Roebuck to Chanel and Versace. She and Richard are a regular fixture in the social pages, the mainstays of the symphony, opera and multiple charities. Ann has far more to lose if Hughie's death is ever revealed. Charlie and Sabrina live a more private and more bohemian life. And Sabrina knows that in the theater, people expect her to be weird.

Ann grabs Sabrina by the shoulders, pulling her out of her reverie. "Enough. This is not a fantasy. It is not going away. We've got to find that body even if we have to dig up every inch of the forest to do it."

They fill up the holes they've dug, pack up the shovels, the wheelbarrow and the hoist. Ann drives to the next clump of redwoods, but they cannot find a large tree resembling the rearing bear. They spend more than an hour driving through three more groves, growing increasingly more desperate until finally Sabrina spots it, looming in a clearing some distance away, the large standing trunk with the outstretched branches, the smaller stump crouched before it.

"That's it," Sabrina shouts. "That's why it was a mother bear. Because of the cub."

It's unmistakable, almost as if carved by a human hand. Ann turns the Jeep sharply in the direction of the clearing. But as they approach, they hear a strange grating noise. It is the crunch of gravel beneath the tires of the Jeep. They are on a road, a newly paved road. Someone has built a road over Hughie's grave. Ann brakes to a halt. The women jump out of the car.

"Oh my God," Sabrina gasps. "Now we'll never be able to get to the body."

"We can't dig up the whole road," Ann agrees.

"Now what?"

Ann paces, thinking hard, her mental legal pad at work. "If we can't get to it, no one else can either. Hughie is under the tar, under the gravel, bulldozed into oblivion. Gone. Leveled. We're saved!" Ann cries. She turns to Sabrina and the women hug hard.

"It just proves it was only an accident," Sabrina says with relief. "We didn't do anything that bad."

"It just proves we're damn lucky," Ann says. "Let's get out of here."

They drive back to the cabin in an exhausted and reflective silence. They head swiftly for their respective bedrooms, peel off their clothes, take long hot showers and climb under the lavender-scented sheets.

The simple joys of living, Sabrina thinks, the basic creature comforts. We never fully appreciate what we have until we're in danger of losing it. Just before she falls asleep, Sabrina recalls the Buddhist definition of nirvana—release from the karmic wheel of fear and desire.

Ann takes her usual sleeping pill and before surrendering to its dependable effect makes a vow to never lose control of her life again.

The next morning, Sabrina awakes well rested and relaxed for the first time since that awful night. She suggests they reward themselves with a calorie-rich breakfast at the Mendocino Bakery.

As they climb into the car, Sabrina muses, "You were right not to bring Deb and Maria into it."

"Simpler is always better," Ann says.

"And it wasn't necessary. We handled it ourselves."

"We're a good team," Ann says.

Sabrina is pleased at the compliment. "I think this will just make our friendship stronger."

"Definitely," Ann agrees. And they vow never to talk about the event again. It will be as if it never happened.

When they arrive at the restaurant, they are ushered to a sunny window table. A pitcher of freshly squeezed organic orange juice, a pot of Jamaican blue mountain coffee and a basket of home-baked breads are placed before them. They both decide on the newest entrée, a fresh fruit and ricotta breakfast torte. The food arrives fragrant and steaming hot, on huge white china plates garnished with golden papaya slices. They dig in with relish and toast each other with goblets of dense, sweet juice.

"Order is restored," Ann sighs. "Peace of mind. This is how life is supposed to be."

"We will never take it for granted again," Sabrina pledges as they clink glasses.

The waiter appears, "Is everything all right here, ladies? Anything else I can do for you?" He lingers, flashing them an inviting smile.

"Not a thing," Ann says curtly, and shoots Sabrina a warning glance. The waiter is a piece of work, a Michelangelo *David* in a tight white T-shirt. An artist, no doubt, Ann thinks. Mendocino is full of them, young

poets and painters living on trust funds or the odd con-
struction job, their supple bodies and sensitive minds
toned by Bikram yoga, herbal medicine and tantric sex.
These boy toys are tempting, but even a flirtation is off-
limits. Men are off-limits...forever...or at least for a good
while. She and Sabrina have had a bad scare and a fortu-
itous reprieve. It is time to behave impeccably.

"May I bring you ladies more bread?" the waiter asks,
nodding toward the empty reed basket. They have de-
voured the two mini loaves, not to mention a muffin and
a brioche.

"Just a check, please," Ann says, slapping down her plat-
inum card. "It's on me. We're celebrating."

"Okay," Sabrina agrees, "but the next one is on me. I'm
going to the bathroom. You don't have to, right?" Ann
nods. She has the bladder of a camel. Sabrina wonders if
it's biology or just another example of her friend's iron
will.

As Sabrina makes her way to the ladies' room, she passes
a free stack of *Mendocino Times*. She picks one up and takes
it with her into the stall.

Settling onto the seat, she scans the front page. The lead
story is the usual stuff, a zoning law fight. The locals want
to build hotels and restaurants and make a bundle while
the weekenders want to preserve the pristine folksiness of
their rural retreat. She reads on: whale spotting, amateur
theatrics, wedding announcements, Little League. And
then she gets to page three. The headline reads: Body
Found on Logging Road. Sabrina stops peeing midstream.

A shallow grave containing the body of a white male was uncovered last Saturday by a work crew constructing a logging road through Headlands Forest. The Mendocino Sheriff's Office is awaiting a coroner's report for the cause of death. A significant wound in the victim's cranium could be evidence of foul play. The body was found naked, wrapped in a pink cashmere blanket.

Sabrina forgets about peeing, zips up her jeans and races into the dining room. Ann is figuring out the tip; she likes to leave it in cash. "Eighteen percent of thirty-five is..."

Sabrina throws down ten dollars. "That's too much," Ann says.

"Never mind," Sabrina says. "Let's get out of here."

"What's wrong?"

"It's bad."

Ann blanches. "How bad?"

Sabrina waits until they're back in the safety of the van to speak. "Why the hell do you need cashmere blankets?"

She reads the article out loud as Ann pulls out of the parking lot. At first Ann listens in stunned silence. But she soon recovers and hotly retorts, "Of course we should have removed the blanket. I knew it then, but none of you could bear to touch him, to expose his naked body."

"It was a mistake," Sabrina admits.

"Hardly our first," Ann says. "And we can't afford any more."

"I know," Sabrina says as she opens the bag of muffins

she was bringing home for Charlie and shoves an entire lemon-crunch topping into her mouth. She offers one to Ann who refuses. That's why she's still a size eight, Sabrina thinks, both admiring and resenting her friend's restraint. "It's a given that they'll trace the blanket," Sabrina says. "How many people buy cashmere throws from Porthault at a thousand dollars a pop?"

"It wasn't my doing," Ann says. "It was Ann Number One's."

"You could have sold them."

"Don't get self-righteous on me. You loved them, remember? *Soft as a cloud.*"

Sabrina relents, "Well, you're not the only one with dough in Mendocino. The town has its share of movie stars and software magnates. There are probably other Porthault blankets."

"Not Provençal pink. They have to be specially ordered."

"When did you last order one?"

"A year ago, when Richard insisted I replace one that wore out. I couldn't get it. They'd discontinued the color."

"That's good," Sabrina says. "No record."

"I wrote to the company, though," Ann says, her hands tight on the steering wheel. "Made a big fuss. They could find the correspondence, put two and two together and trace it to me. Oh God, Sabrina."

"It's just a blanket," Sabrina soothes. "No one knows it's yours."

To reassure her, Sabrina opens the newspaper and

rereads the article. *Continued on back page.* She hadn't noticed that before. She turns the paper over and gasps.

"What?" Ann cries.

"'Police report that the pink blanket had a laundry tag stapled to its satin binding bearing the initials AS.'"

"Jesus Christ," Ann cries. "I told you so."

"God damn it, why can't you do your own laundry?" Sabrina explodes.

"Me? What about you? You're the one who forgot the car keys. You're the one who gave him the ride."

She's right, Sabrina thinks, and now is not the time for recriminations; they must stay calm and figure this one out. "Okay," Sabrina says, "say they trace the blanket. Say they come to you. Then what?"

"Then what?" Ann says. "They'll arrest me and then they'll come for you. And Deb. And Maria."

"Just because they trace the blanket to you doesn't mean you've had anything to do with his death."

"He's wrapped in the bloodstained blanket that came off my bed and I had nothing to do with it!" Ann cries. "How the hell did he get it?"

"You gave it to him, of course."

"Oh, great," Ann shouts with irritation.

"The point is, when."

"You know when," Ann cries as she spins out to pass a car and nearly collides with a truck. The van sways wildly as she screeches back into their lane.

"Don't kill us!"

"Don't be such a baby," Ann scolds. "When?"

"When we dropped him off at the campground. Remember, it was cold. It was raining. Out of the goodness of your patrician heart, you threw him your pink Porthault blanket, which you were planning to bring back to the city to launder. You gave it to him and that's the last time you saw it."

"I would give a vagrant a thousand-dollar blanket?"

"You've got a million of them."

"I do not."

"You were compassionate," Sabrina reasons. "Profligate. Dumb. You pick it."

"Wasn't I planning to get it back?"

"No. It was bread on the waters."

"That doesn't seem logical."

"Look," Sabrina snaps, "you were the one who wrapped his goddamn body in it."

"You were the one who gave him to Deb."

"But afterward, I wanted to call the police. Come clean. Get it over with."

"It wouldn't have been over with," Ann shouts. "It would have been worse."

"For you," Sabrina says.

"For all of us," Ann retorts. "Believe me, I'm the lawyer here. All right, we'll go with your story. The simpler the better. Don't overstrategize, airtight is suspicious. We picked him up. We gave him a ride. We dropped him at the campground with the blanket. That's the last we saw of him. Now the only thing is to make sure we all tell the same story, all four of us. I'll call Maria. You call Deb."

"Will they do it?" Sabrina is doubtful.

"It's their necks, too. We'll stick together. Woman power. Solidarity. Now, let's go over the details."

They spend the next hour into the city polishing their story. "It's going to be all right," Ann assures, placing her hand upon her friend's.

Sabrina clasps the proffered hand. "You're right," she says. "All they have is the blanket. We've got each other."

CHAPTER SIX

"Ladies, do we have this straight? We felt sorry for him, it was raining, so we gave him a ride. We dropped him off at the campground. We didn't even get his name. It was the last we saw of him. That's all we know."

Ann is standing in the middle of Maria's tiny kitchen, elegant in her gray three-piece business suit. The room is warm and softly lit, Maria's well-used copper pots hanging from the low ceiling. Maria, Deb and Sabrina are seated around the small table, watching Ann. The aroma of a long-simmering stew, tangy and rich, hangs in the air. The room, which previously has embraced these four women like a warm cocoon, tonight feels claustrophobic.

Deb's eyes are wide with fear. "But don't you remember," she whispers. "I danced with him at the bar before everything happened. People must have seen."

"I've thought about that," Ann says. "It doesn't have to

be a problem. Don't volunteer the information unless you're asked directly. Then say something like, 'Everyone was dancing,' like it was a group thing."

"But you know I'm no good at that. I can evade maybe but…if they ask me things directly, right to my face, I can't lie." Deb's cheeks are flushed; she is breathing hard. Ann puts her hand gently on Deb's shoulder, struggling for the right tone.

"Deb," she says quietly, "just remember it's not your fault. You didn't do anything wrong. Just think of your boys. Keep your cool for them." Christ, Ann thinks. Here's our loose cannon. Got to get her in line. One angry word or look and she'll spill her guts. Ann remembers her criminal-law professor, Bo Bernstein, a big shambling guy with a lopsided grin that made him look deceptively harmless. "Rehearse your witness," he had urged his students. "Drill them. Drill them until they've forgotten any truth but yours."

Ann tries again. "Deb, I want you to practice saying it to me. Tell me what happened. From the beginning."

Deb looks bewildered. "What beginning?"

"Listen, my dear," Ann says softly but firmly, a therapist's voice. "You remember. The bar where we all had a drink and then did a little line dancing…all very innocent…"

"But that's when he came up to me. Remember it was me he came to. I was the one who danced with him."

Despite her struggles to keep her tone low and even, Ann's voice rises harshly. "Forget about that, don't say he picked you out, say he was one of the crowd, say we were line dancing. Can't you just say that?"

Deb lowers her head into her hands. The kitchen is silent. Only the muffled roar of a distant siren can be heard. Sabrina is leaning against the back of her chair, her arms folded, her eyes narrowed. Maria is staring straight ahead, her olive skin unhealthily pale, her chin slack and sagging, like an old woman's.

"Friends," Ann says in an exasperated voice, "you've got to help me out here. We've got to help each other. I can't talk for all of us. I won't be there when they come!"

"What do you mean, when *they* come," Sabrina says, "Who the hell is coming? J. Edgar Hoover?"

Sabrina had grown up in a family where J. Edgar Hoover was a lurking presence. Her uncle Harold had been convicted for tax fraud and spent three years in a federal prison. She remembers the day he returned. She hardly recognized him. He looked so old and battered. He described the prison: open toilet, iron bed and the constant threat of violence. For weeks she couldn't sleep.

Ann pauses. "I don't expect anyone is coming. This is just a precaution. I told you that. But if they do somehow trace the blanket to us, they're going to question us one by one. That's why we have to get our stories straight."

"Stories!" Sabrina says. "They're not *stories,* they're lies. Look, I've been thinking. Enough already. The longer we wait the worse it's going to look. I say we go to the police right now."

"Are you crazy?" Ann cries.

"We should have gone when it first happened," Sabrina insists.

"Maybe we should have," Ann snaps, "but we didn't."

"Because of you," Sabrina accuses, "protecting your damn society reputation."

"It wasn't just Ann. It was me, too," Deb says staunchly. "How could I explain to Donald why I was in a hot tub with another man?"

"Deb's right. Richard divorced the first Ann because she was playing around. I'd be dead meat if he thought I was doing the same thing." Ann's voice struggles for calm. "So let's not panic. What we're doing here is damage control. The police only have the blanket. Without more evidence that's nothing. As long as we stick to our story we're fine. Trust me. Just for once, Sabrina, try to think of someone other than yourself. Try not to be such a damn drama queen."

In agitation, Sabrina rakes her fingers through her black and silver curls. The mass of hair swells, Medusa-like, into a large dark cloud. "Trust you!" she says. "Why should I? You've got more money than God. You can hire the slickest lawyers in town. You'll get off without a scratch. I'll be the one whose life is ruined."

"You've got it made," Ann retorts. "You've got Charlie wrapped around your little finger. He's a fucking wimp. Or more to the point...a nonfucking wimp. That's why we went to that bar in the first place."

"My Charlie's a saint," Sabrina cries. "Don't you dare say anything about him, you bitch." She strides angrily toward Ann, eyes blazing, chin clenched.

Maria holds up her hands in dismay, but it is Deb who steps between the women. "Stop this bickering right now," she says in an unaccustomedly strong voice. "We're all in this together."

The three women turn toward Deb, startled. "I mean it," she continues. "We haven't got time to fool around here. I promised Donald I would be home by nine. So let's do what Ann says. Let's practice saying our lines for each other. I don't see that we have any other choice now that they've found the body and the blanket."

This is a Deb they have never seen before, clear, confident, assertive. It's like a wolf pack, Ann thinks, the leaders fight each other to the ground and the next in line takes over, stepping over the bloody bodies.

Maria sits up straight in her chair and obediently begins. "We were just going out to get a little air, an after-dinner drink," she says solemnly, as if reciting a poem in third grade. "This place was supposed to have good drinks. Then when we were leaving, this guy—"

"No," Ann interrupts. "Tell them about the dancing, say we just joined in the fun, didn't really know anyone."

"We saw people dancing," Maria adds. "And had a little fun."

"But tell them we were not drunk," Ann instructs.

"We were definitely not drunk, Officer, we only had a pitcher of sangria, three bottles of wine, four margaritas. Just normal social drinking. You know how city gals are." She winks broadly and flirtatiously at an imaginary police officer.

In spite of themselves, none of them can resist a small smile. Here is Maria, trying to bring them together again with gentle humor. She looks more like her old self at this moment, Ann thinks, the grayness of her skin tempered by a soft flush.

Thanks to Deb's intervention, things go more smoothly. Ann regains her authority. She marches them through their lines, one by one. Sabrina begins her recitation sullenly, but quickly yields to her own theatrical urges as she warms to the story. "The bar was lively, colorful, it had a sense of community like the Old West. The dancing brought us all together like a barn raising or a hoedown."

Christ, Ann thinks. She makes it sound like a scene from *Oklahoma!* When her own turn comes Ann recites carefully, as if giving a deposition. "The man who asked us for a ride was about six feet, weighed about a hundred eighty pounds. Ruddy skin, dark brown hair. He was wearing glasses."

At that moment Ann realizes that he was not wearing glasses when they buried him. His bloated moon face was naked. Were the glasses in the bedroom by the massage table? With his clothes that they threw in the city dump? She stores away the question and forces herself to go on. She makes each of the women repeat the story, using their own words. She insists they use simple phrases and chastises them if they repeat each other's line. They finish in less than an hour.

Maria smiles at them. "Now, ladies, I say we need a drink. This is the first time you have sat in my kitchen empty-handed."

"Sorry, I promised I'd be home," Deb says as she picks up her jacket from the back of her chair.

The others follow her lead. This is an awkward moment, Ann thinks. Usually there are fond farewells, promises to meet soon. But not today. The truth is, they don't want to see each other again, Ann realizes. Not until this whole thing goes away.

They do, however, manage halfhearted hugs, more genuine for Maria than for each other. Sabrina and Ann look away when they touch briefly; it is a stiff, unfriendly embrace.

Behind the wheel high up in her Jeep Cherokee, Ann tries to sort out her thoughts. First things first. Her own vulnerability. She thinks about Wing Lee's Elite Laundry and Dry Clean, a tiny storefront on the main street of Mendocino with a sewing machine in the window where Mrs. Lee works on repairs and alterations. All the weekend people take their clothes there; the Lees are fast, thorough and they know your name. Christ, they know your name. Mr. Lee always called her Mrs. Richard. But will they recognize the blanket? Do they keep records? Probably. She imagines a stack of carefully hand-written accounts in Cantonese piled neatly on a shelf in the back room. It's that kind of place. What are the odds the police will find them? Sixty percent. No...seventy. She always tries to be precise about odds, especially when the situation is out of her control.

Maybe I can hold the line, she thinks, protect the others from the police. Even though they've rehearsed their stories, someone's likely to reveal information that isn't in the script. What chance does she have of stopping the cops from interrogating the others? Twenty percent, she reasons. Not good.

And when the information comes out about the week-end "incident" at Nirvana, will Richard leave her? She feels her breath catch in her throat, her stomach clench. She is awash in a familiar wave of fear, the dread of being alone in the world again. Is this what it was all about...the hasty burial, the dangerous cover-up, the incrimination of her friends...just to protect her role as Mrs. Richard Salant? She knows that is what Sabrina thinks.

There is much that she values about being Mrs. Richard Salant. She likes the way waiters snap to attention when they walk into a restaurant, likes the box seats at the opera, likes knowing she can quit work anytime she wants. She likes Nirvana. No...she loves Nirvana.

But does she love Richard? Ann is uncertain how to define love. She knew she wanted to marry him; that was enough. But now how well does she really *know* him? She tries to envision Richard's face and cannot. She realizes she is not even sure where he is tonight. Did he say New York or Chicago? Is he at a business dinner or attending a performance at the Met? Richard was the one who introduced her to opera. "Imagine singing that beautifully as you die," he had said, smiling. He will probably call tonight at eleven. She looks forward to those late-night chats. In fact, she feels closer to Richard when he is away than when he's at home. They can let down their guard and become two disembodied voices in darkened rooms, three thousand miles apart, sleepily sharing the events of their separate days.

Driving home, Sabrina is so angry that she has difficulty concentrating on the road. Damn that Ann, trying to save her own neck at the expense of her friends. Sabrina feels exploited, used. She never should have agreed to bury the body. Never should have gone on that weekend. Never should have courted that friendship. Ann is in a different league. Her money insulates her.

And yet Sabrina can't forget being drawn to many aspects of Ann in the beginning, her quick intelligence, her steely resolve, her surprising skills at observation. And how she supported The Edge and their friendship. Sabrina feels a ripple of forgiveness. She does not want to lose her best friend. They are going through a bad patch and with luck and determination they will survive it. She will forget how mean Ann was about Charlie. It was probably just jealousy. After all, Richard has never made lunch for Ann. And never would.

Deb opens the back door and strides quickly through the kitchen. She feels energized, empowered. She knows she has done something useful. The ground floor is quiet; the older boys must be upstairs watching TV. She promised to be home to put them to bed so that Donald could finish his paperwork. Sometimes they needed repeated shouts and warnings before they finally settled down. She finds Donald at work at his desk in their bedroom. When their third son, Danny, was born he gave up his study.

"Hi! I'm back. You're off duty," she says.

Donald looks up. "You must have had fun, you look good."

She stands tall under his appraisal. "Really. Why?"

"I don't know. You just look...different. So what did you ladies talk about?"

"Nothing much. The usual."

"The usual what?" he probes.

"Never mind, Donald," she says firmly. "That's my business."

He can't take his eyes off her.

"I'll go into the other room so you can work," she offers.

"What's your hurry?" Donald says. He crosses the room and slips his arms around her waist.

She is startled but pleased. She can't remember the last time he did anything that spontaneous. Donald looks closely at her face as he presses his body to hers.

"How about an early to bed?" he whispers.

"What about your work...I thought..."

"Don't think, just get undressed. I'll be right there."

He leaves the room, strides to the landing. "Boys, do you hear me?" he shouts. Several grunts in response. "Your mother is tired, and we are going to bed early. If either of you dares to leave your room, you'll get garbage duty for six months. Do you understand?" More grunts follow. Donald returns to the master bedroom and carefully locks the door.

He quickly casts off his clothes and climbs under the sheets. He pulls her close; she can feel the throb of his erection. Gently her hand traces circles on his stomach, moves lower. "I thought you didn't love me anymore," she says.

"Whatever gave you that idea?" he murmurs, his mouth seeking her breast.

"You worked late so many nights."

"Oh, that." His hand moves between her legs.

"That." She guides his hand.

"I didn't want to worry you, but if you really want to know..." He moans.

And he proceeds to tell her, his reticence melted by his growing ardor.

Oh my God, Deb thinks as he enters her. If he had only told her before, Hughie would still be alive.

Maria swallows her pain pills, turns out the light in her small kitchen and heads immediately for bed. She thinks about calling her sister but decides to wait until morning when she will have more energy. The fatigue in her voice now will only alarm Consuela. She has told no one of the latest test findings. She has placed her future in the hands of God. In one corner of the bedroom is a small shrine with a ceramic statue of the Virgin Mary. Her niece made it for her in fifth-grade art class. Recently Maria has taken to lighting a votive candle before the statue. It burns most of the night, casting a warm glow through its red glass holder. It comforts her when she awakes in the dark, which she knows she will do several times that night.

CHAPTER
SEVEN

Ann is lying curled up in bed when she hears the door-bell ring. Swaddled in her white terry-cloth comfort robe, she is trying to concentrate on her latest intellectual-property case. "Can someone get that?" she shouts. But Richard is in his study with the door closed. And Kim is in the shower.

It's probably one of the neighborhood kids selling chocolate bars or Girl Scout cookies, Ann thinks as she pads barefoot down the long staircase. She stops to rifle in her purse for a ten-dollar bill. But as she opens the front door she is confronted by a large African-American man in a dark raincoat who abruptly thrusts a piece of shiny metal toward her face. Startled, she tries to shut the door, but the man is too quick for her. He curtails her motion like a football player defending a pass.

"Good evening, Mrs. Salant. I'm Agent Rod Curt,

FBI," the man in the raincoat says. "I'm here on a murder investigation and I believe you might have some information that could help with the case. May I come in?" Without waiting for a reply, Curt steps into the house and heads for the lighted kitchen. Ann follows him silently. She has expected this moment and has prepared for it. But still her pulse is racing and her throat is dry. Her mind returns to Maria's kitchen a week ago when they had been rehearsing their stories.

She forces herself to concentrate on the agent's long broad back, his thick gray hair cut close and precisely. Curt walks directly to the kitchen table where he sets down a large shopping bag. He peels off his coat, hangs it carefully on the back of a chair.

"Would you like some coffee, Detective?" she asks.

He refuses politely, all business.

She pours herself a mug of leftover coffee and leans against the opposite wall, as far away from him as she can get.

With elaborate care, he opens the large shopping bag. "Mind if I ask you a few questions?"

She shakes her head, trying not to stare at the bag.

"Good," he says, bending to his task. He places one large hand inside the bag and slowly pulls up the contents, like a magician unfurling silks. "Recognize this, Mrs. Salant?" he asks.

She glances at the strip of fabric bound in stained satin. "No, I don't."

"Maybe this will help," he says, removing the entire piece of material from the bag. He holds it up, outstretched between his hands. It is longer and wider than he is, a mottled grayish pink, bearing several large dark stains. Bits of earth and leaves cling to it in sodden clumps.

Ann forces herself not to turn from the filthy cloth and the rotting odor that it exudes, although even Curt recoils slightly from the powerful stench of decay.

"I know this doesn't look like something you would own, Mrs. Salant."

"What is it?" she asks.

He ignores her question. "It must have looked a lot better when Mr. Lee cleaned it."

"Mr. Lee?" she echoes faintly.

"Wing Lee's Elite Laundry and Dry Clean? Mendocino? Do you patronize the store?"

"Yes" she says. "It's the only one in town. Everyone uses him."

"He identified this blanket as yours. It has your laundry code."

She examines the markings. "Perhaps? What of it?"

In answer, Curt thrusts his hand again into the shopping bag. This time he produces a plastic laminated card that looks like a driver's license. He walks across the kitchen to Ann and presents her with the card. Looking directly into her eyes, he asks, "Look like anyone you know, Mrs. Salant?"

Ann concentrates on holding the card steady. At the top in bold letters it states United States Drug Enforcement Agency. Below there is a picture of a man with a crew cut and regular features who looks about forty. Although the man they brought home had long shaggy hair and wore

glasses, there is a distinct resemblance. Was the DEA looking for Hughie? It's possible. He was suspiciously elusive,
a man who could have done time, could have been on
the run. Ann looks more closely. Beneath the picture, the
card reads Agent Dennis Curran. She stares at it in confusion. Was that Hughie's real name? She runs through her
legal pad list. That's the only explanation that makes sense.
Hughie wasn't Hughie. Hughie was Dennis Curran. A
DEA agent. A narc. Her body stiffens in fear.

"Ann, what's going on there?" She hears Richard's
worried call as he hurries down the hallway. He must have
heard Curt's voice.

Curt looks up as Richard appears. "Mr. Salant, I was
hoping to meet you. Come in, come in." He gestures
broadly, inviting Richard into his own kitchen.

Richard remains at the kitchen door, as if uncertain
whether to fight or flee. Curt places a large firm hand on
his shoulder and pulls him gently into the room.

"I was just asking your wife about some small details
we're trying to clear up regarding the death of a fellow
law enforcement officer, DEA Agent Dennis Curran. I'm
sure you've heard about it. They found his body not far
from your country place."

"Really?" Richard says, his voice deliberately low and
calm.

"Really," Curt echoes in the same offhand tone. "And
I'm just having a few words with your wife. About this
blanket. You must recognize it." Curt picks up the blanket by its two corners and approaches Richard, who turns
away from the smell.

"We found it wrapped around the body of Agent Curran. He'd been buried in it for a couple of weeks. Corpse was quite deteriorated, some animal intervention, but not enough to destroy the physical evidence. There was still plenty of flesh on his bones, which is a good thing from our point of view. Anyway, this blanket turns out to be our number one clue. And, according to a laundry tag, the blanket belongs to your wife, or at least, she's the one who brought it to the Elite laundry."

Richard looks at Ann in confusion. His reading glasses have slipped to the tip of his nose. Wrapped in his tartan bathrobe, his feet bare, hair awry, he looks at the moment more like a befuddled sleepwalker than a captain of industry.

"Anyway, this blanket is, as I am sure you know, just circumstantial evidence," Curt continues. "There are probably a number of good explanations as to how it found its way onto the body. No doubt your wife has one of those right now."

This is Ann's cue. She can say she lost the blanket. It must have fallen out of her car as she was bringing in the laundry to the Elite. Someone must have picked it up. Maybe that's all it will take. That way, the other women will never be implicated. She won't have to worry about Deb's loose tongue or Sabrina's emotional outbursts.

But before she can respond, Curt adds, "And there is another small detail I've got to check out." He turns toward Richard. "It may just be a coincidence, but it seems as if your wife was one of the last people to see Agent Curran alive, at least as far as we can trace his activities.

Your wife and three of her women friends were with him in the Last Roundup."

"What?" Richard says, shaking his head as if to clear it.

"Maybe you don't know the place," Curt continues. "I guess it's more for the locals than folks like yourself. Anyway, I understand from the bartender the ladies were having a pretty good time. You know a normal Saturday-night kind of thing, a little drinking, a little dancing, I'm sure all very innocent. Well, anyway, the bartender says Agent Curran left with them." Curt looks pointedly at Ann. She feels her tongue cleave to her mouth. So he's found a witness. It's inevitable now that the others will be questioned as well. She must lay down the framework for the story, present her case.

As she composes her recitation, Curt adds, "One more thing, Mrs. Salant, I'd like your permission to look around a bit at your country house. Nirvana, I think you call it? Tomorrow, say?"

"I'm afraid that would be difficult," Richard says.

"Just a routine investigation."

"Perhaps in a few days," Richard offers.

"It's important."

"Look, this has gone far enough," Richard bristles. "I want you out of my house right now. My attorney is Sam Parker. You can deal with him."

Ann looks at Richard, surprised. Sam Parker is a flamboyant, nationally known criminal defense attorney, famed for taking celebrity cases. Ann had no idea that Richard even knew him. Unless he is just using the name to intimidate Curt.

Unfazed, Curt continues. "As you wish, Mr. Salant. That just means we'll have to get the cooperation of our good friend, Judge Tollet, for a search warrant. We'll be careful with your things, I assure you." He turns to Ann. "Now, Mrs. Salant, just one last thing. Are these the correct addresses and phone numbers of your friends?"

Ann looks at the list. "Yes," she says weakly, realizing this is the first word she has uttered since Richard appeared.

Curt carefully refolds the fetid blanket and puts it back in the shopping bag. He takes Agent Curran's identity card from the kitchen counter where Ann has dropped it and slips it into his raincoat pocket. "'Night, folks, have a good evening. Don't worry about me, I can let myself out." He strides to the front door with a light step.

As the door closes, Richard quickly crosses the kitchen to Ann, his face a mask of white-lipped fury. He grabs her, digging his fingers into her shoulders. She tries to pull away but he holds on, shaking her hard. His anger is so intense that small drops of spittle fly from his mouth. "What the hell were you doing up there?" he hisses. "How dare you jeopardize my life! Do you want to see me in jail?"

Ann is frightened by Richard's anger; he has never laid a hand on her before. But greater than her fear is her puzzlement. Why should this investigation jeopardize Richard's life? Why should he go to jail? When she has considered the possible consequences of "the incident," she has pictured herself being imprisoned, but the worst that she has imagined for Richard was public embarrassment.

She places her hand gently on Richard's cheek, drawing his gaze down toward hers. She speaks slowly, softly. "I'm so sorry, darling. It was just a foolish mistake. We meant no harm." Her fingers stroke his face. "Please, let me explain."

He releases his grip from her shoulders and allows her to guide him to a kitchen chair. Ann is relieved; Richard is still amenable to her touch. She must remember the dichotomy that works with him, Grace Kelly by day and dominatrix at night.

"Sorry," he says, his voice tight but under control. "Naturally I'm upset and concerned. I'm your husband. Tell me what happened. I'm sure there's a good explanation."

Although still unnerved, Ann begins to tell the story that she and the Coven have carefully rehearsed. They have agreed that, if the time came, they would tell the same story to their husbands as to the police. Ann wonders if Deb is capable of withholding the truth from Donald, but there is nothing to do but hope.

In the version Ann now carefully relates to Richard she minimizes the amount of alcohol they had consumed and omits entirely their bringing "Hughie" to Nirvana. "We were getting cabin fever," she begins, "so we went out for a little break. We had a drink at the Roundup, listened to the cowboy music for about an hour, and when we were ready to leave, this guy asked us for a ride to the campground. It was dumb, I guess, but you know what a softie Deb is. It was raining hard, so when we dropped him off we gave him the blanket." Ann is feeling more relaxed; the story almost sounds plausible, not half-bad.

Richard, however, does not look convinced. "You picked up a drifter? Gave him a thousand-dollar blanket?"

"We just weren't thinking," Ann says.

Richard looks skeptically at his keen-minded wife. In his opinion, Ann is always thinking. But Richard is equally pragmatic; it is one of the traits they value in each other. "Forget it, we can't do anything about that now. What else is there at Nirvana we should worry about?"

Ann is taken aback at the question. She thinks about the cleanup she and Sabrina did when they returned to rebury the body. Were they completely thorough? Were there any traces of that night, or Hughie, his clothes, his backpack, anything that would indicate that he had been there, danced with them, massaged them, flirted with each of them as if she were the most desirable. But that can't be what Richard is asking. He doesn't know Hughie was there. He must mean the marijuana. There's not that much. The FBI couldn't possibly care about a little weed.

"There's that small stash of pot. We used a bit," she confesses, although she doesn't reveal that they shared it with Hughie, that it heightened their senses, evoked a wildness in the Coven.

"You didn't mess around downstairs, did you? In my workroom?"

What was he talking about? Why would they go down there? Ann knows that Richard has a room downstairs where she assumes he keeps his files on the Northern California clients who meet with him at Nirvana. The room is always locked, and she has never been inside. She has always respected Richard's privacy; it is part of their deal. All couples have agreements, she guesses, written or unwritten. Her nonnegotiable demand, although never voiced, is her autonomy. She maintains her own career, her own friends, and is adamant about not being considered by anyone, including Richard, as just Mrs. Richard Salant. She remembers that Agent Curt called her Mrs. Salant and directed most of his comments to Richard. Did he do this to throw her off guard? Was he trying to undermine her sense of self so that she would be a less confident witness? He was a dangerously skillful man. If she has performed so badly, never even getting to tell her story, imagine how the others would do.

"We've got to drive up to Nirvana before they get the warrant," Richard says. "I've got to clean the place up. I need your help. We'll take the Jeep." He looks at his watch. "Get ready. We'll leave in thirty minutes."

Ann does not argue. She understands that Richard is talking about his basement office. He has something there that he does not want Agent Curt to find, and he is not going to tell her what it is, at least not yet. No matter; she is already carrying around enough secrets. She doesn't need the burden of Richard's as well. She thinks how far apart they've become, each in a private world of lies and evasions. Ann trudges wearily up the stairs. She feels as if her life is unraveling and she is helpless to stop it.

"Mom?" Ann hears Kim's throaty whisper as she passes her daughter's bedroom. She peers into the darkened room. "Come in," Kim urges. Ann has not been asked in there for a long time. Kim is fully dressed, under the covers, her cheeks wet with tears. She pulls Ann down next to her. "What did he do to you?"

"The detective? He was just asking some questions."

"No, Richard."

Ann hears the fear in her daughter's voice.

"He was yelling at you. I heard him," Kim says. "Did he hurt you?"

Ann is moved by her daughter's concern. "No, honey, he was just upset." She lays what she hopes is a reassuring hand on her daughter's shoulder.

Surprisingly, Kim moves into the embrace, burrowing her head against her mother's side. Ann is flooded by memories of how they were once so close, of the cherished bedtime ritual of hugs and butterfly kisses, the delicate brush of eyelashes on her cheek that Kim had devised. She remembers the dreamy replaying of Kim's day before she would drift off to sleep, the challenges of long division, the shifting barometer of friendships, tales of hope and desire and confusion. Ann recalls how Kim would turn to her for advice and comfort and how much she misses that time.

When did it shift? When did Kim stop confiding in her? Probably about the same time Kim became estranged from Richard. Had Ann sided with her husband against her own child? Not intentionally, she reflects, but she had defended Richard against Kim's accusations of arbitrary control. It seemed important to present a united front. And after all, she had married Richard as much for her daughter's future as for her own.

But now nestled against her daughter's side, she feels

close to tears herself. She takes a deep shuddering breath. Kim cuddles closer and pats her mother's back. After a few minutes, Ann's breathing steadies and Kim whispers, "Are you sure you're okay?"

"Positive." Ann sniffles.

"Then can I ask you something important?"

Ann tenses for the question.

Kim is silent for a long moment. Then she blurts, "Can cowboys really dance?"

"What?" Ann is bewildered.

"Or do they just throw the bull?" Kim smiles hopefully.

Kim has revived "silly joke time," the method that Ann had invented to cheer up an unhappy Kim. Ann remembers all the riddles and goofy rhymes she has concocted. But this time she is the recipient. She bursts out laughing and Kim joins in. It is the best moment they have experienced together in a long time.

Kim takes her mother's hand. "What really happened?" she asks. "You didn't tell Richard everything, I know you didn't. You can trust me. Tell me. Please."

Ann considers the request, sorely tempted. She longs to share with Kim what it's like to be a responsible wife and mother but still have occasional wild urges. She would like to tell her how older women still feel the need for adventure and sensuality and how they try to exercise that desire in ways that will not hurt themselves or their families. How can she explain the dynamic of four women together, their behavior going beyond what any of them would have done alone? It was not intended, and yet it was not entirely accidental, powerful feelings arising from primordial instincts.

She thinks of Hughie, the charming, mysterious stranger. She remembers his strong hands massaging her back and neck. She wanted that touch to continue. She imagines each of the Coven desired it as well, each in her own way. Four women performing a ritual competition for the attention of one man. He had danced discreetly with her. Wildly, with Sabrina. Romantically, with Deb. With Maria, like an old friend. For each of the women he became someone different, mirroring their desires.

Ann thinks her daughter might understand this. She is almost a woman now and knows about the bonds that women have with each other, the shared wisdom, but also the fierce competition for a man they desire. She would like to explore these feelings with Kim, to welcome her to the truths of womanhood. Above all, she would like her daughter's compassion, her reassurance that her mother's actions that night were understandable, forgivable.

But she feels it is both premature and unfair to unburden herself, and instead says, "Don't worry, sweetheart. It is all just a big mistake. Nothing is going to happen. We gave this guy a ride and dropped him off. Most likely someone in the campground, another drifter, killed him for his wallet and then got scared and tried to hide the body."

"But then why is Richard going to Nirvana tonight? I don't get it."

Ann tries to think of an appropriate response to this question. She can only speculate about what Richard is so desperate to clean up. His Mendocino investment dealings were always a mystery to her. The only in-dustries in that rugged, wild county are logging and marijuana, and she doubts the clients he brought to Nirvana were forestry executives. Only once did she ac-tually see a client, or someone she thought might be a client. A young guy with a ponytail arrived in a beat-up truck and spent several hours with Richard down-stairs in his basement office. When she asked about it, Richard said he was arranging for some work to be done on the property. Although Ann usually took care of hiring maintenance workers, she didn't question him further. But she never saw the young man again nor did Richard ever speak again of the work that needed to be done. And now she has learned from Curt that Hughie is a DEA agent.

That fact is just starting to sink in. Hughie's scruffy look meant he was undercover. But why would he pick up four older women and manipulate them to taking him to Nirvana? Was he just horny, or was there something else on his mind? If he were a drifter, a warm night in a fancy place with free booze made sense, but for a DEA agent, it didn't. Ann is too tired to try to think this through. Her usual logical reason-ing has deserted her. Secrets and lies. That's all there is now.

Ann rises from Kim's bed. "I think Richard is con-cerned about his property. He doesn't want the police to ransack it."

Even in the dark Ann can tell that this answer does not satisfy Kim, but the girl is silent. "'Night, my sweet," Ann says quickly, kissing her on the forehead. "We'll probably spend the night up there. Will you be okay on your own?"

"I'll be fine," Kim mumbles as she turns her face to the wall. "'Night, Mommy. Drive safe."

Ann has one final task before getting ready to leave with Richard. She turns on the computer in her office and brings up the e-mail address for the Coven, the group address for Sabrina, Maria and Deb. This is the address she has used to arrange their annual meetings, to decide who brings salad and who's in charge of dessert, all the details of shared friendship. Now she must send the message she has dreaded. In Maria's kitchen, she made the women agree that if any of them were approached about the incident, whether by a snoopy journalist or the police, they would alert the others but not meet or talk together. "Leave no trail," she had warned, drawing on her legal experience.

Slowly she types, "Double, double, toil and trouble." Will they pick up this message? Will they understand? Sabrina is a Luddite when it comes to computers; she hates e-mail. Most of the time Ann has to follow up by phone. She switches off the computer and heads for the bedroom to change clothes for the trip to Nirvana. As she is pulling on her pants, she hears the door close downstairs.

"Kim, is that you?" she calls out. There is no answer. She zips up her pants and rushes to her daughter's bedroom. The light is on, the bed is empty and two discarded black T-shirts are on the floor, one with the logo Suck You, the other decorated with indecipherable Gothic lettering. But Kim is gone.

Ann reaches for the phone and punches in Kim's cell-phone number. She gets Kim's recording and leaves a crisp message "Be home by midnight, young lady." Then softly adds, "Love you."

CHAPTER
EIGHT

Kim heads down to the garage. Richard's Mercedes and Ann's Jeep are parked there, but both are off-limits without permission. And tonight is not a night to "push the river." She climbs on her bike, presses the automatic garage-door button and speeds off.

Her destination is just minutes away. Chris's house, locally known as the Punk Pad. She remembers how cool she used to think it was. Chris's parents appeared only when it was time to deliver pizza and beer to the candlelit basement room. Anyone could stay the night, and many kids took advantage of that hospitality, particularly street punks with no other place to go. Chris had a mean temper though, and sometimes he'd drink too much and patrol the room with a broom, swatting at kids' heads until they left. Kim has never stayed all night. Her mother would freak out. It wasn't worth it.

Tonight she intends to stay for only a few minutes, just long enough to get the information she needs. The front door is unlocked as usual. She makes her way down the darkened steps to the basement. There are only a few kids in the room, and by their languid postures she can tell they're already stoned. No one greets her. She locates Chris in the half dark and sidles up to him. "Hey, pal. It's me. Kim."

"Long time no see, baby," he says, planting a smacking wet kiss on her lips.

Resisting the impulse to wipe it away, she forces a smile. "Been busy."

"Missed you." He wraps his arm around her waist. "Want to get high?"

"Not tonight," she says. "I can't. I'm on business."

"Oh yeah?" Chris asks, suddenly alert.

"I'm looking for Jerry Sanchez."

Chris looks at her blankly. "Who?"

"You know Jerry. Used to be a dealer. Used to be my boyfriend."

"Oh, yeah, 'the Dude.' Used to be very cool. Not so cool anymore." Chris wrinkles his nose in disdain. "He's got a job."

"What kind of job?"

Chris flashes a wicked half grin. "Hey, lady, you want fries with that?"

"Where?" she asks.

"In the mall. The Veggie Whopper."

"Thanks," she says, extricating herself from his grip.

Well, at least the restaurant is environmentally correct,

she thinks, picking her way among the languid teens, happily marooned in their own heads.

As Kim pedals toward the mall, her knees are shaking and her palms are wet. She and Jerry hadn't exactly parted on good terms. Richard had forbidden her to see him, said she was too young. But Kim had trouble believing that. Most girls had boyfriends by the time they were fifteen. And Jerry was a gentleman, not at all rough or pushy. But Richard had insisted, and when she disregarded his order, Jerry was ambushed in an alley and badly beaten.

Although the assault was never linked to Richard, Jerry broke up with her shortly after that. "I really love you," he said. "But you don't mess with The Boss." That had stuck with her even though she had tried to push it to the back of her mind. Although Jerry had never said explicitly, he gave her the impression that Richard wielded a lot of power, much more than just a protective father. She needs to know more about that connection. She feels it has something to do with her Mom's tears.

Kim stands outside the window at Veggie Whopper until she catches a glimpse of Jerry. He is not flipping burgers but manning the cash register. And he looks good, real good. People used to say he looked like Tom Cruise, but she could never see it. His eyes weren't blue. From this distance, she can't see his eyes, but she can see his sculpted muscles, his powerful neck, his clean-cut profile…actually, a lot like Tom Cruise. She stands there for a long time, afraid to go in. Then Jerry looks up and sees her standing there. He smiles at her with wide-eyed delight. Just like in *Top Gun,* Kim thinks, smiling back.

CHAPTER NINE

"If we make good time, we'll get there by one-thirty," Richard says as he drives quickly through the wet city streets toward the Golden Gate Bridge. He says nothing more and puts on a Willy Nelson CD.

Ann leans back in her seat, closes her eyes and pretends she is dozing. She thinks about their first trip to Nirvana together, more than ten years ago. They had been dating for only a few weeks, and Richard was doing his best to impress her. That day, she recalled, he played only opera on the drive up. They didn't talk much; Richard didn't like to talk when he drove. He had rested his hand on her knee, however, for most of the drive. Ann had never experienced such erotic feelings from a simple touch, even a prolonged one.

At the time, she'd wondered if it meant she was falling in love with Richard or if it was just that he knew more about women's sensuality than most men. She had almost suggested they drive off the road for a bit of quick love-making, recapturing teenage car-passion, steamy windows, elbows and knees against the dash. But dating was a power game, and Ann knew that her strength lay in Richard's desire for her. He held the cards in all other ways: money, status, self-assurance. If she let him know her sexual desire was equal to his, she might concede her advantage, make the game less interesting. Men still needed to pursue, to feel they were winning a coveted prize.

When she first saw Nirvana, the elegant, wildly beautiful house had frightened her. She had felt herself regress to the yearning ten-year-old from the bad part of town that she had once been, staring at the children in Upper Terrace, the best neighborhood in Tulsa. Every day she passed through Upper Terrace on her way to her grandmother's house where she stayed after school while her mother worked as a waitress. She thought of the children of Upper Terrace as being of a different species, like royalty in fairy tales. It was not just that the children in Upper Terrace had better bikes, or better clothes, but they seemed to Ann to have a sense of belonging, of entitlement that she could barely imagine. Once she saw a girl her age fall off a bike and three or four adults came rushing from neighboring homes to help her. Ann, if she were lucky, would be returning to an empty house. If she weren't, her father would be there, already halfway through his bottle of Jack Daniel's, in which case she would try to sneak quietly into her room and lock the door.

It was that first weekend at Nirvana that Ann decided she would marry Richard. She wandered through the spacious rooms, mesmerized by the wild sea pounding outside the windows. It was still clearly Richard's first wife's house; her imprint was everywhere, from the choice of gold-rimmed china to the pink Porthault blankets. And yet Ann felt she could live with that presence. She might never own Nirvana, but she could be its mistress. She made love to Richard that night, but it was Nirvana that enveloped her, welcomed her into its vast chambers.

Tonight is different. She pretends to still be dozing as they turn into the cypress-lined driveway. She does not feel the joyful anticipation that usually fills her when the headlights wash across the craggy exterior. In its place tonight is cold fear.

Richard stops the car and jostles her shoulder firmly. "Ann, we're here."

She pretends to come awake. "Okay," she says thickly. "I'm up."

"Good. I need your help," Richard says, his voice urgent. "We've got to get rid of the pot before Curt gets here."

Ann is perplexed. Is Richard talking about the little stash in the kitchen they sometimes enjoy before making love? Why would Curt care about that? She imagines most weekend cabins in Mendocino harbor a larger array of recreational drugs than that. Christ, most of California probably does.

"I think it's in the kitchen," she says dully. "Above the refrigerator."

"No, not that," he says impatiently. "I need your help getting rid of a great deal of pot. We'll have to burn it in the fireplace."

"What pot? What are you talking about?"

Richard reaches into the back seat, grabs a roll of black plastic trash bags and thrusts it into Ann's hands. "Take this. You'll need it to load the stuff." He reaches back again and pulls out a large can of lighter fluid.

"I'm not getting out of this car until you tell me what this is all about," Ann demands, although she's not sure she really wants to know.

Richard hesitates before opening the car door. "I didn't ask for your explanation, don't ask for mine. I'm trying to save both our asses."

"What do you mean? I have nothing to hide," Ann says in what she hopes is a convincing tone.

Richard glares at her. "God knows what you and your friends do when you're off together. What do you call yourselves, the Coven? An appropriate name, but did you have to mess around with a DEA agent?"

Ann is silent. There is nothing she can say that will make Richard believe a story that is, in fact, only partially true. It seems the whole truth is something neither of them is prepared to offer.

"But what are you doing with all that pot?" she persists.

He glares at her, his eyebrows raised in disbelief. "Come on now. Don't be naive. We haven't got time for this."

She feels a rush of anger toward Richard as she finally grasps what he's telling her. He has betrayed her. The ten years of respectability and wealth that he has offered her are a sham, based on lies and criminal behavior. He is no different than her father; a small-time con man who brought in occasional cash from shady deals. "Mrs. Richard Salant." What a joke. She has become a gangster's moll. If she had taken up hooking in Tulsa, an offer she had considered at seventeen to escape from home, she would be in about the same place now. She blinks hard to staunch the tears. The outline of the house shimmers and blurs. Nirvana is a mirage after all.

Richard comes around and pulls her out of the car. "Come on," he says, shaking her for the second time that night. "We have work to do and we've got to move fast. Do you understand me?"

They enter the house and head down to the basement. Richard unlocks the door to a small room behind a wine cellar that Ann didn't know existed. It is nearly filled with neatly stacked bundles of large-leafed grass bound in twine. The dry leaves give off a strong musty odor. Richard lifts one of the towering bundles and thrusts it at Ann.

"Stuff it in the garbage bag and don't spill the seeds on the floor," he orders.

In a short time, Ann is able to make three trips carrying the heavy bundles from the basement to the giant fireplace in the living room. Her legs are weary from the climb, and she feels light-headed. She is relieved when Richard announces that he'll get the rest and she is to watch the fire. He piles two bundles into the fireplace, pours the charcoal lighter fluid on top and strikes a match.

Orange tongues of fire leap from the hearth and attack the dry grass. Richard draws back quickly and shoves the fire screen in front of the opening. Just as quickly as the fire springs up, it subsides, the dried leaves burning into charred wisps. But the pungent odor of the burning grass invades the room, causing them both to gasp for air.

Richard hurries to open the glass doors as Ann throws open all the windows except for the largest, which is fixed and looks out at the sea. She grows dizzier as she works. Is it smoke inhalation, she wonders, or is she getting stoned? She decides the latter might be a blessing under the circumstances.

Richard shoves the remaining bundles into the fireplace. They burn less quickly, not accelerated by the lighter fluid. In spite of the damp night air rushing through the open windows, the sweet smoky smell of marijuana still dominates the room.

"I'll be back with the rest. Watch the fire," Richard barks.

Ann stares at the crackling flames. Her thoughts wander giddily. It's like burning dollar bills, perhaps hundred-dollar bills. How much have they destroyed? A thousand dollars? Ten thousand? A hundred thousand? Maybe they could start a new game show. Dialing for Drugs; guess the value of what you burn and win its weight in gold. Which would she choose? The money or the pot? She smiles broadly, realizing she is sliding into a decidedly altered state. Digging her fingernails into her palms, she fights for control. She must stay alert; she is in the middle of committing a crime. Make that another crime, she thinks. She is racking up quite a criminal record. Christ, she is turning into Lizzie Borden or Bonnie and Clyde, she giggles, corpses in the hot tub, a ransom in pot burning in the fireplace.

"Enough," Richard says sharply. "I think we've finished here. Go back and give the stairway and the storeroom a good sweep. Don't leave a trace."

Ann dutifully finds the broom and dustpan and sweeps her way down the staircase, step by step. By the time she gets to the small room where the marijuana has been kept, her head is clearer. She takes her time, teasing every seed and stray twig from the corners. When she returns to the living room, dustpan in hand, a sharp new acrid smell has replaced the sweet smoky odor of pot. Richard is feeding black floppy disks into the fire and dousing them with lighter fluid. They are melting into a puddle of black gel.

"I blew the brains out of the computer and now I'm frying these," he says by way of explanation, although Ann has not asked for one. "They won't vaporize, but no one will be able to read these fuckers," he says with a manic laugh. This does not sound at all like Richard. Ann guesses the pot has gotten to him, too.

They stand there quietly, watching the black ooze of what had been stored information bubble and spread. The room reeks of a mixture of acrid and undecipherable odors, overlaid by the sweet smell of dope.

"What about a steak fry?" Richard says, an almost merry twinkle in his eye. "I'm starving and it'll help to kill the odor."

Ann is glad to escape the smell and Richard. She fo-
cuses on finding the steaks in the freezer, buried under
piles of frozen packages. She identifies them by their big
blue stickers, each with a termination date, the tags a sou-
venir from her previously well-organized life. She pulls
them out from their frozen grave and thaws them briefly
in the microwave. When she returns to the living room,
the wet, bloody steaks on a platter, barbecue fork in hand,
Richard has opened a bottle of red wine. He passes her a
filled wineglass.

"To us, my dear," he says, touching her glass with his.
The crystal rings like a small bell. "We did it."

Did what? she thinks. He is clearly still stoned. All they
have done is incinerate tens of thousands of dollars' worth
of marijuana. The liquid black computer disks have
mostly vaporized; only a tarlike scum covers the bottom
of the fireplace. She watches as he grills the steaks. The
room now smells of meat, smoke, sweat and burnt plastic, but it has lost its hazy pot fragrance.

They eat their steaks in silence. The meat is thickly
charred on the outside, but tender and juicy inside. Ann
is surprised by her appetite. She hardly ever eats red meat,
but clearly this is a night for engaging in the unusual.

Morning light is beginning to filter through the open
windows as they finish their steaks and the last of the wine.
Ann feels her eyes grow heavy and fights to keep them
open. She must confront Richard and find out exactly
what's going on and what she has to do to protect herself and Kim, but she can't seem to stay awake. Fatigue
laced with pot, wine and a heavy meal are a soporific

combination. Her chin falls heavily on her chest. The next thing she knows, Richard is lifting her onto the couch. He gently places a pillow under her head and covers her with a blanket. She murmurs her gratitude and surrenders to sleep.

Ann drifts in and out of her dreams. They are the wild Technicolor visions she has not experienced since her heavier pot-smoking days with Steve. One particular dream seems to be a musical. The lead singer is a naked bloated corpse singing "Some Enchanted Evening" in a deep baritone. He is standing tall, gesturing broadly, his eyes sunken in his pale moon face. His limp penis swings merrily in rhythm to his movements. A chorus line, garbed in crisp police blues with polished gold badges, backs him up.

One tall black dancer-cum-policeman towers over the others. Ann recognizes Agent Curt. He is dancing the tango with the female lead who turns out to be Sabrina. Her signature black and silver locks are covered in billows of soapsuds. She is singing, "'I'm gonna wash that man right out of my hair'" in the throaty, slightly off-key manner that Ann knows well. At the end of each line, Sabrina grabs a handful of suds and flings them at the corpse. The suds land on various parts of his body, melting the flesh. The corpse screams in pain.

Ann muffles her own cry as she bolts awake. She rubs at her eyes trying to bring the room into focus. She hears the sound of a masculine throat clearing and turns to find Agent Curt standing in full daylight beside the couch on which she is lying.

"Good morning, Mrs. Salant. Didn't mean to startle you, but we've got some business to take care of."

Ann lies back and closes her eyes. This is another of those crazy dreams. She has to get some sleep; she needs her strength.

"Mrs. Salant," Agent Curt says more insistently. "Sorry to bother you so early, well, not so early, but we need your cooperation. These are my assistants, Agents Ramirez and Kelly."

Ann sits up. Richard is standing behind Curt, small and slight by comparison to the towering agent. He is flanked by a youngish man and woman in ordinary business clothes. It is not obvious which of them is Ramirez and which Kelly. They nod gravely. Curt also is dressed in a plain gray suit: no raincoat, no badge that she can see.

"Dear, these agents have a warrant," Richard says quickly. "I've promised them full cooperation. I explained to them that we drove up late last night to take advantage of a long-planned weekend."

His set smile and even tone signal her to back up the story.

She nods in agreement, then murmurs, "I need to use the bathroom."

"Of course, Mrs. Salant," Curt says. "But before you do, can you tell us where the key to the hot-tub cover is? I'd hate to damage the lock, such a nice piece of equipment."

"Just let me go to the bathroom," she says, and stumbles past the waiting group. The young agents watch her with narrowed eyes.

She shuts the bathroom door behind her and peers into

the mirror, examining her haggard face. She looks like hell, and there are no clean clothes or makeup in there. But she simply can't go out and face them again, not yet. She steps into the slate-tiled shower and stares out through the wide porthole at the ocean. By the look of the sun on the horizon, it must be nearly noon. She commands herself not to rush, she'll only make mistakes, and turns on the water for a long, slow shower.

Why are the police examining the hot tub? Ann wonders as the steamy shower water pummels her back. They must know something. When she and Sabrina had come up for the intended reburial, Sabrina swore she checked both the outside and the inside of the tub. Ann also reasoned that the elaborate continuous filter system and the chemicals that constantly fed through the tub, even when no one was there, would destroy any human traces.

Out of the shower, she puts on her rumpled clothing, still smelling of smoke, and combs her wet hair into some semblance of its usual sleek cap. Her face is red and shiny from the hot shower, and her eyes, pale without makeup, look small and frightened.

When she returns from the bathroom, Curt and his assistants are still in the living room. The younger man is scraping ashes and fragments of petrified black plastic into Ziploc bags while Curt and the young woman watch. Richard is sitting glumly on the sofa, as if he was already in custody.

"You guys sure had yourself some fire," Curt greets her with a chuckle. "I love barbecue. They used to call me Mr. Smoke when I played ball for USC. Not that I burned up the field, I was only middlin' fast. But afterward, at Delta Phi, I cooked up the best ribs those white boys ever 'et."

"Delta Phi" and "ever 'et," an odd juxtaposition, Ann thinks. Who is this Curt with his fabricated shuck and jive? Not just a foot soldier, but someone fairly high up. And no doubt he's a lawyer; most of the FBI are. She can't afford to make any mistakes.

"These bones look like great T-bone steaks, my favorite, except for baby back ribs, of course. But what's all this other stuff?" Curt lifts a poker and stabs at the solid black ooze lining the bottom of the fireplace.

Ann shrugs. The most important thing she has learned as a lawyer is when to keep your mouth shut. She learned that from her first boss at legal aid, Janet Brown. Janet had been a street policewoman who went to law school at night. She was tough talking, no-nonsense and highly respected. At legal aid, they didn't do hard criminal cases, but mostly landlord/tenant problems, employment disputes and a good deal of domestic violence. Janet's advice to clients and to her stable of young attorneys just out of law school was the same: don't offer information to the other side unless it's asked for. And when it is asked for, remember the Fifth Amendment. They have to make their case; you don't have to make it for them. This basic advice works well in Ann's current job as a software contract negotiator where clients were sometimes too eager to reveal potential bugs in their products.

"Well, I guess we've got enough to get started on," Curt says, pointing to the dozen or so Ziploc bags with different-colored ashes in them. He puts them all into a larger plastic bag and marks it "fireplace stuff." He turns to Ann. "Now, Mrs. Salant. I trust you remembered where the key to the hot-tub cover is? That's the last place we need to check. We've collected seeds and such from the stairs, and there's that big wreck of a computer with its brains blown out. I checked your pink blankets in the hall closet; we borrowed one of those, for a possible match. We'll be running some tests on it at the crime lab. But don't worry, we'll return it, although, you might want to send it back to Wing Lee's Elite Laundry before you use it again."

He holds out his hand for the hot-tub key. Ann walks to the audio/video center, a series of high-tech cabinets and speakers next to the terrace door, and produces a key ring laden with a dozen keys. "I think it's this one," she says as she separates a key from the pack but does not remove it from the ring. She knows it's not the right one, but figures it will take Curt a while to try them all. She needs that time alone with Richard.

All three agents march out onto the windy deck. Ramirez and Kelly bend over the hot-tub cover, their suit jackets flapping wildly, as they take turns trying the key. Curt positions himself so he can see Ann and Richard on the couch. They are clearly under surveillance.

As soon as the agents go outside, Richard seizes her hand and holds it tightly. "Sugar, we have to be honest with each other," he whispers. "We've got to present a united front."

"Sugar" is not a term Richard has used since their courtship. He is pulling out all the stops, Ann thinks. He is in battle mode. He knows he's outflanked and out-numbered. Time to rally the troops, and that means her.

"I'm sorry, Ann," he begins. "I never meant you to be involved in this. I've always tried to protect you."

"Protect me? By dealing drugs?"

His voice rises in anger. "None of this would have happened if you'd stayed out of that goddamn bar."

"Me?" she cries. "How is a roomful of pot my fault?"

He battles for control. "Never mind, we can't undo that now. I owe you the truth, so here it is. I was doing a favor for a client. His son-in-law is a small-scale pot farmer up the coast. The guy believed he was being watched by the DEA, and he needed someplace to store his crop until he figured out a safe way to get it out. The police were watching the local boats like a hawk. He was trying to find one they didn't know. He promised it would be no more than a month. I didn't want to do it, but my client insisted, and he is my biggest client. I figured the risk was small. No one would be watching Nirvana. I was wrong. Somehow they found out that the crop was here. That's why they set up the scam, sugar, so they could get a look in the house."

What is Richard talking about, Ann wonders. What scam? Does he believe there is no Hughie, or at least no dead Hughie? That must be it. He thinks the DEA and the FBI invented the murder just to be able to search the house. He believes Ann's story that they had dropped Hughie off at the campground and that the FBI has made up the rest.

Richard puts his arm around her shoulder and pulls her

closer. "Sugar, I'm so sorry that you got caught up in this little business mess. I know it'll all work out, as long as we can be a team. I called Sam Parker. He should be here any minute. He advised us not to say anything. Is that okay with you?"

Ann wishes her head were clearer. She wants to believe Richard, that this is just a small business favor gone wrong. She longs to return to the days when he called her sugar, and she admired and respected him. Even Kim liked him during those years. But what about the blown-out computer and all the disks he tried to burn? It just doesn't make sense.

"Saying nothing is fine with me," Ann answers truthfully. She allows herself the comfort of leaning back into Richard's arms, letting him stroke her back. She notices from the corner of her eye that Curt and his crew have figured out how to open the hot tub. They've removed the cover and pushed it to one side of the deck. Curt and the male agent, Ramirez or Kelly, are sitting on the edge of the sunken tub. Curt is fishing in the tub with the net they use to filter out leaves. The female agent is taking off her shoes. She turns around to discreetly slide down her panty hose.

My God, thinks Ann, she doesn't want to wait for it to drain. She's going in.

"Before Sam arrives," Richard continues, "is there anything more you want to tell me about that night? About picking up that guy? Anything at all that Sam should know about?"

This is the moment, Ann thinks. He's made his confession and she should make hers. After all, they're a team, aren't they? She weighs her answer; it would be a relief to tell Richard everything, to trust him to make things right. In many important ways he has protected her over the years; given her and Kim a secure haven. But her own hard-won survival strategy of making independent, judicious decisions is too strongly ingrained. She and Richard have entangled themselves in separate webs of lies and evasions. It is too late to join forces. She must save herself.

She smoothes the silver-gray hair at his temple, allowing her hand to rest there. "No, there's nothing."

As if on cue, the doorbell chimes. They both flinch. "Must be Parker," Richard murmurs. As he walks to the door, Ann sees Curt look up from the deck, monitoring Richard's movement. The female agent, Ann notes, has one bare foot over the edge of the hot tub. She can step onto the ledge inside the tub, Ann reasons, without totally immersing herself.

Richard returns with a man about his own age, but with none of his good looks and polish. Parker is short, balding and overweight. Although the day is cool and windy, he is as red-faced and breathless as if he were battling a heat wave.

Richard introduces them, and they shake hands, coolly appraising each other. Ann knows of Parker's reputation as a criminal defense attorney for country club scofflaws and Mafia types. She wonders what Richard has told him about her and the Coven's escapades. Parker looks at her with equal wariness. No doubt he can tell she isn't exactly ready to sign on to the team.

"Let me see the search warrant," Parker demands. For such a stocky man, his voice is surprisingly high and thin, almost a falsetto. Richard hands him the document.

"It says here they have the right to search the premises for any information regarding the presence of Agent Curran," Parker says. "Did they go down to the basement?"

He knows about the basement, Ann thinks. What else does he know? Probably a lot more than she does.

"Yeah, but they only found a few seeds and my burnt-out computer," Richard says with confidence. "I told you we cleaned out everything."

"Are you real sure about the computer?" Parker asks. "They can restore these fuckers now, they have special people who do that."

"It would take divine intervention to raise that computer from the dead," Richard says.

Parker looks skeptical. "You should have thrown it into the ocean and reported it stolen. What about the backup disks?"

Richard points at the black scum in the fireplace.

Parker walks to the fireplace, runs his finger over the black tarlike surface and smiles. "Where are the cops now?" he asks.

"Wading in the hot tub," Richard answers with a scowl. "They're going over the house with a magnifying glass."

"Well, of course," Parker says. "It's a goddamn fishing expedition. Isn't it?"

Ann realizes that Richard and his attorney still think that Curt is just looking for illegal drugs. If it were only that, she thinks. But she can still visualize the body floating in the hot tub, bloated, unearthly. She pictures the horrifying human remains that she and her friends had literally tried to bury. How could she have done something like that? She must have been mad.

Parker continues speaking to Richard in his high-pitched voice. "So they found a few seeds, so what? If the computer files are as dead as you say, I can't see that they've got anything important. If they do, I'll claim it's tainted evidence, that the warrant didn't include your files, so they can't be admitted. But I don't think it'll get to that." Parker's face grows redder and his sizable paunch heaves with the effort of his reasoning.

There must be a lot of evidence on the computer that Parker hopes is now dead, Ann thinks. The files seem far more important to him than the marijuana bonfire.

Just then Agent Curt opens the glass door and enters the living room. "Mrs. Salant, I'm sorry to inconvenience you, but Agent Ramirez has had a slight accident." He continues with a slightly embarrassed grin. "She fell into the hot tub."

So Ramirez is the female, Ann thinks as they all look through the glass doors. Agent Ramirez is standing shivering on the deck, pulling her dry suit jacket around her shoulders. Water drips from the hem of her skirt.

"Could we trouble you for a towel, and if you can spare it, a sweat suit or something?" Curt looks Ann up and down. "You two look about the same size." From Curt, the remark seems a purely professional observation.

"Certainly," Ann says, rising quickly. She is relieved to leave the smoky room filled with dangerous secrets and to play the familiar, comfortable role of hostess. She goes to the hall closet, pulls out a thick emerald-green beach towel and takes it out to the deck. Ramirez nods gratefully as Ann wraps it around her shoulders and leads the young woman to the bathroom where she instructs her on the use of the shower.

Ann then enters the huge walk-in closet, just off the master bedroom. One side is all open shelves and cubicles, the other reserved for hanging clothes. On the shelves, neatly folded, are dozens of sport-specific outfits: tennis shorts, golf skirts, biking shorts, riding pants. There is a shelf of jeans and one of sweat suits of myriad hues. At the far end of the shelves are several cubicles of lingerie and socks.

Considering Ramirez's dark hair and eyes, Ann decides powder blue would be good. She picks out the appropriate sweatpants and sweatshirt, adds a conservative pair of beige underpants and a pair of thin socks that can fit into the agent's pumps. She won't presume to offer a bra. She thinks about changing her own dirty, smoky clothes, but that would probably be noticed by the ever-vigilant Detective Curt. He might think she was destroying evidence. Would he ask her to bring him the clothes so he could put them in a tagged plastic bag? What would he write with his Magic Marker? "Suspected Murderer's Cover-up"?

She leaves the clothes for Ramirez outside the bathroom door and reluctantly returns to the living room. Parker and Curt have apparently been arguing over the search warrant during her mission of mercy. They are nearly nose-to-nose, or would be if Curt were not six inches taller.

Parker waves the piece of paper in agitation. "You can take your goddamn fishing expedition and shove it where the sun don't shine. Wait until a real judge throws out your so-called evidence and slaps sanctions on you besides. I'll make sure your bosses and the press hear about it, too. Mr. Salant has friends in very high places. You're taking on more than you can handle. This is the big time, my friend." His whine sputters to a stop.

For once, Curt is not sporting his half grin. His fists are clenched and his lips thin. Still he speaks in a calm low voice. "Don't threaten me," he says evenly, "or the only big time you'll be seeing will be in jail." Curt and Parker glare at each other for a moment, like two boys about to begin a schoolyard fight.

They hold the stalemate until Parker steps back. It is only a miniscule step, but it releases the tension. Curt brushes invisible dust from his hands and says, "I believe we've found something interesting." He carefully removes a shiny object from a Ziploc bag: a pair of glasses with steel frames. He turns toward Ann. His half smile returns. "Mrs. Salant," he says cheerfully, "perhaps you recognize these? After our intrepid Agent Ramirez sacrificed her dignity and a good suit, we decided it would be better to drain your hot tub. We retrieved these from their watery grave."

What watery grave? Ann thinks. Then it comes to her. She pictures Hughie as she last saw him alive. There he was in the hot tub, his longish hair dripping, slightly steamed glasses perched on the tip of his nose. The corpse wasn't wearing glasses; they must have slipped off. Yes, those are Hughie's distinctive Ben Franklin glasses. Her stomach clenches in fear. She can feel the sweat break out under her arms. The pink blanket can be explained. This cannot. She leans heavily upon the arm of the couch.

Damn! Sabrina had sworn she'd checked the hot tub. Just like Sabrina, careless and slipshod. Ann recalls their last meeting, Sabrina's hostility and meanness, blaming Ann for their predicament. She can feel righteous anger rising.

"Mrs. Salant, the glasses?" Curt continues.

"They're either mine or my husband's." She fights for calm, reaching out her hand for them.

"That's easily checked," Curt says, returning the glasses to the plastic bag. "They're prescription."

Richard and Parker stare at the glasses, not comprehending that the "fishing expedition" has found what it is looking for.

Ann feels sick to her stomach. She needs to get out of there; she needs to think. She turns to Richard. "Can we go home now?" she says, heading for the door.

"You go right ahead, Mrs. Salant. We'll lock up nice and tight. But remember to stay where you can be easily reached," Curt says. "We may have a few more questions for you...and your friends."

Richard rises and puts his hand on Ann's arm to stop her. "Dear," he says with bare civility, "we don't want to leave before the detectives. It wouldn't be polite."

She pushes his hand away. "I'll take the Jeep. You can

get a ride with your lawyer." She walks out the door as calmly as she can manage. She feels Curt's gaze burning into her back as she walks along the path to her Jeep. As she starts the engine, she wants nothing more than to drive south all the way to the Mexican border and disappear.

CHAPTER

TEN

Sabrina's rehearsal is going badly. If a production is an army, she thinks, then the director is the general. No, make that the dictator. She knows that any creative endeavor is fraught with peril, too many decisions and too little time. One has to be decisive, even arbitrary. Confidence is everything. After the mixed reviews on the brothel version of *Macbeth*, she should have chosen something simple. Why on earth, she wonders, has she picked *The Bacchae* for their next play? The parallels with the Nirvana weekend are frighteningly close, and her memories are besieging her. All she can think of is *Hamlet* and how the guilty Claudius is found out when he is shown a scene similar to the murder he has committed. But the Coven hasn't committed murder, she reasons. It was an accident, wasn't it?

"Sabrina, which one?" her lead actress shouts.

"Which...what?" she asks.

"Which take do you like better? Ironic or straight?"

Sabrina hasn't heard a word of the actress's speech, and there is no way to fake it with Jasmine. "So sorry, darling," she says. "I've got a raging headache. Let's take a break."

The actors disperse for their caffeine and nicotine fix. Sabrina reaches for her voluminous purse to extract her heavy-duty painkillers. She is digging into its dark interior, vowing once again to get organized, when her lighting designer and stage manager approaches. "There's someone to see you, Bri," Tony announces.

"You know I never see anyone when I'm working." Sabrina finds her pills.

Tony hands her some bottled water. "I know, but this guy's got a badge and he's been waiting for twenty minutes."

Sabrina swallows two pills and then another for good measure. "I'll see him in my office."

"He's already there. I gave him the newspaper and some coffee."

"Thanks, love." Sabrina smiles to ease Tony's concern. Thank God for theater people, she thinks. Quick instincts and tender hearts.

Sabrina makes a detour into the bathroom before entering her office. She stares into the pockmarked mirror willing herself into a state of calm. "You have nothing to hide," she whispers. She remembers her acting coach's chief axiom, "Do the act and the feeling will follow." Emotion doesn't have to begin from inside; it can be evoked by taking the proper stance. Courting confidence, she relaxes her shoulders, quiets her breathing and enters her office.

"Rod Curt, Mrs. Berman," the man says, standing as she enters. He is forty-something. A Harry Belafonte type, same café au lait skin, same leonine grace but tougher. A lot tougher. This guy is not about to sing *Day-o.* He dwarfs the small office, his bulk ludicrous next to Sabrina's dainty red velvet settee. He flicks open his black leather wallet and flashes an FBI badge. Sabrina feels her stomach flip. This is serious business. Hughie was a drifter. Why should the FBI care?

Curt answers her unspoken question. "You probably want to know what this is all about, Mrs. Berman," he says.

"Well, yes, Officer, but I'm in rehearsal. I wonder if we could do this later?"

"Afraid not, Mrs. Berman."

This "Mrs. Berman" stuff is unnerving her. "Call me Sabrina."

He nods but ignores the suggestion. "You see, there's been a murder, Mrs. Berman."

"A murder! Who?"

"A man identified as Dennis Curran," he says.

Sabrina is relieved to be able to tell the truth. "Sorry. I don't know anyone by that name." She longs for a drink, though, something to hold in her hand. There is a bottle of white wine in the tiny refrigerator. Better not, she thinks.

"His body was found wrapped in a pink blanket on the old logging road on the Mendocino coast."

"Really?" Her voice is low, controlled.

"Really, Mrs. Berman, and I believe you and your friends were the last people to see him alive."

"I have no idea what you're talking about," Sabrina says, reminding herself to breathe, deeply and slowly.

"There are eyewitnesses that place you at the Last Roundup, so let's cut to the chase here, shall we? I've already met with your friend Ann—Mrs. Salant, that is. The blanket the body was wrapped in has been traced to her."

"Blanket?" Sabrina muses, as if just summoning memory. "Oh, it must have been the one we gave to that drifter. It was raining. We gave the guy a lift, took pity on him and gave him the extra blanket from Ann's trunk. It was a Porthault cashmere. Imagine keeping a blanket like that in the trunk of your car. Some people just have too much money." She tries for lightness but Curt isn't laughing. "We gave him the blanket," she adds hurriedly, "and then we dropped him off at the campsite."

"Was he wearing glasses, Mrs. Berman?"

Sabrina takes a moment. She remembers Ann's admonition not to offer any information. "I'm sorry. I can't remember."

"Let me help you." Curt pulls out a plastic evidence bag from his jacket pocket. He carefully extracts a pair of wire-framed Ben Franklin glasses. "These look familiar?"

"Not really," she says.

"We found them this morning in the bottom of your friend's hot tub."

The police searched the hot tub? Why didn't Ann tell her? Why didn't she call? Trying to save her own neck, that's why. Sabrina goes to the refrigerator and pours herself a glass of wine. She needs it. Damn appearances. She takes a quick slug.

Curt watches her, then, "More news, Mrs. Berman. These glasses match Dennis Curran's prescription."

"Dennis?" she says. "He told us his name was Hughie."

"It's to correct a very rare astigmatism. Seen in only one percent of the population," Curt continues.

"Why would you know the eye prescription of a drifter?" Sabrina asks.

"Because he wasn't a drifter."

"Then what was he?"

"A DEA agent, Sabrina." He pronounces her first name quickly, loudly, like a threat. "A former agent, that is. He was on probation, trying to get reinstated. Working as a freelancer."

"But h-he never said," she stammers.

"No, he wouldn't have. He was undercover."

"Doing what?" Sabrina stares into the empty glass. She has drunk the wine as if it were water. That and the pills are making the room spin. She sits down heavily on the velvet sofa.

"His job, Sabrina."

There is a knock on the door. It's Tony. "Ten minutes are up, Bri. We're waiting."

"I've got to get back to work," she says, rising.

Curt places his hands firmly on her shoulders, guiding her back down to the sofa. "I suggest we finish our business first." He looks deadly serious. "You and your friends are in big trouble, Sabrina." This time he sounds her name like the hiss of a cobra. "We have enough evidence to lock you up for the rest of your lives."

She quickly weighs her alternatives. Should she insist on calling her attorney or should she try to play it cool, for at least a little longer? She decides on the latter, forces herself to speak calmly as she calls to Tony, assuring him that everything is fine. "That's it for today," she tells him. "We'll begin at the top of act two tomorrow." She adds in a firm voice, "Make sure everyone is off book."

Agent Curt takes the chair opposite Sabrina. His tone is once more disarmingly light. "Amazes me how you theater folk memorize all those lines. Get them letter perfect every time. What's the secret?"

"It's all about context. You tie the speeches into motivation," she explains, "into what your character wants. Then they're easy to remember."

"Just like in real life," he says, relaxing back into his chair. "Mind if I smoke?"

"Not at all," she says. "I used to smoke myself."

Curt taps out a filter tip from a nearly full pack and lights up. He drops the rest of the pack into the trash can. "I admit it's wasteful," he offers with a reluctant shrug, "but it's the only way I can keep it down. Three cigarettes a day is my limit."

"I admire your discipline, Agent Curt," Sabrina says.

"And I yours. Acting, that is," he clarifies. He lights a cigarette, inhales deeply. "So tell me, how do you think

Agent Curran's glasses wound up taking a dive in your friend's hot tub?"

"I have no idea," Sabrina says. "Would you like a glass of wine?"

"Can't drink on duty," Curt says, "but you go right ahead."

"I rarely drink myself, but..." Sabrina says, pouring herself another glass.

"But a visit from the law can put anyone on edge," Curt exhales companionably. "So how about telling me the whole story from the beginning?"

"What beginning?" she asks.

"When you ladies first met Agent Curran?" He settles back in his chair, pen and notebook at the ready.

Sabrina repeats the story that the Coven has prepared; the drinking, dancing and flirtation at the Last Roundup; Deb's offering Hughie a ride to his campsite; the rain. Then taking pity upon him, giving him Ann's pink blanket.

"And then?" Officer Curt asks. Sabrina's thoughts race frantically. How the hell did those glasses get into the hot tub? What if the whole thing is a frame-up? What if those aren't Curran's glasses at all? But, she reasons, that FBI badge is legit. And something about Curt's self-assurance tells her he has the goods, that it would be foolish to stick to the prepared story. The investigation has moved beyond it. Curt knows that Hughie was at Nirvana. He has the glasses. And under his questioning, Ann must have admitted as much already.

Curt meets her gaze levelly. "If you're wondering

whether your friend has already told me her version of the story, she has, including how those glasses got into the hot tub."

Damn! Why didn't Ann stick to the story they'd agreed on? Why didn't she stonewall Curt, claim ignorance about the glasses? Because she was trying to save her own neck, Sabrina thinks bitterly. Then a charitable thought intervenes. Or maybe...just maybe...it was damage control. Ann is a lawyer after all. They hadn't gotten to rehearse that part in Maria's kitchen. But Ann had said, as they parted, that if something went terribly wrong and all else failed, just say they found him dead in the tub that morning. Say that he must have died of natural causes.

It'll be better if both their accounts of the evening are the same, Sabrina quickly reasons. She decides to tell Curt what happened, or most of what happened.

"Okay," Sabrina says with a deep sigh, grateful to release the burden of deception. "I'll tell you everything." She proceeds to describe how they couldn't bear to leave Curran at a deserted campsite in the cold and driving rain. Instead, they decided to bring him back to Nirvana for a few hours until the storm cleared.

"We probably shouldn't have done it," she says. "But it felt perfectly safe. After all, there were four of us and only one of him."

"He probably thought it was his lucky night," Curt says.

"He was happy enough and it turned out so were we. He had an unexpected talent."

"And what was that?" Curt asks.

"He was a certified masseur."

"No kidding? Didn't include it on his CV."

"He gave us each a massage. We soaked in the hot tub until it was our turn. It was perfectly legit. Just a massage." This isn't that hard, Sabrina thinks. The successful lie sticks close to the truth.

"And then?" Curt asks.

"It was still raining. Even harder. So we decided to let him sleep on the couch, and we all went to bed."

"Then what happened?" Curt prods.

"That's the awful part." Sabrina reaches for the bottle and pours the last inch of wine into her glass. She can feel her eyes fill with tears, not all feigned. "When we got up the next morning, Hughie was floating in the hot tub, facedown. Dead." She rises to get a tissue, blows her nose, dabs at her eyes. "We were horrified."

"I'm sure you were. But there was a working phone, right? Did you call the police?"

"That was our first impulse, believe me," Sabrina says. "As soon as we stopped screaming. None of us had ever seen a dead body before. But then..."

"Then what?" he asks.

"We knew we couldn't."

"And why was that?" Curt looks longingly at his discarded cigarette pack. This slow spinning of the story may be as trying for him as it is for her, Sabrina reflects.

"We were afraid, Rod," Sabrina says, deciding to go for the familiar. "After all, we're respectable wives and mothers. What would our husbands think? Our children? Our community? What were we doing letting a strange man in the house?"

"Alive or dead," Curt adds.

"That's right," Sabrina says. "I wasn't really worried about myself because Charlie, my husband, and I trust each other. Completely. But Ann's husband, I hate to divulge this, but under the circumstances I guess I have to, Richard is insanely jealous and has a violent temper. And our other friend, Deb, her marriage is very rocky. This was not the time to take chances."

"So you decided to dispose of the body," Curt says.

"We decided to bury him. That was going to happen, sooner or later, anyway."

"The law demands you report a death...accidental or not."

"We were going to, Rod. Believe me we were. But have you ever tried to get four women to agree on the best way to do something? It's very hard."

"I'm sure it is," he agrees amiably. "But this time it's going to be easier. I suggest you call your lawyer and don't plan on leaving town. We'll be coming by within an hour with an arrest warrant to pick up you and your friends."

"Arrest warrant? Why?" Sabrina cries.

"For murder in the first degree." Curt rises, fishes a cigarette out of his discarded pack, shakes his head in a "see what you make me do" manner. He lights the cigarette, takes a deep drag. He stands in the doorway for a moment. "Don't do anything foolish," he warns before he leaves.

Sabrina sits frozen in her chair watching the minute hand sweep around the face of her dressing-room clock. If only she could move it backward. How did she ever get into this? Because of Ann. Sabrina replays that morning at Nirvana. She had wanted to call the police. It was Ann who insisted that they bury the body. Ann was sure she could maneuver her way out of anything. So devious, Sabrina thinks, so self-serving. It's all Ann's fault.

Sabrina lifts the phone and punches in the familiar number. Ann picks up on the first ring.

"Thank God," Ann says. "I was hoping it was you. I have something important to tell you."

"I'll bet you do," Sabrina counters.

Ann rushes ahead. "They found the glasses."

"I know," Sabrina says. "Curt was just here. Why didn't you call me?"

"I've been trying to reach you for hours. Why don't you pick up your goddamn messages?"

Sabrina glances down at the answering machine. It shows ten messages. "I was in rehearsal," she retorts angrily. "Now it's my fault?"

"Just calm down. It's no one's fault. They drained the hot tub and found the goddamn glasses. It was an oversight, that's all."

"An oversight." Sabrina's voice grows shrill. "The oversight was not reporting a dead body to the police."

"The oversight—" Ann's voice is chilly "—was not finding the glasses. That was *your* job, Sabrina. You were supposed to check the hot tub, remember?"

"I did check it," Sabrina declares.

"Sure," Ann says, "some of it. But not all of it. What about the bottom? You could have found those glasses as easily as Curt. But no, you are always in such a goddamn hurry. You are so sloppy, never think anything through. You may have gotten away with it before, but this time it's going to cost. Big time."

Sabrina is awash with emotions. Angry and defensive at Ann's diatribe. Miserable and guilty as charged. She struggles for calm, for equanimity. She and Ann have clashed this way before. It is the natural difference between an artistic and a analytic temperament. It is time to rise above it, to be conciliatory. She remembers the words of Martin Luther King: *You cannot cure anger with more anger; only love can stop anger.*

"I'm so sorry, Annie," she says. "It's my fault. I should have looked more carefully."

Ann's voice drops a decibel level. "It's okay. We were both upset. The important thing is how we handle it now."

Sabrina is puzzled. "What do you mean? Handle it? It's over."

"What's over?" Ann demands.

"I told the truth. At least most of it." Sabrina says.

"What?" Ann shouts.

"Well, what else could I do? He was holding the goddamn glasses!"

"Just what did you tell him, Sabrina?" Ann's voice is venomous.

Sabrina repeats verbatim what she told Curt, the discovery of the body floating in the hot tub, the hasty burial.

"Oh, my God. He didn't know any of that. All he knew was that the glasses were the same prescription as Hughie's. They could have been anyone's."

"But..." Sabrina sputters.

"But nothing. We agreed that none of us would talk without the others."

"I thought you had talked already," Sabrina says weakly.

"You didn't think. You panicked. What a stupid thing to do!"

"Don't call me stupid." Sabrina's voice breaks. "You were the one who insisted on breaking the law. If we hadn't buried that body, none of this would have ever happened."

"Who got us to go to the Last Roundup in the first place? Who agreed to give that guy a ride? Who likes to play around, Sabrina?"

Sabrina collapses onto her settee. Was this the price she was going to pay for kicking up her heels, for wanting to bring some fun and adventure into the lives of her friends? Was this the price of wanting a bit of drama, a few moments of surprise? Of wanting to feel young and attractive again? Sabrina pulls her scarlet pashmina shawl over her head. It is the softest, finest wool, outrageously expensive, a gift from Ann for her last birthday. Her voice is muffled. "We're in big trouble, aren't we?"

"The biggest," Ann says.

"What are we going to do?" Sabrina asks.

"We? There's no 'we' right now. There's you and there's me. And you will now call Deb and Maria and tell them what you've done. Tell them the police are coming to arrest them because you can't keep your big mouth shut."

"Goddammit, Ann! I said I was sorry. I don't know my way around the police. I was scared."

"I'm not interested in your excuses. Just make those calls and make them fast." Ann slams down the phone.

Sabrina sits with the dead receiver in her hand. Her mind fills with fearful images of her family's shock, the community's censure, a life in prison. But the strongest sensation, to her surprise, is an enormous sense of emptiness. This time she is sure the breach is irremediable. She has lost her best friend.

CHAPTER ELEVEN

"You have the right to remain silent. Anything you say may be used against you." True to his word, Curt sent the squad car for her within an hour, and Sabrina now stands in line with two prostitutes and a drunk driver as she is read her Miranda rights at the San Francisco County Jail. She is booked, fingerprinted and given a number to hold as she is photographed front face and in profile. She attempts a feeble joke with the stern deputy. "Can't I just use my VISA number? I've memorized that one." The officer gives her a blank stare and leads her to a large holding room, its green walls peeling paint and sporting a dozen Most Wanted posters.

Sabrina has tried to alert Deb and Maria, but they were already in custody. The police must have been staked outside their homes, she reasons. How long have they been suspects, she wonders. The grim-faced officer ushers in the rest of the Coven and positions himself at the door. Deb and Maria each greet her with a hug. Ann maintains a chilly distance. Each is dressed true to form. There was no time to change. Deb is wearing her gardening overalls; Maria is wrapped in a colorful Guatemalan poncho; Ann is elegant in a silk business suit. Sabrina realizes she is still in her rehearsal clothes, a black leotard that fit fifteen pounds ago.

Why didn't I change? she thinks. What if there are photographers? She quickly chides herself on her vanity. Here she is facing a life behind bars, and all she's thinking about are her thighs. Where's Charlie? She needs Charlie. He must be waiting outside by now. She called his office, told Rose, his dental tech, to have Charlie meet her at 960 Brannan Street. She neglected to add that it was the central police station.

"What did you tell Donald?" Sabrina asks Deb. She realizes she is as concerned about Deb's faltering marriage as she is about her own situation. She and Charlie have worked their way through twenty years of major and minor crises; they'll get through this one. At least she hopes they will, and without too much scar tissue.

"Donald is away on a business trip," Deb says. "He doesn't get back until tomorrow."

"That's a break," Maria says. "What about the boys?" They are all protective of Deb.

"The sitter can stay the night, and my mom promised to drive the boys to school tomorrow—" Deb's voice wavers "—if I don't come home."

Maria turns to Ann. "What about Richard?"

"He's out front trying to buy off the press," Ann says.

"What press?" Sabrina asks.

Ann pointedly ignores Sabrina, addressing her answer to the other women. "When they came to get me, there was a *Chronicle* photographer on my front lawn."

"Front page or society?" Sabrina snipes.

The two women glare at each other.

"Hey you two, cut it out," Maria says. "We need to be a team."

"It was humiliating," Ann says. "A squad car and hand-cuffs."

"Why did they need handcuffs?" Sabrina asks.

"Because Richard slammed the front door on them when I was leaving through the back. The police thought I was trying to escape...but I was just trying to get away from the press."

"I know," Deb says. "They came for me with sirens howling. The whole neighborhood was watching. And Danny's school bus was just pulling in."

Maria commiserates, and then adds, "Didn't cause a rip-ple in my 'hood, someone's always getting arrested."

"It's completely unreal," Sabrina says. "I can't believe we're here."

"We wouldn't be, if not for you, Miss Drama Queen," Ann hisses. "I thought we had agreed on what happened."

"Never mind," Maria whispers sternly, eyeing the of-ficer at the door. "We were all part of it then. We're all part of it now."

Grateful for Maria's intervention, Sabrina holds out her hand in truce. Although Ann refuses to take it, she does nod in grudging acquiescence and turns her attention toward the policeman.

Coolly, Ann checks the man's badge. "Officer...Rooney, if you're finished, I'd like to get us out of here as soon as possible."

"Well, ma'am. I certainly understand that. Nobody likes being in a police station."

"Especially when we've done nothing wrong. We have families and jobs to get back to, Officer. So if you'll excuse me, I'm going to see about setting bail." Ann starts walking to the door.

For a pudgy sixty-year-old, Rooney moves fast. He crosses the room and bars the door. "Sorry, ma'am, but I suggest you talk to your lawyer."

Ann straightens her shoulders, sets her jaw. "I *am* a lawyer."

"A software tax lawyer," Sabrina amends.

"I've handled criminal cases," Ann declares.

"We need someone from outside," Sabrina says, her voice rising. "Someone who can represent us all. *Impartially.*"

"I resent that," Ann snaps.

"Why don't I leave you ladies to talk it over. I'll be right outside." The door shuts behind Rooney with the finality of a coffin lid.

There is a long moment of silence as the women look around the room, at the ceiling, the floor. Anywhere but at each other, Sabrina notes. The last time the four were together, it was Deb who saved the day, stopping Ann and Sabrina's vicious fight. This time it is Maria.

"Now, Ann," Maria says softly, "that is a very generous

offer, and we thank you for it. But you know it wouldn't be in your best interests. I've got another suggestion. Someone I think you'll approve of."

"Who?" Ann demands.

"Gloria Okimoto."

"I know that name," Ann muses. "But from where?"

"She knows you, too," Maria says. "She was one year behind you at law school."

"Oh, right," Ann recalls. "A bleeding-heart liberal with a great sense of style. A true oxymoron."

"It's easier for Asian women," Deb reflects. "Their coloring is dramatic, they're naturally small-boned, and it's impossible for them to get a bad haircut."

"Excuse me, darlin'." Maria puts a hand on Deb's shoulder. "Let's do *Vogue* later."

"Sorry," Deb says.

"Gloria's certainly smart," Ann admits. "But why do you think she's right for us?"

"She's fierce on women's issues. Her firm won the class action suit against Dow Chemical on silicone implants."

Ann is impressed. "That *was* a big case. Why would she want to take ours?"

"Because Gloria and I are friends. We go way back. We're used to doing favors for each other."

"How do you know her?" Sabrina asks.

"We'll talk about it some other time," Maria says, softening the deflection with a smile.

Sabrina lets it go. Just another little Maria mystery. She reflects that there's actually quite a bit of her friend's history that is veiled, more so than with the other women.

But the agreement of the Coven is not to probe. Each woman offers what and when she wishes, and of course nothing shared in confidence is ever to be revealed. And yet, Sabrina thinks, for all their assumed closeness, each behaved very differently that night at Nirvana, just as each is behaving very differently now.

Deb, whom Sabrina believed was the weak link, is holding up surprisingly well, probably summoning her marine father's credo: Never complain, never explain. Ann, whom Sabrina thought she could always count on, has turned against her. It is only Maria who remains her old dependable self, levelheaded and compassionate. And yet, wasn't it Maria's actions that night that had brought them to this terrible time? The women have pointedly never discussed it.

"So what do you say, ladies?" Maria asks. "Shall we go with Gloria? All those in favor?"

Deb's hand raises first, then Sabrina's, then reluctantly Ann's. "All right, but I'm still going to be very involved," Ann says, glaring at Sabrina. "You can't trust anyone these days."

"Great," Maria says, checking her watch, "Gloria should be here by now."

"When did you call her?" Deb asks.

"As soon as they arrested me," Maria says.

"Wasn't that a bit premature?" Ann asks.

Maria shrugs. "It sure saved time."

Maria raps on the door and Rooney returns. The four women leave the darkened holding room for the glaring lights of the main station. Amidst the throng of cops and other felons being booked, Sabrina spots Charlie. He is standing in a corner in deep conversation with Richard. Charlie is mostly listening and nodding as Richard gesticulates wildly. Charlie spots her and leaves Richard in midsentence. He races to Sabrina's side and hugs her hard. His familiar form, his sweet round belly fitting against her hips, his aftershave, the same one he's used since college, make her knees weak. "Take me home, Charlie," she whispers.

Leaning against him, Sabrina wonders why she ever wanted to be a "liberated" woman. What was so great about freedom and independence? If she didn't want to be taken care of, why get married? All this hype about risk taking is fine when nothing bad happens. But when disaster strikes...what then? Who was it who said, "Most of our troubles come from not being able to sit quietly in a room?" She would give anything to be sitting quietly in her own living room. Her own safe haven, her own cherished family. It is then that Sabrina sees Tamar. She is standing in the doorway with Ann's daughter, Kim.

What are the girls doing here? For God's sake, this is no place for children. And imagine, seeing their mothers, arrested. Their mothers, supposed pillars of virtue, alleged sources of all nurturing, their mothers whose heinous misdeeds will be revealed imminently. Next stop, "The Jerry Springer Show." The Coven will be sitting on a soundstage opposite their devastated husbands and children. "You ruined my life," the daughters will cry. "I'm an unwed mother on crack cocaine now."

"Tamar," Sabrina calls, and her daughter anxiously hurries to her side.

She takes her mother's hand. "Are you okay?"

"I'm so sorry, sweetie."

"Did you really do it?"

"Do what?"

"Kill him?"

Sabrina is astonished. "Do you think I could kill someone?"

"Well," Tamar reflects, "there were four of you."

"Of course we didn't," Sabrina declares.

Tamar shrugs. "I just know what I read in the papers, Mom."

"You watch too much TV." Charlie raps his daughter lightly on the head. "Your mother is innocent, and we're going to get her out of here as fast as we can." He signals to a beautiful Japanese woman who is standing nearby. Sabrina doesn't know many designers, but she recognizes the gold buttons and braiding of Chanel anywhere. The tailoring is as streamlined and distinctive as the Concorde and shows off Gloria Okimoto's slender, toned body to subtle perfection.

As Gloria heads her way, Sabrina notices Richard greeting Ann. He murmurs something but does not embrace her. Even Kim keeps a formal distance. Sabrina is grateful for the closeness of her own family and feels a twinge of pity for Ann's isolation. She notices that Maria has her hand upon Deb's shoulder. Everyone has someone to comfort them except for Ann, Sabrina thinks. Her heart goes out to her estranged friend but she takes no action. Let Ann make the first move.

The women repair to the holding room to meet briefly

with Gloria, who in her own soft-spoken way is as incisive and no-nonsense as Ann. "So, ladies," she says, "are you all agreed that I will represent you?"

The women nod.

"Please say yes in turn, giving your name." Gloria whips out a tiny state-of-the-art tape recorder.

They each do. Gloria rapidly gives her dossier, outlines her regular fee, and while Sabrina is figuring that she will have to mortgage her house to pay it, Gloria adds that she is taking the case pro bono. Why? As a favor to Maria. Again Sabrina wonders what that debt of kindness was occasioned by. No doubt, something big.

"Okay, ladies, here's my advice. Don't ask and don't tell. When they question you, take the Fifth, and wait until I'm with you before saying anything." Gloria Okimoto flips open her Gucci briefcase, slips the tape recorder inside. "Have a good night," she says and heads for the door.

"Just a minute," Deb cries. "What about us?"

"I'll have you out by tomorrow," Gloria assures.

"You mean we're going to spend the night in jail?" Sabrina asks, horrified.

"It's too late to have you arraigned tonight. I'll schedule your appearances in court first thing tomorrow."

"And then?" Sabrina's voice is tight with fear.

Gloria's voice is reassuringly confident. "We set bail, and you go home." She smiles at the women. "And, ladies, I've gotten a special dispensation. You'll all be in the same cell." Gloria turns and heads out the door. Her stiletto heels tap out an enigmatic Morse code as she walks down the tiled hallway and into the night.

CHAPTER
TWELVE

This is just like the movies, Sabrina thinks, when minutes later she is led into a small room and told to strip to her underwear and remove all jewelry. She stands barefoot and shivering on the cold tile. Taking off her wristwatch and silver hoop earrings, she hands them to the deputy who places them in a manila envelope. The deputy's name badge reads Delores O'Hearn. She holds out her hand. "The ring," she says.

"What ring?" Sabrina asks.

"The one on your *finger*," the woman drawls, the subtext being "duh."

"My wedding ring? Why?"

"Them's the rules," Delores says.

"But I never take it off," she protests.

"You want me to do it?"

"Do you think I'll hammer it into a knife? Trade it as

a bribe? Swallow it to commit suicide?" Sabrina's voice is careening out of control.

"You need a sedative or something?" Delores asks.

"No drugs," Sabrina says as she struggles to pull the ring off her finger.

Delores hands her a bit of soap. It smells like lye. Sabrina rubs it on her finger, and her wedding ring slides off. She holds the small circle of gold in her hand, reading the inscription carved on the inside: More than yesterday. Less than tomorrow. Charlie has one just like it. They'd bought those rings twenty years ago from a distant cousin of hers, a Hassidic jeweler, who had escaped the Holocaust. Charlie had chosen the saying and the jeweler had carved it in Hebrew.

Placing the ring in the deputy's palm, Sabrina feels violated and helpless. She puts on the baggy orange prison pajamas she is handed, slips her feet into oversize canvas shoes. She forfeits her purse and is given a toothbrush, a tiny tube of toothpaste, a bar of the same strong soap and a rough towel. Delores leads her down the long echoing hall. The light is harsh, the walls damp and gray. Sabrina passes barred cells filled with women lying on their bunks, staring blankly at the walls. A few jeer at her.

Finally they reach the end cell. Delores extracts a key from the dozens dangling around her waist and opens the heavy metal door. She turns on the single overhead light. It illuminates the four stacked bunks, the open toilet and rusty sink. The cell is empty; Sabrina is the first to arrive. She sits upon the lower bunk. The smell. The bed. Somehow this is familiar. Then the memory comes flooding back. Summer camp. But summer camp from hell. The worn bedsprings sag under her weight. The mattress is lumpy. The blanket is rough. The air smells of cabbage and urine. Out of the corner of her eye she sees something scurry. A dust ball? A cockroach? Oh, God, not a rat.

Get me out of here. I'll turn stoolie. I'll squeal, Sabrina's thoughts rage. Out loud all she does is whisper, "Where are the others?"

"I'm going to get them right now," Delores says and clangs the door shut.

In a few minutes the others appear, walking in a single line, each escorted by a deputy, each in matching orange pajamas.

The barred door is opened and the women enter, one by one. First Deb, looking like a lost child, in her overly large prison uniform. Then Maria, relaxed and confident, as if the pajamas were her routine leisure wear. And lastly Ann, who somehow has managed to find a good fit and looks defiantly chic.

The women settle in. Ann clambers agilely to one of the upper bunks. Sabrina takes the lower. Deb offers Maria the remaining lower bunk, but Maria adamantly refuses and grunting a bit with the effort, slowly climbs to the other upper bunk.

The women pound their pillows, shake out their blankets, groan about the thin lumpy mattresses. Deb examines the plumbing. "Oh, no," she says, jiggling the handle of the toilet, "it won't flush. And of course there's no cover."

"Now you know why I'm up here," Maria says.

"What time is it?" Ann asks.

There is no clock. Their watches have been taken from them. No windows either.

"Must be dinnertime," Sabrina says. "Let's send out for pizza." They all attempt a smile. Even Ann, Sabrina is relieved to see.

"It's a blessing there's no fridge," Deb says. "Otherwise, I'd be pigging out. I always eat when I'm anxious."

"Me, too," Ann agrees. "I just shovel it in. Fat, sugar and salt. When I was a kid, my favorite snack was a chocolate malted and a thick pretzel. I'd time it so the last taste was a swallow of chocolate through salty lips."

"Talk about salty lips," says Sabrina, "that's what got us in here in the first place."

"Margaritas *grandes*," Maria says. "*Mucho* tequila."

"Shh," Ann cautions. She points to the ceiling, to several plastic spheres. The women fall silent. Of course, Sabrina thinks, that's why the police have agreed to put them all in one cell. They're counting on the women revealing themselves. But they won't, not with Ann's vigilance. Once again Sabrina feels grateful for Ann's legal mind, her ever-ready paranoia. Even if the cell isn't being bugged, there's nothing to be gained in going over the horrors of that weekend again. And if they are being bugged, nothing must be revealed until Gloria sanitizes it.

"So what are we going to do?" Deb moans. "We can't eat. Can't drink. No TV."

"We can always talk," Sabrina says. "Just not about—" She points to the alleged bugging devices. They're probably just sprinklers, she thinks, but by the power of suggestion, they now seem to be plugged directly into FBI headquarters.

"Not a good idea to talk about anything," Ann whispers. "Remember, what you say may be used against you, including anything that might shed light on your character or anyone else's." She raises her voice. "We are four upstanding citizens, respectable wives and mothers. We have done nothing to be ashamed of."

"Hallelujah, sister," Maria says, clapping her hands in a steady beat. "'I once was lost but now I'm found.'"

"'Was blind but now I see,'" adds Deb, leading the others in a rousing version of *Amazing Grace.*

And that's how they spend the night, singing gospel, blues and rock 'n' roll. One song leading associatively to another by theme, by lyrics, by era. When they forget the words, they make them up. Deb's lilting soprano and Maria's rich alto anchor Ann's and Sabrina's indeterminate pitch through rounds of Elvis, the Beatles, Stevie Wonder, Leonard Cohen and Johnny Cash until, exhausted, they fall upon their prison cots and sleep until morning light streaks through the bars.

They are woken by Delores bringing mugs of watery black coffee.

"That's funny," Sabrina says. "I'm sure I ordered a double latte."

Maria peers at the unused toilet. "Can you believe we all made it through the night without a potty stop?"

"Just like camping," Ann says. "Aversion strengthens the bladder."

Delores brings in four metal trays heaped with reconstituted eggs. Ann refuses hers, as does Deb. Sabrina tries one mouthful, but Maria finishes all of hers. "The trouble with you, girlfriends, is you've never gone hungry," she says.

Another tantalizing bit of Maria's biography that we'll never know, Sabrina muses. No point in asking, but she does anyway. "When was that, Mare?"

"Not at Nirvana," Maria says. "That's for sure."

Ann catches Sabrina's eye in a little wink of recognition, same old elusive Maria. Sabrina is warmed by Ann's contact. Maybe everything is going to be all right. Once again they're all in this together, and they do have the smartest feminist lawyer in town.

Delores removes the breakfast trays and coffee mugs and returns with their clothing, shoes and purses. The women dress hurriedly. Sabrina slips into her black leotard, relieved to be a theater director again and appreciative of the strength and authority of a costume. Her hair is a wreck, though. It needs washing and she badly needs a shower. There's a stale musky odor that her deodorant barely masks. It's a familiar smell...one she associates with opening night...the acrid smell of fear.

Sabrina spends a long time with her makeup, as do Ann and Deb. Poor Deb can't even put on her lipstick straight, her hand is shaking so hard, yet she applies three layers of mascara. It is only Maria who merely washes her face in the rusty sink, ties back her thick dark hair and still musters the majesty of Cleopatra summoning her royal barge.

"Are you ladies presentable?" Delores calls from down the hall. "Your lawyer's here."

Delores opens the heavy door and lets Gloria into the cell. "*Vogue* visits The Vanquished," Sabrina whispers. Gloria enters trailing a cloud of expensive scent, wearing yet another Chanel suit, this time pale yellow, her shoes exactly the same shade of glove leather, her purse a matching quilted envelope. Her hair is a cascade of black silk. She stands in the doorway like a runway model, but when she speaks, she's all business. She perches on the nearest bunk and pulls out her miniature tape recorder.

"Okay, ladies, how did it happen?" Gloria asks.

Sabrina points to the ceiling, enacts a "we may be bugged" mime.

"The smoke alarms? Not to worry," Gloria scoffs, recrossing her legs. At the ankles, Sabrina notes, and elegant racehorse ankles they are. Sabrina's own, she reflects, are more Clydesdale; the kind Birkenstocks are made for.

"And anyway," Gloria continues with a meaningful glance, "you have nothing to hide. So let's start at the Last Roundup. That's where you met him, right?"

For the next half hour the women take turns sketching out the story, filling in the details. Gloria makes note of any discrepancies and irons them out before moving on.

She summarizes the events succinctly. "So you went to the Last Roundup at nine-thirty, had a few drinks, danced with the locals and left at midnight. You gave this Hughie, who appeared to be a drifter, a ride to his campsite. Because of the heavy rain, you took pity on him, brought him home, let him sleep on the couch."

"Do we have to tell about the massage part?" Deb's voice is quavering.

"Did it happen?" Gloria asks.

"Yes," Deb says. "But my husband can't find out."

"You should have thought of that before." Gloria's voice is crisp, merciless. "Whom did Hughie massage?"

"Everyone," Sabrina says.

"Just massage?" Gloria asks.

"Yes," Ann says. "First Maria. Then me. Then Sabrina. Then Deb."

"And while each of you was being massaged, where were the others?"

"In the hot tub," Sabrina says, "waiting our turn."

"And after all the massages were done, what happened then?"

"We each went to bed," Maria says.

"Were you in separate rooms?"

"I was in the master bedroom," Ann explains. "Sabrina was in the guest room next door. Maria and Deb shared Kim's room downstairs."

"What time did you all get to bed?" Gloria asks.

"It was very late," Ann says. "I didn't look at the clock."

"About three?" Gloria suggests.

"Almost four," Deb says, adding hurriedly, "by the time I got to sleep."

"And the next thing you remember?" Gloria asks.

The women all talk at once now, their voices spilling over each other.

"We got up the next morning and found him floating in the hot tub."

"It was horrible."

"That disgusting bloated face!"

"No idea how it happened."

"We pulled him out of the water."

"He weighed a ton."

"We tried CPR."

"He was dead."

"From alcohol," Ann says.

"From drugs," Maria chimes in.

"It was a heart attack," Deb cries.

"Death by hot tub. How very California!" Gloria Okimoto smiles mischievously. Another good old bad girl, Sabrina thinks. The Coven has found their defender.

"So who found the body first?" Gloria asks.

"I did," Ann says. "I got up to make the coffee, saw him, screamed…"

"And we all came running," Sabrina adds.

"And then what?" Gloria asks. "When you determined he was good and dead. What did you do?"

"We were in a panic," Deb says.

"Why didn't you call the police?" Gloria asks.

"We didn't want anyone find to out we'd picked up a guy and brought him home. What would people think?" Deb cries.

"So you buried him instead," Gloria says flatly.

"Until we could come up with something better," Ann admits.

"It was a dumb thing to do," Gloria says. "Makes you look guilty as hell, but maybe we can attribute it to group hysteria. So you wrapped him up in that cashmere blanket. Don't know why you couldn't have used a sheet. Drove into the woods, dug a grave and threw him in."

"We prayed," Deb says, "in three religions."

"Very ecumenical," Gloria says. "But you should have called 911."

"Do we have a case?" Ann asks.

"I think I can make a fair defense. Accidental death by drowning. You had no idea who the guy was. You took a little walk on the wild side. Four respectable women way out of your league and you got into hot water. No pun intended. Oh, and by the way, you've been getting quite a bit of press." Gloria zips open her Louis Vuitton briefcase and holds up two of this morning's papers.

Ann reads the *New York Times* headline out loud. "San Francisco Matrons Suspects in DEA Agent Murder."

Sabrina reads from the more colorful *San Francisco Bay Guardian*. "Menopausal Babes Cook Narc."

"I am not menopausal," Deb protests.

"Guilt by association," Sabrina says.

"I didn't say I wasn't guilty," Deb says. "I just said I'm still menstruating."

Maria pats Deb's arm comfortingly and turns to Gloria. "Is that it? Are we ready to go?"

"That's it." Gloria returns the newspapers to her briefcase, stowing them expertly. She can probably refold those gigantic road maps, Sabrina thinks. She watches as Gloria stands and smooths her skirt. Damn, she thinks, not even one wrinkle.

Gloria calls for Delores, who opens the cell door. The five women walk toward the courtroom. "Since none of you has a criminal record," Gloria says, "I'm going to ask that the judge waive bail and you each be released under your own recognizance."

"That will be good," Maria says, "because my bank balance is below sea level."

"That's because you give it all away." Gloria slips her arm briefly around Maria's shoulders as they enter the courtroom.

Sabrina is shocked by the level of noise. The room is packed. She spots Charlie right up front looking very worried, next to a grim-faced Richard and a furious Donald. The rest of the room is filled with strangers, most of them sporting press badges.

"All rise," the bailiff intones, and the judge enters.

The judge could come from central casting, Sabrina notes. He is tall, imposing, white-haired. He scrutinizes them impassively through thick horn-rimmed glasses. Solomon-like or just near-sighted?

It's the D.A. who looks like trouble, Sabrina thinks. Dark, feral. Short. Short men often compensate by being either macho or boyish. He looks more Napoleon than Peter Pan. He's also too thin, she notes. Way too thin. Shakespeare got it right. Sabrina whispers to Ann, "'Yon Cassius has a lean and hungry look.'"

Ann raises her eyebrows and whispers, "Will you just pay attention, for God's sake!"

"I am," she whispers back, defensively. "'Such men are dangerous.'"

It's small comfort to Sabrina when she proves to be right. District Attorney Cornelius Hawn from Baton Rouge is one tough cookie, a Harvard-educated good ol' boy and a super-cagey Cajun. He calls Gloria Okimoto's suggestion for release without bail ludicrous.

"If you please, Your Honor," he says, his words heavy and slow as grits and molasses, "we have here a respected government agent who has died on the job and under suspicious circumstances. And we have incontrovertible evidence that his corpse was buried surreptitiously and illegally without benefit of religious or civic rites by the four women you see before you. They are, Your Honor, suspects for first-degree murder."

Deb cries out as if she's been struck.

"Dios mio," Maria says, crossing her heart.

Sabrina searches for Charlie, while Ann stares straight ahead.

"The state asks a million dollars bail each, Your Honor," the D.A. says. "They might run."

"They are upstanding citizens...wives and mothers," Gloria Okimoto retorts. "They're not going anywhere. It's a serious charge, but it is their first offense."

The judge reduces the bail to fifty thousand each and sets a court date for three weeks later. He bangs the gavel, and exits. The courtroom bursts into noise and motion. Reporters rush out to file their stories. The families of the accused move forward. Richard is the first to reach them.

He grabs Ann's arm. "You are not using Madame Butterfly," he says, referring to Gloria, Ann assumes. "I checked out her credits. She's never done a criminal case. Nothing but transplants."

"Implants," Ann corrects. "Silicone implants."

"I want you to use Sam Parker."

"Oh, great, the mouthpiece of the Mob," Ann hisses. "Just walking in with that guy makes us look guilty. No way."

Richard's fingers dig into her arm. "Look, I'm in this, too. You'll do what I say."

"We've agreed to use Gloria. She's representing the four of us," Ann insists.

"That's crazy," Richard growls.

"It is, Deb," Donald says, picking up the refrain. "You need your own lawyer. I know you. You had nothing to do with this."

"But I did," Deb says softly, "as much as anyone."

"I don't want to hear about it," Donald cries. "I'm taking you home. Now."

"There's a small matter of paying bail," Charlie intervenes, pulling out his checkbook.

"And for Maria," Sabrina says. "Divided three ways."

"I can get someone to put up the money for me," Maria protests.

"You already have someone. Us. It evens out. You're saving us a bundle in legal fees." Charlie writes a check for a third of Maria's bail. Ann does the same. And so does Donald. Sabrina notes that of the three couples, only hers and Charlie's is a joint checking account.

Sabrina takes Charlie's hand and slips her fingers into his. She feels the touch of his wedding band and remembers her own. Taking the ring from the envelope Delores has returned, she places it back on her finger, where it belongs. She feels her eyes mist in tears. How she values that simple gold band.

She exits the courtroom to a phalanx of exploding flashbulbs. "Sabrina, over here. A little hot nookie, eh?"

"Annie, Annie. Is that what women want?"

"Hey, Deb. Give us a smile."

"Hola, Maria. Aquí. Aquí."

Each time their names are called, the women instinctively turn and another photographer captures his prey. The reporters swarm over the four women like yellow-jackets at a picnic.

"Did you know he was a narc?"

"Was there a five-way?"

Gloria ushers her clients swiftly to a waiting limo, tucks them inside. "Keep a low profile. All of you," she says. "I'll be in touch as soon as I have something. The driver will take each of you home."

Sabrina is the first to be dropped off. She takes a long hot bath, climbs into fresh sheets and falls into a troubled sleep. Still groggy and disoriented, she is awakened at noon by a phone call from Ann. Hearing her friend's familiar voice, she is filled with hope. Perhaps Ann is calling to reconcile.

"Have you seen the papers?" Ann asks.

"I saw the *Chron* and the *Examiner*. We're on the front page," Sabrina says. Then trying for levity, she adds, "Must be a slow news day."

"You sell yourself short." Ann's voice is icy.

So much for rapprochement, Sabrina thinks. "Well, if we're an international sensation, might as well lie back and enjoy it."

"That's fine for you to say," Ann retorts. "Richard is going ballistic."

"About Gloria?"

"About everything."

"Like what?" Sabrina asks.

"Never mind." Ann cuts her off tersely. "Is Tamar home?"

"Not yet. Why?"

"Kim wants to talk to her."

"Kim? What about?"

"She won't tell me. Just have Tamar call her. Kim says it's important. That it can help us." Ann hangs up.

And God knows we need it, Sabrina thinks. We're not helping each other. But Kim and Tamar? What can the two girls possibly have to do with this? She needs to discuss this with Charlie. His good analytic mind will help to shed some light.

She can hear him walking about downstairs. He must have skipped his morning conference.

"Honey?" she calls.

She hears his muffled reply.

"Can we talk?" She knows that her habit of starting a conversation when they are in separate rooms annoys Charlie. She expects the usual gentle reprimand and then his appearance. Instead, there is silence. She waits a few minutes, calls again, more loudly. Still no Charlie. She pads out of the bedroom and down the stairs to find him sitting in the living room reading the newspaper.

"Didn't you hear me?" she asks.

"I heard you."

"Then why didn't you answer?"

"I figured if you wanted to talk, you could come in here."

"I was in bed, Charlie."

"So now you're out of bed."

"Is something wrong?" she asks.

"What could possibly be wrong?" he counters flatly.

"Are you upset about that whole Nirvana thing?"

"My wife goes off on a weekend with her girlfriends. Picks up a guy. Fools around with him in a hot tub. And murders him. Why should I be upset?"

"Charlie, it was an accident. You know that." She reaches out to take his hand, but he gets up and walks quickly to the other side of the room.

"Look, Charlie, I know how bad it looks."

"Looks? What the hell do I care about looks?"

"I'm sorry. I never meant to hurt you. You're my anchor. My rock."

"Did it ever occur to you that I don't want to be a rock? That I have feelings, too?"

She reaches out to him again, but he evades her touch. "I love you," she says.

"What the hell does that mean?"

"That you're the most important person in my life."

"Then why wasn't I enough for you? Why did you need other men?" His voice is tight with anger. "You betrayed me. You betrayed our marriage."

The magnitude of her action strikes her now, for the first time. She wasn't simply acting alone. She has wounded Charlie, deeply, destroyed his trust. Her voice catches in her throat. "Can you ever forgive me?"

He is silent for a long moment. "Things are going to have to change."

"They will. I promise." Then softly, "Come back to bed?"

He reaches for his jacket. "It's not that easy."

"Charlie, wait. Will you be home for dinner?"

He turns and strides quickly out the door. It is the first time he has ever left without a goodbye, without a kiss.

Sabrina leans against the kitchen counter listening as his car pulls out of the driveway. She stands motionless until the sound dies.

The ground has shifted under her feet. She remembers the Loma Prieta earthquake. The grinding rumble. The thudding impact. The walls swaying. The floor rippling. Plates crashing from shelves. Windows shattering. She had hidden under the dining room table, trembling, until, after an eternity, it had mercifully stopped.

She wonders what Hughie and the Coven would register on the Richter scale of her marriage. Is this the "big one" that will destroy them? Or can the shock possibly bring them closer, grateful for a restored life together? For now though, all she knows is that she is deeply shaken and sadly undone.

CHAPTER THIRTEEN

Tamar looks for Kim in the darkened, half-empty coffee shop on Haight Street. Classic hippie, she thinks; psychedelic murals, scarred wooden furniture, the smell of stale smoke and burnt coffee. Just Kim's kind of place. Tamar isn't sure which persona Kim will be sporting from her repertoire of vamp to vampire. Finally she spots her at a dimly lit table in the rear. Today Kim is dressed in conservative Goth: black hair, black clothes, but no heavy metal jewelry or ghoulish makeup; only her own pale skin and wide, unpainted eyes. Tamar is disappointed as she herself had gone to considerable trouble to dress for this meeting. She didn't want to look too "GAP." She is wearing her new high platform boots, a see-through black sweater with a flesh-colored spaghetti-strap tank top underneath and fake eyelashes. Kim just looks ordinary.

"What's up?" Tamar asks as she seats herself. "It sounded important."

"Caffeine first," Kim says.

The girls study the menu, both order cappuccinos and stare at the table in an awkward silence until the drinks arrive. The years have transformed them into strangers.

"How's your mom doing?" Kim finally asks.

"She's become the boudoir queen," Tamar says wryly. "She holds court in her bedroom, says she can't leave because of the 'paparazzi.' Her theater people come to visit every day with comfort food and flowers. They watch the soaps. 'Indigenous Americana,' they call it. She finally gets to play Camille and she's not even dying."

Kim smiles at this account. "My mom's exactly the opposite. She's set up her study as a war room for the Nirvana Four. She's on the phone constantly, either to Gloria or Donald."

"Who's Donald?"

"He's Kevin's dad. Kevin from the Blue House? His mom was arrested with ours. His dad is some college professor, but he used to do public relations."

"Why do they need a PR guy? Are they going to write a book or something?"

"I don't think so, at least not for now, but my mom says they have to manage their image. If they go to trial, they have to appear as respectable wives and mothers, pillars of the community and all that shit."

Tamar snorts. "No wonder the PR guy isn't dealing with my mother. She'd put them on the cover of the *National Inquirer*."

They stare at the table again.

Tamar spoons up the foam from her cappuccino. "So...what gives?"

"I asked you to come because I think maybe we can help our moms."

"How?"

"I know some things about Richard."

"Richard?" asks Tamar with a puzzled look.

"Yeah, Richard, my wicked stepfather. I used to think he was cool, and then I found out what he was really like."

"What do you mean?"

"I just talked to Jerry. You remember him? Jerry was, like, my first real boyfriend. When Richard found out we were dating, he went ballistic. Beat him up and threatened to do worse."

"I didn't know that," Tamar gasps.

"I just found out for sure myself. But I thought something like that might have happened. Jerry just kind of disappeared. Real fast. And then when all this Coven stuff happened and I saw Richard act real mean to my mom, I just put two and two together. And I went to see Jerry."

Tamar listens, her eyebrows drawn together in puzzlement.

"I know this is going to sound like bad TV," Kim continues, "but Jerry knows all kinds of stuff about Richard. Jerry was actually working for him. That's why he got beat up. Jerry says that Richard is a big-time dope dealer, the biggest in California. They call him the The Boss. What he does is give money to the growers in advance, sort of buys their crop. The growers are always broke and willing to sell for quick cash. Then when the crop comes in, Richard sells it for a big profit and gives the growers money to plant for next year."

"No shit!"

"Yeah, and all those years when I was little, I thought Richard was the perfect gentleman, like James Bond. Boy, was I taken. He's really the Godfather."

Tamar is impressed. "Why did your mom marry him? Is she like in the Mob, too?"

"No," Kim says, dismissing the idea. "She didn't know anything about it. But I think that's why she got into trouble, and your mom, too."

"You mean they weren't really fooling around with that agent?" Tamar asks.

"I think they were fooling around, all right. But they were also set up."

"You mean, the dead guy was part of the Mob?" Tamar asks.

"No, the dead guy was an agent, but he was really looking for Richard and the dope. That's why he picked up our moms."

"And they thought they were so hot," Tamar says.

The girls laugh.

"Well, I don't see how this helps our moms. Sounds like they still took the guy home and stuff," Tamar says.

"Listen, here's the thing. Jerry's scared. Says he's still being watched, threatened by Richard's thugs. He wants to go straight, but he knows too much. Anyway, he thinks maybe he can save our moms, and they can save him. If he can get into one of those witness protection programs, he says he'll tell the narcs everything he knows about Richard."

"But Richard didn't kill the narc!" Tamar says with exasperation.

"I know that!" Kim answers with equal irritation. "But the cops want evidence against Richard, and Jerry can give it to them. And that will help our mothers get off."

"I still don't get it. Why will that help them?" Tamar asks, her voice rising.

"Because we make the deal for them. Jerry is afraid to go to the cops on his own. He figures they'll just nail him. If we go and serve as his brokers, then he'll tell everything. So we ask to get our moms off in exchange for his information."

Kim waits nervously for Tamar's response. Tamar is silent.

"Don't you want to help your mom?" Kim presses.

"Well, sure, but..."

"I can't do this all by myself. If you go, it'll seem more kosher."

"Kosher?"

"Yeah, like they won't think I'm just this freaked-out punk who doesn't know what she's talking about. You'd make it seem more respectable, because of how you look and everything." She gives Tamar the once-over. "Although not today especially."

"I dressed that way for you," Tamar says a bit sheepishly.

"Gee, thanks," Kim says. Her tone is ironic, but her smile is warm.

Tamar is uncertain. Is this just another crazy scam? She

has enough trouble trying to deal with her flaky mother's exploits without buying into Kim's bizarre drug story. Yet she remembers their childhood friendship with affection. Although Kim was often stubborn and moody, she was equally generous and loyal. Kim never gossiped about her like the other girls did about their best friends. She has always trusted Kim and she still does.

But what about her mom? Would this really help her? And even if it did, why should Tamar care? Sabrina doesn't deserve help. Tamar is furious with her. What kind of stupid game was her mom playing, picking up some guy and getting involved in a murder? Her dad was being a good sport about it, as always, but how could her mom do that to him? She doesn't appreciate him, Tamar thinks. But I do. I'll do it for my dad. Tamar takes a deep breath. "Okay," she says. "Let's talk to your friend Jerry."

"I was hoping you'd say that," Kim says, pointing out the window. "That's him leaning against the phone booth." She races out the café door.

A moment later she reappears with a reluctant Jerry in tow. Tamar sits up straight as they near the table. Jerry is really cute, she thinks. Great dark eyes, good body. Probably Hispanic. Looks like a Mexican Tom Cruise. A little old for Kim. Early twenties, she guesses. She can see why Richard would have been pissed. Especially since Kim had only been fourteen. Somehow Tamar cannot see Jerry disappearing anywhere. Women will always notice him.

As Kim introduces them, Tamar smiles warmly.

Jerry responds with polite shyness, his eyes not meeting hers. "Pleased to meet you," he says.

Kim fusses over him, pulling up a scruffy chair with a cracked wooden seat and placing it between theirs, summoning the waiter to serve him. She keeps her hand on his arm at all times. To keep him from bolting? Tamar wonders. Or is she laying claim?

"Jerry knows you're on board. Now we can move on." Kim looks at her expectantly.

"Move on how?" Tamar asks.

"Go to the police, I guess." Kim pauses uncertainly. "What do you think?"

Tamar realizes that Kim has no real plan. She is counting on Tamar to take charge just as she did when they were children. Whether it was for a Band-Aid or a math problem, Kim has always looked to Tamar.

Tamar scrapes the chocolate flakes from her cappuccino cup reflectively. "I guess we should go to Gloria first. After all, she is our moms' lawyer. But then Gloria will have to tell our mothers, and they may have problems with this. Especially your mom, Kim. Like, is she really going to sell her husband up the river?"

Kim considers this. She doesn't pretend to understand Ann's relationship with Richard, but her mother would not betray a friend, much less her husband. Her mom may be rigid and tight-assed in some ways, but she is not a rat. Even her real dad has never accused Ann of that. He just says she was too ambitious for his blood.

"No, Gloria's no good," Kim agrees. "How about the FBI?"

"You know how to reach the FBI?" Tamar asks.

"Sure," Kim says as she pulls out a cellular phone from her bulging backpack. Jerry sits nervously clutching his coffee, not saying a word.

To Tamar's great surprise, Kim dials a number and asks for a Detective Curt, identifies herself and gets through immediately. It's almost as if he was waiting for her phone call. Kim speaks a few terse words, mostly "okays," and hangs up the phone.

"His driver will be here in ten minutes," she says. "Her name is Ramirez."

"Wow," Tamar says.

Kim basks in her friend's admiration and decides not to tell her how she knows Curt. Let Tamar be impressed for once.

They have just enough time to order another round of cappuccinos. They drink them in the back of the black Mercedes that speeds them to Curt's office.

As they enter Curt's beige-walled, no frills government office, he rises to greet them. "You must be Ann Salant's daughter," he says, holding out his hand to Tamar.

Tamar points to Kim. "You got it wrong. But nearly everybody does." Even at the Blue House many parents instinctively picked out Ann and Tamar as mother and daughter. There was something in their erect posture, their sure style. And many believed Kim, with her unruly black hair and mischievous eyes, was Sabrina's daughter.

Curt smiles at Kim. "Sorry, I never would have thought you belonged to Mrs. Richard Salant." Kim smiles back, not sure if she has received a compliment.

Finally, Curt looks at Jerry. He holds out his hand, "I'm Chief Detective Rod Curt."

"Jerry," he says softly.

As the three of them settle in and decline anything to drink, Tamar thinks through her strategy. They can't give up anything too soon. Jerry's information is all they have. She will have to play her cards right, negotiate, work out a deal. Above all, be cool.

"Mr. Curt," Tamar begins, "you may wonder why we've come?"

"Not for a moment, young lady," Curt interrupts, "and please call me Curt. Everyone does. My only real surprise is why your mothers aren't here. I thought they'd be the ones making the deal, not sending out the youth brigade."

"You've got it wrong, Mr. Curt," Kim says. "We came here on our own. Our mothers don't know anything, but my friend Jerry does."

Surprised, Curt turns toward Jerry, studies him carefully. "Well, Jerry, I got you wrong, I thought you were just the boyfriend along for the ride. But now I recognize you. Yes sir, Jerry Sanchez, you did two for dealing when you were eighteen, as I recall. I guess the rumors about you were true. You were working for The Boss."

Jerry looks to Tamar for guidance.

"Jerry has things to tell you," Tamar says in a business-like manner. "But first we've got to make a deal. He'll tell you everything if you let our moms go and put him in a witness protection program."

Jerry leans over and whispers in Tamar's ear. "He wants Florida," she says.

"Florida!" Curt says in mock surprise. "Those Miami Cubans will chew up a sweet boy like him for breakfast. I think he's too pretty for Florida. What about Minnesota? No, on second thought, he's too, shall we say, 'exotic' for Minnesota. Detroit. Yeah, Detroit's the place, but he'll need an overcoat."

Tamar is growing angry; Curt is playing with them. "Mr. Curt," she says firmly. "Clearly we are wasting your time." She stands up and gestures to the others. "We're out of here."

"Not so fast," Curt chuckles. "Forgive an old man a little fun." He turns to Jerry and says soberly, "I don't know what kind of game you're playing, or why you're playing it. But if you do know anything, we'd like to hear it. And maybe we can do something for you and the girls."

"We need more than that," Tamar cries. "We need our mothers to go free. Jerry won't talk unless you promise us that. How do we know you won't rough him up for his information and give us nothing in return?"

"That only happens in the movies. Here in the real world we are all slaves of the Mother Bureau. We behave ourselves. And the truth is, we want Richard Salant more that we want your mothers. In fact, your mothers are becoming a royal pain. Have you seen the latest missives from abroad?"

Curt holds up to a copy of the *London Sun*. On the front page is a picture of the Nirvana Four blinking into the explosion of camera lights as they left the federal building following their arraignment. A bold headline proclaims:

Murdered FBI Agent Caught With Pants Down

The two girls and Jerry lower their eyes with embarrassment. "You notice how they never fail to trash the bureau," Curt says with irritation. "And Curran wasn't even one of ours!" He spreads out a number of foreign and domestic papers for their appraisal.

The *New York Times*:

Federal Agent Murdered in California Hot-Tub Orgy

France Soir:

Les meurtrières américaines—C'est formidable!

Rolling Stone:

Drugs, Dames and Death by Jacuzzi

"This doesn't do the bureau any good in Peoria or in Paris. I want to bury this story. Forgive that poorly chosen verb." Curt's half smile emerges. "But you get the gist. It's gotten totally out of hand. We need to get rid of your mothers as soon as we can and not make this into an O.J. We do not want the FBI and the DEA dragged across America's living rooms for months. Jay Leno is already talking about...the Federal Bureau of Incompetence."

Tamar glances at Kim. She looks as scared as I feel, thinks Tamar. Get rid of our mothers? Are they going to put out hit men or stage an accident? She supposes the FBI can do anything they want to.

Curt notices their alarm. "Girls, girls," he says soothingly. "This is good news for you. Not to worry. If your friend," he says, looking sternly at Jerry, "has some real stuff to give, we can deal. You understand it's not just up to me. We need to have some important negotiations with several locals, including the mayor. He's enjoying this publicity as much as we hate it. Says it puts San Francisco back on the map, just when it was losing its weirdo image. Brings in the tourists. Everybody's got to get something for this to go away. I'm not promising we can get your moms off squeaky clean, but we can lessen the pain, and get them off the goddamn front page!"

He's talking about some kind of a plea bargain, Tamar thinks. But couldn't people still go to jail with a plea bargain?

"Mr. Curt," she says firmly, "we will not give you any information unless we can be certain our mothers won't go to jail!"

"I promise you that I will do my very best."

Tamar is uncertain. She realizes they are not getting any kind of a firm deal. They are being treated like the amateurs they are. She tries a last tactic. "If it doesn't work out, we'll tell everyone that you forced us into giving up Jerry. We'll claim police harassment," she cries.

"Young lady," he says calmly, "you will tell no one that I have harassed you. Think about it. I know you are a smart girl. First of all no one would believe you, and secondly, what good would that do your mothers?"

Tamar is silent. She narrows her eyes and clenches her teeth, as she always does when faced with what she considers unreasonable adult authority. Her father calls it her Joan of Arc look.

"In fact," Curt goes on, "this conversation never happened. You girls are underage. You shouldn't be here. Jerry, on the other hand, is not a minor, he has already seen more of the world than I hope you ever will. He talks to us, and you were never here. That's the only way this works. Got it?"

Tamar and Kim look at each other. Jerry keeps his head lowered.

"Mr. Curt," Kim says. "You may think we're just kids, but I want you to know that if anything bad happens to our mothers..." She hesitates, searching for a consequence, then settles for a menacing, "Just remember we'll be watching you."

"I'll count on that," Curt says gently, half grin solidly in place. "And now," he announces, "it is time for me and Jerry to have a talk on our own. Have a good day, ladies. I think you can find your way out."

The three young people stand. Kim is the first to act. She turns toward Jerry and pulls him into a fierce hug. Jerry returns the embrace, tenderly stroking Kim's hair. Embarrassed, Tamar fidgets with her purse, looking away. But when Kim and Jerry break apart, Tamar is surprised to feel Jerry pull her in close as well. Jerry's body feels lean and hard, just the way Tamar imagined it would. He smells like worn leather and shaving lotion, a strong, heady male aroma.

"Take care, Jerry," Tamar whispers softly. When they separate she steals a last long look. Will she ever see him again? Maybe someday she'll go to Detroit, walk into a restaurant, and there he'll be, tossing a pizza. Will he be altered, disguised? Will he have dyed his hair? Grown a beard? She is saddened to think that this beautiful young man might become someone else, someone she may not even recognize.

The two girls leave Curt's office and walk in silence for a few blocks. When they reach a small park, Kim stops and fumbles in her backpack for a cigarette. "Want a smoke?" she asks.

"No thanks, I'm trying to quit. But I'll sit with you." The two girls perch on a slatted bench. The late-afternoon fog rushes through the streets, borne by the usual cold wind. The sun peeks in and out of the thickening dampness. They huddle closer together, hugging themselves for warmth.

"I think that went pretty well," Kim says. "Don't you?"

"Who knows?" Tamar replies glumly. "Jerry could wind up doing time with our moms." She imagines Jerry behind bars. Would they shave off his great wavy hair? What color were prison suits? Orange? Not a great color. And being so good-looking, wasn't that a problem in prison? Didn't some of the older guys treat them like women? She could write to him in jail. Maybe she would go to law school and help him get out.

"You don't think Curt will go back on his word, do you? It wouldn't be fair." Kim is clearly alarmed.

"Life isn't fair," Tamar says in a worldly tone. "The truth is, Curt can do anything he damn well pleases. We're just children playing."

Kim is silent, puffing hard on her cigarette.

Tamar notices that Kim's eyes are brimming with tears. She puts her arm around her friend's shoulder, and Kim begins to cry in earnest.

"Hey, don't do that. You know me. Eternal pessimist. I feel better if I go through the worst-case scenario."

"It's all my fault," Kim sobs. "I talked Jerry into turning himself in. Now he'll go to jail and so will my mom."

"Kimmy-Cat," says Tamar, retrieving the childhood name. "It's not your fault."

"It is. I messed up," Kim insists.

"You didn't mess up. Our mothers did. And Jerry did. You just tried to help. It was the right thing to do."

"But what's going to happen now?"

"We'll just have to wait and see," Tamar says. Then, recalling Sabrina's favorite adage, she adds, "It's in the lap of the gods." Sometimes it helps to have a literary mom.

Kim squints at Tamar through her tears. "You really think so?" she says hopefully.

"Sure."

"So you think everything is going to be all right?"

"Absolutely," Tamar lies.

CHAPTER
FOURTEEN

Two weeks later, Donald is driving the van he has hired to transport the Nirvana Four to the courthouse for their pretrial hearing. As the newly appointed public relations agent for the group he has carefully planned their entrance. "You can't afford to walk in separately," he has warned them. "The pack will pounce on you and tear you to pieces." He has chosen a flying-wedge approach. He will lead the way with Deb; Charlie and Sabrina will flank Maria in the next line, followed by Gloria and Ann. Originally, he had Richard marching in the third line, until he learned that Richard would not be with them.

As the van approaches the courthouse, Ann feels a growing wave of fear. She knew there would be reporters but hadn't imagined there would be so many. Yet now, even with the courthouse dome still small against the horizon, she can already see a mass of large vans, attached by long black umbilical cords to the video and sound equipment, set up in clumps on the sidewalk and in the adjoining park. Three giant cranes support cameramen who are pointing their TV cameras from on high, like sharpshooters, at the steps of the building. A milling mob of men and women, many sporting earphones and microphones, pick their way among the black cords.

The low chat in the van stops as its occupants see what Ann has spotted. Donald pulls the van over to the curb. "Time for an adjustment," he says, straining for a confident tone. "I think Charlie and I should go out there and bring in some backup." He pauses. "Will you women be all right without us?"

"We'll manage somehow," Deb demurs.

Donald glances at Deb, unsure whether to gauge her remark as serious or ironic. Just as well, Ann thinks, it keeps him on his toes. Deb confessed to them that it's nice not to be taken for granted anymore, just as she newly appreciates Donald now that he's reclaimed his former expertise. He never should have left public relations, she told them; it's much sexier. The university has made him boring.

"Don't worry," Gloria adds. "You've got me, the fastest tongue in the West. Never met a man I couldn't outdraw." Gloria is armored for battle in a black Armani power suit, the skirt short enough to display her sleek and shapely legs yet long enough to pass as business wear.

"Donald's right," says Ann. "It would be good to have a police escort." She is feeling particularly vulnerable today. Deb has Donald. Sabrina has Charlie, even though he does seem a bit distant. Maria has Gloria. And she has no one. Richard disappeared the very evening he bailed her out of jail. He phoned later in the week to say he had business in New York. It was not a friendly call, not their usual leisurely long-distance chatter. The conversation was short, chilly and impersonal. When she hung up she realized he hadn't left a contact number. And when she called his cell phone a moment later, there was no answer. She heard nothing for another week, and then just a few days ago, his lawyer, slippery Sam Parker, called.

"Mrs. Salant," he said formally, "I want you to know that I have advised my client not to be present at your up-coming court date. After the incident at Nirvana, we feel he needs to separate himself from your...issues."

Ann expected as much, but it still troubles her deeply. Were she and Richard ending a more-than-ten-year re-lationship like this...with a call from a sleazy lawyer? She studies the women in the van. Aside from Gloria, with her professional composure, they are a frightened group. Maria's golden face is pale and her bright red dress seems several sizes too big. Sabrina, though carefully made up, her wild hair artfully arranged, sits with her hands so tightly clasped that her knuckles are white. Deb stares fixedly at the retreating figures of Donald and Charlie as they are swallowed up by the crowd.

"You know, when I was a little girl growing up in Kansas," Deb says wistfully, "I used to dream that someday I'd be a star, that my picture would be on magazine covers, that I'd be known to millions." She sighs. "And now I am."

"Time to wake up, Dorothy," Sabrina says glumly. "This sure ain't Oz."

"Well, it still beats Kansas," Gloria says. "Look at it this way. We all like attention, and now we're getting some. Fifteen minutes of fame. Might as well lie back and enjoy it."

"Excuse me, Gloria," Sabrina says hotly. "You can damn well enjoy it because you will be admired for your terrific suit and your great legs. You'll give a dynamite press conference and get proposals from horny guys all across the country. But what you will not do is go to jail with us."

Gloria puts her well-manicured hand on Sabrina's shoulder. "I know you're frightened, Sabrina, but I can assure you that you will not be going to jail."

Sabrina and Ann exchange a look of surprise. Have they heard Gloria correctly? Did she just promise that they wouldn't be convicted? What does she know that she is not telling them?

There is a loud knock at the van's front window. A large male face crowned with a dark blue police cap bends close to the glass and shouts, "Ladies, time to go. We're going to leave the vehicle right here."

Ann looks out the window and sees nothing but a forest of blue-uniformed legs, dozens of them. The car door opens and a male hand reaches out to her. She accepts it gratefully.

The Nirvana Four, employing a flying wedge, moves forward, but not as Donald planned. A small army of uniformed cops, spearheaded by their captain, surrounds the four defendants and their lawyer. Ann guesses their police escorts have been chosen for their height since she can see nothing but blue shoulders around her. She can hear the desperate voices outside the blue wedge, however.

"Come on, ladies, give us a break. We've got jobs to do, too."

"Yo, Gloria, how are your girls going to plead?"

"Over here, sweetheart, just one shot."

Looking up, Ann can see the long-necked cranes bending down toward them, the shiny lenses holding the women in their crosshairs. Deb and Maria hurry forward, walking arm in arm. That leaves her and Sabrina. She would find comfort in linking arms with Sabrina, but she cannot make the first move. Her pride will not permit it. And her estranged friend keeps her distance, as if the space between them is strewn with land mines.

Gloria, marching in front of the four, turns around and whispers, "Now remember, ladies, loose lips sink ships." Gloria has prepped them several times about today's procedure. "The prosecution has to show their cards, we hold ours close to our chests. Remember the Miranda ruling. Anything you say or do may be held against you. Let's just see blank faces. Attentive, serious, but blank. No matter what they ask, stick to the script."

Ann has had little experience in criminal court, and none in murder cases. Murder is the criminal big time she has always avoided as a lawyer and never imagined that she would experience as a defendant. She knows the pretrial hearing is the time for the prosecution to show their stuff, or at least enough of their stuff to convince a judge that the case should go forward to trial. Most often this was a formality, and the judge passed it on to trial. Criminal prosecutors were not going to mess with cases that were losers; they had their reputations and their conviction batting averages to maintain. Usually the hearing was short and the witnesses few. Rarely did defendants testify, but then defense lawyers almost never let their clients testify; they were considered loose cannons, even in the rare cases when the lawyer believed they were innocent.

What does Gloria really think, Ann wonders. The Nirvana Four have told her the official version, or rather, the second official version, where they came down in the morning and were shocked to see their cowboy floating like a beached whale in the hot tub. There was no mention of how he died, and Gloria has not questioned them further.

Inside the courthouse the wedge of cops disperses, and only three or four remain to escort the women to their seats. In spite of the high media interest, the judge, Mary Hayes, is allowing only a small pool of reporters in the courtroom and two sketch artists; no TV, no photographs. One hundred spectators are let in on a first-come, first-served basis, and designated family members are given seats. Because of the small number of spectators, the large high-domed courtroom is hushed and quiet as the women take their seats at a long table to the right of the judge.

Ann scans the huge dim room and spots the family row directly behind their table. Donald is sitting on one end beside two large adolescent boys, awkwardly outfitted in jackets and ties. Danny must be home, too young to see his mother on trial for murder. When do children become old enough for that? Ann wonders. Next to the boys are Kim and Tamar, somberly dressed in black, looking years older than the adolescent boys. Charlie is at the end next to Tamar. The family members are all sitting up straight, holding fixed smiles on their faces. No doubt Donald's order to show support and solidarity to the world. Kim gives a little wave when she sees Ann. Ann waves back and attempts a reassuring smile. She is saddened that her daughter has no parent to sit beside her.

On the prosecution side of the courtroom two tables are filled with men and women whispering to one another and brandishing yellow lined notepads. The same familiar notepad that Ann relies on herself. It is this simple detail that underlines the surrealism of her situation. How did she get on the wrong side of this proceeding?

Behind the lawyers' tables a row of dark-suited men sit silently. She glimpses the large frame of Rod Curt among them.

"All rise, court is in session, Judge Mary Hayes presiding," the bailiff booms.

At first glance, the judge, a small gray-haired woman dwarfed by her heavy black robes, looks to Ann like a sweet, middle-aged librarian. But when Mary Hayes puts on her steel-rimmed glasses and sternly surveys the courtroom, Ann reconsiders. Maybe not so sweet. And furthermore, women are not always kind to other women. A man might have been better. But then, a conservative male judge might have found the whole situation of Hughie and the cowboy bar too threatening; he might consider the Nirvana Four disreputable, sluttish. Maybe this middle-aged woman can better understand a girls' night out.

The D.A. stands up to deliver his opening remarks. He is a different D.A. than the one who arraigned them. He looks experienced, sophisticated and is better dressed than most public lawyers. Must be bringing out the big guns now, Ann thinks. The world is watching.

"Good morning, Your Honor," the D.A. begins. "My name is Guy Fallows." His voice is low and soothing. "The state is confident that we have more than sufficient evidence to present a case for second degree murder. We will show you the physical evidence, which places the defendants at the scene of the murder. We will present evidence of the blow on the head that murdered the deceased. And we will show you the evidence, which proves that the defendants physically removed the body from the scene and buried it four miles away in an isolated forest. Moreover, Your Honor, we will explain their motive. This was not just an act of random violence committed by dangerously inebriated women. Not at all. This was part of a deliberate cover-up, which has widespread and sinister implications. The victim was killed because he was a drug agent about to expose the vast criminal empire of the owners of the house, Richard and Ann Salant."

"I object, Your Honor," Gloria says sharply, rising to her feet. "Mr. Fallows is referring to unproved allegations, which are not in evidence here. His remarks are both misleading and irrelevant and they may interfere, as I understand it, with an ongoing federal investigation." Judge Hayes pauses for several seconds, looking back and forth between Gloria and Guy Fallows. And, Ann thinks, also briefly at Agent Curt.

"Sustained," Judge Hayes says. "Mr. Fallows, please keep your remarks to the evidence presented in this case."

Ann is stunned. What is this ongoing investigation? As far as she knows, Richard has not been arrested. Did Curt find things at Nirvana she didn't know about? She has tried to focus on the murder charge and not think about Richard and his possible criminal connections. She has accepted Richard's explanation that he was storing marijuana for the son of a client, but wonders if she's deluding herself.

She notices that Deb is looking at her with surprise and Sabrina with suspicion. Only Maria is facing forward without expression as Gloria has instructed them to do.

Guy Fallows is winding up. "In short, Your Honor, the state believes we have more than met the standard of evidence to proceed to trial on the charges of second degree murder against all four defendants. They had clear opportunity and motive. They may look like ordinary citizens with no clear criminal past, but that illusion will be dispelled at trial."

At this comment, all four defendants disregard Gloria's orders and jerk their heads up in astonishment. What the hell is he talking about? Ann thinks. What criminal past? Ann reviews her own history: a shoplifting arrest when she was fourteen, which was dismissed; two speeding violations. There couldn't be anything on the record. But what about the others?

She doesn't have time to consider the matter further as Gloria approaches the judge for her opening remarks.

"Your Honor, I believe the evidence will show there has been a major misunderstanding here," she says in an authoritative voice. "This is not second degree murder, but simply a tragic accident. These women went away to the country for a long-planned quiet weekend. A well-deserved getaway. We all know life can get terribly pressured for working mothers." Gloria glances empathetically at the judge, hoping, Ann suspects, that she is also a working mother.

"They met former Agent Curran at the Last Roundup where they had gone to listen to some music," Gloria continues. "But Dennis Curran had his own agenda. In hopes of reinstating himself in the DEA, he was working as a freelancer. He was on a fishing expedition to find out more about drug activities in Mendocino, and Nirvana, because of its remoteness and access to the coast, was one of the houses he wanted to investigate. When he learned the women were staying there, he played on their sympathies by pretending he had no place to sleep on a stormy night. In their compassion, they allowed him to spend the night. On the couch. They woke in the morning to find him floating in the hot tub. Dead. The evidence will show that there is no valid complaint for murder here, that Agent Curran died accidentally. His diseased body simply could not handle the combination of heat and alcohol to which he was exposed."

Ann relaxes slightly, and she can tell the others are relieved. This is more like it. No surprises here.

Gloria concludes, "When the defendants found his body they understandably panicked. Instead of calling the proper authorities, they decided to bury the body themselves. That, Your Honor, may be very bad judgment, but it is not murder. To allow this case to go forward would be a gross miscarriage of justice."

Ann searches Judge Hayes's face. Is she impressed by Gloria's argument? Do they have a chance? She quickly runs through the possible scenarios. No, she decides glumly, there's a ninety percent chance they are dead ducks. If Judge Hayes refuses to send this hot case forward she may as well hang up her robes. As long as the prosecution is insistent and has a shred of evidence, Judge Hayes will pass it on to the next judge to do the dirty work.

The prosecution presents its case first. The pink Porthault blanket with its incriminating laundry tag is offered into evidence. Mr. Wing Lee from the Elite Laundry and Dry Clean testifies that Ann is the owner of the blanket. Agent Ramirez is called to the stand. She testifies that the eyeglasses, exhibit B, were found at the bottom of the Nirvana hot tub. The defense stipulates that a report from an optometrist in New Jersey, identifies the eyeglasses as belonging to Agent Curran.

All this testimony goes quickly. None of it is new or unexpected, but to Ann, each public recitation feels like another nail pounded into her coffin. She glances at Deb, who has lowered her head, no longer eager to be noticed by the world. Sabrina is chewing on her white-knuckled hand, and Maria is slouching lower and lower into her chair.

Ann knows that the prosecution's critical witness is the coroner. Gloria has told them that she has arranged for an expert witness to question the coroner's report. But she has not given them any details. This has frustrated Ann, who when she asked, has been told repeatedly by Gloria, "Your job is to hold yourself together, my job is to save your ass."

Guy Fallows calls on the coroner, Dr. Wong. He is a short, squarely built man. He wears a shiny gray suit that is at least a size too small, his shoulders straining against the seams. His shirt collar digs into his second chin. He looks more like a sumo wrestler than a doctor, Ann thinks. Dr. Wong responds patiently to dozens of routine questions: his credentials as coroner, the approximate date and time of death, the rate of decomposition and so forth. At last Fallows touches on the critical issues.

"Dr. Wong, tell us about the condition of the body. Were there any signs of physical assault?"

Dr. Wong answers slowly. Clearly he has been waiting for this question. "Yes, there was an indication of a blow to the back of the head at the very base of the skull."

"Could this blow have killed the victim?"

"I don't know. The body was too decomposed to determine the extent of the trauma. All the tissue had separated from the head."

"I see," says Fallows quickly. "But you can't rule out that this blow killed the victim?"

"Well, no," Wong says. "But there are signs that his lungs—"

"Thank you, Dr. Wong. One more question along this line. Is it possible that the blow to the head merely rendered the victim unconscious and that afterward he drowned?"

"That is, I think, far more likely, since there was water in his lungs and dead men do not breathe when immersed in water."

"So you are saying that Agent Curran may have been rendered unconscious by a blow to the head and then drowned?"

"Yes. That is one possibility. But—"

"Thank you, Dr. Wong," says Fallows. "No more questions."

Gloria approaches the witness. She smiles warmly, confidently. "Dr. Wong, I don't think we need to take up a lot of your time. Just two questions. We would all appreciate brief answers."

Wong smiles slightly. Is he charmed? Ann wonders. Or is he just relieved that he may be able to leave before lunch?

"My first question. Could Agent Curran have died from drowning alone, without the blow to the head?"

"Oh, yes," says Wong eagerly. "That is most probable."

"And here is the second. Is it possible that the blow to the head could have occurred in the hot tub? Say Agent Curt passed out in the hot tub and hit his head as he was sliding into the water."

"Yes, that is very possible," says Wong. "As I say, the tissue was too decomposed to correctly evaluate the trauma to the head."

Is Ann imagining this, or does Wong glance toward Curt as he delivers this information?

"No more questions. Thank you," says Gloria.

Gloria next calls Dr. Norman Spencer as an expert witness. Dr. Spencer recites his credentials. He is a vascular specialist, has published many journal articles, has hospital privileges at the University of California Hospital, and has testified at least fifty times in cases involving vascular disease, usually dealing with high blood pressure.

"Have you ever testified in hot-tub death cases?" Gloria asks.

Dr. Spencer smiles slightly. "I wouldn't say it is my specialty, but yes, I have testified in about a dozen hot-tub deaths."

"Have you ever testified regarding the effects of high blood pressure combined with alcohol?" Gloria asks.

"Yes, that is the most common case."

"And what are the effects of high blood pressure and alcohol in the event of hot-tub deaths?"

"Generally, water temperatures of more than a hundred degrees combined with high blood pressure and an alcohol level of more than .08 make the chances of passing out very high. If no one is around to help the person, that person has a good chance of drowning. I call it 'hot-tub suicide.'"

"But you don't really mean suicide, do you, Dr. Spencer?" Gloria asks.

"Well, not literally. I just mean that people are asking for trouble if they step into a hot tub with those conditions, and I don't think the hot tub manufacturers—"

"Thank you, Dr. Spencer."

Bravo, Ann thinks. Gloria is getting her points across perfectly. Maybe she is more than a designer suit, after all.

"And have you examined the medical and coroner's records regarding Agent Curran?"

"Yes, I have."

"And would you say former Agent Curran is a victim of hot-tub suicide?"

"Of course, I can't say for sure. But his medical records show he was hypertensive, and the bartender at the Last Roundup testified that he was drinking heavily. He was a great candidate for hot-tub suicide."

"Thank you. No further questions."

Guy Fallows slowly walks over to the witness stand. His well-tailored jacket accentuates the breadth of his athletic shoulders. "Death by hot-tub suicide." He chuckles. "That's a new one for me. Is that a medical term, Dr. Spencer?"

Dr. Spencer does not answer.

"I asked you a question, Dr. Spencer. Are you using medical terminology?"

"No, that's my own term," Dr. Spencer says quietly.

"Well, what about 'murder by hot tub'? That's not a medical term either, but I suspect it is more accurate in this case. Think on this, Dr. Spencer. If Agent Curran were quite drunk, as you have testified, it wouldn't take much force for a person, or perhaps more than one person, to hit him on the back of the head with a blunt instrument and then, when he was dazed, or perhaps unconscious, simply hold him underwater for a minute or two."

"Well, I don't think—"

"Bear with me, Dr. Spencer. Consider the angle. If one or more persons were pushing down on Agent Curran from above, say, standing or kneeling outside the tub, they would have additional leverage, would they not?"

Spencer is again silent.

"It is a simple question, Dr. Spencer. If someone were pushing down, wouldn't she have good leverage, even a person lighter than the deceased?"

"Yes, I suppose so," Spencer mumbles.

"Now, this is a trickier question, Dr. Spencer."

Spencer sits up, his eyes alert.

"Who is paying for your testimony today? I am not asking how much, but I assume you are not here out of the goodness of your heart. Did the check not come from the bank account of Richard Salant?"

Spencer looks confused. "Well, it came from Mrs. Salant, but his name is on it, too."

Gloria leaps up. "This is irrelevant, Your Honor."

"Give me a moment, Your Honor, and you will see it is quite relevant," says Fallows in a soothing tone.

Judge Hayes looks at him warningly. "It had better be."

"Don't you consider it odd that a drug agent dies by accident in the home of a drug lord?" Fallows continues, addressing the jury. "Isn't it far more logical that a drug agent is murdered in the home of a drug lord?"

Gloria rises again. "Your Honor, I must approach the bench!" She steps up quickly, and Fallows comes in a languid stroll. There is a whispered consultation.

"We will take a ten-minute recess," announces the judge. "Do not leave the room unless accompanied by a bailiff."

Gloria, Fallows and the judge exit toward the judges' chambers. Ann is surprised to see Curt heading in that direction, too. Why is Curt allowed to talk to the judge?

She wonders if it has to do with Richard and the marijuana they burned. What kind of trouble is Richard in?

Ann forces herself not to think about Richard. She has her own neck to save, and right now she does not feel at all confident about that prospect. Granted, the evidence is circumstantial, but there is a lot of it. Fallows is right; it looks bad for them. Death by hot-tub suicide? It sounded plausible when Spencer first took the stand, but now it seems ridiculous.

She glances over at her friends; the Nirvana Four appear to be a very frightened group of middle-aged women. Maria looks faint and is leaning heavily against Deb's shoulder. Sabrina is staring at Ann coldly. Ann can't really blame her. Sabrina hadn't known about the Richard drug connection, but then, neither had Ann. How could she have been so misguided all these years? There were rumors and allegations. That incident with Kim's boyfriend. Richard's off-limits office. Some of the company he kept. It's become clear she just didn't want to know.

Ann glances furtively at the family row, no reason for eyes forward now. The boys look bored, slouched in their seats, but Donald and Charlie are alert, leaning forward. They, too, must sense something unusual is happening. Kim and Tamar are holding each other's hands tightly. This surprises Ann. She didn't think they were close anymore, but, she reasons, the emotions of adolescent girls are notoriously fluid. One moment they hate each other, the next they're best friends and whatever had separated them quickly forgotten. Would that grown-up women could forgive as easily, Ann thinks as she surreptitiously glances at Sabrina. But Sabrina is staring fixedly at the door of the judge's chambers.

The door opens and only Gloria exits. She returns to the defendants' table, her expression inscrutable.

"Ladies, we need to talk," she says tersely. "Follow me."

Gloria herds them into a little meeting room off the main courtroom set up for just such occasions; drab gray walls, a scarred wooden meeting table and an assortment of ill-matched wooden and steel chairs.

"Here's the deal. They drop murder two, we plead guilty for stealing a body and burying it. Your basic body snatching and concealment of corpus. It's usually a felony, but it can be dropped to a misdemeanor in special cases. The special case here is that you are naive women, 'dumb broads' as the D.A. so delicately put it, who lacked real criminal intent."

Sabrina is wild-eyed. "What!" she shrieks. "You're agreeing to our committing a crime! I thought you said this wouldn't happen! I want Charlie. I'm going to get Charlie."

Sabrina starts to rise, but Gloria seizes her wrist and pulls her firmly back into her chair. "Listen, Sabrina, this is as good as it gets. The judge has given us her Girl Scout word of honor that she won't give you jail time."

"Then what will she give us?" Sabrina demands.

"Eighteen months of community service. Believe me, it's a steal."

Sabrina is somewhat mollified; the terror leaves her eyes. "What kind of community service are you talking about? Cleaning toilets in the city jail?"

"I can't promise you, but most likely you'll be picking up litter on the side of the freeway. Hell, it's good exercise and you'll be out of doors."

"Picking up butts...in those orange vests," Ann muses.

"Only on weekends," Gloria adds.

"I'm in the theater on weekends," Sabrina cries. "I can't do it."

Ann stands up, her hands curled into fists. "This is not a play, Sabrina! This is real life. You don't get to write the ending. And you are damn lucky Gloria is saving your over-the-hill ass."

"Over-the-hill," Sabrina shouts angrily. "Just because you're a goddamn anorexic..."

"Stop it!" commands Deb. All eyes turn toward her.

"We want to thank you, Gloria. No one wants to pick up garbage along the highway, but if it's the best we can do..."

Gloria looks straight at Deb. "Believe me, this is the very best we can hope for. You don't want to know what I went through to get it. And if we don't get back in there soon Judge Hayes may change her mind. She's got a lot to lose by giving this up."

"All right, then," Deb says with authority. "Let's have a vote. I say we go along with Gloria and plead guilty to body stealing and concealment."

Ann is stunned by this incredible turn of events. It's amazing to see Deb's newfound confidence and authority. And God knows how Gloria pulled them out of the fire. Ann quickly adds up the pluses and minuses. A criminal record is not a great thing, although if it is only a misdemeanor she won't be disbarred. Will the reporters follow them as they pick up trash on their weekend rounds? Not likely; the press is bound to get bored with them if there are no new developments. They'll be yesterday's joke. On the positive side, it'll all be over and they won't have to fear the trial and what that might expose. They won't go to jail and the truth, thank God, will never come out.

"I vote yes," Ann says decisively.

Maria's face is gray and strained. She says yes so faintly that Gloria can barely hear her.

All eyes are now on Sabrina, who looks directly at Ann. "What choice do I have? I'm caught up in a web of secrecy and lies." Sabrina pauses dramatically, then nods her reluctant acquiescence.

The women are led back to the courtroom, this time directly to the podium. Guy Fallows and Gloria recite the plea bargain they are offering. The women all say yes again. Judge Hayes looks at each of them solemnly and declares their sentence of fourteen months' community service, even better than Gloria has promised. Finally the judge says sternly, "I have shown clemency because I do not believe you are hardened criminals, and I do not believe you pose a threat to society. But I warn you, I will not be as lenient again. Behave yourselves. Act like ladies!"

· The Nirvana Four and Gloria return to the table to pick up their papers and purses. Ann looks around the milling courtroom and sees the members of the family row smiling and waving vigorously at them. Deb's two boys circle their fingers in victory signs. It is all over, Ann thinks; we should be happy; we should celebrate. She looks down the table to the other women who are gathering their things. Maria is holding a handkerchief to her nose; the cloth is growing redder by the second as blood soaks into it. Ann rushes to her side and pulls a small packet of tissues from her own purse.

"It is nothing," says Maria. "Just the excitement." And indeed the flow of blood stops with the wad of tissues.

Aside from the forced cheerfulness of those in the family row, a vague air of disappointment pervades the large courtroom. This is the end of the entertainment. The Nirvana Four are about to fade into oblivion.

Ann can picture that evening's dispirited headlines: *Nirvana Four Confess To Body Snatching. Bad Girls Sentenced To a Year of Butt Picking.*

It could be a lot worse, Ann thinks as she heads toward the family row to greet Kim. Kim runs to meet her and throws her arms around her. "We've won!" she cries jubilantly. Surprised and moved by Kim's enthusiasm, Ann returns her daughter's heartfelt hug.

As they draw apart, Tamar comes rushing up with Sabrina in tow. Tamar grabs Kim by the shoulders and whirls her around in a happy dance. "You did it," she laughs. "Good work."

"Couldn't have done it without you, girlfriend," Kim says, smiling.

The girls give each other high fives as Ann and Sabrina exchange a look of bewilderment.

Sabrina breaks the silence. "As Alice once said…'Things in Wonderland just keep getting curiouser…'"

"'And curiouser,'" Ann agrees.

CHAPTER
FIFTEEN

The four women agree to put Hughie and the hot tub in the past and get on with their lives. It is best, they decide, that they go their separate ways. At least for a while. They even request different times for their highway-sanitation stint. A year passes, and, true to their vow, they neither see nor communicate with each other. Sabrina knows they all manage to stay in touch with Maria, though, via brief e-mail messages. She sends them chatty, cheerful notes about her niece's budding artistic talent and her clients' progress. She briefly reports that although the cancer has spread, she is combating the disease with vigor. She is undergoing chemotherapy and radiation and using the herbal remedies of her Oaxacan healer to help assuage nausea and fatigue.

But a month ago the messages stopped. And two days ago Sabrina received a call from a honey-voiced woman with a warm Spanish accent. "I am Consuela, Maria's sister," the woman explains. "I have sad news." She gave the details of the funeral service. Our Lady of Guadalupe chapel in the Mission, three o'clock Saturday afternoon.

Sabrina and Charlie are the first of the group to arrive, Sabrina teary and leaning on Charlie's arm. Deb and her husband enter the chapel next. Donald greets Sabrina warmly. After his stellar performance as the media manager of the Nirvana Four, creating just the right picture of verve and repentance, Sabrina has employed him as marketing director of The Edge.

Donald gave the definitive blockbuster interview in *Time* magazine. And from the glow on Deb's face, Sabrina notes, it looks as if Donald is scoring in more than one area. Donald has told her that Deb's fear that he was having an affair was completely unfounded. He had been spending his evenings at a second job. His university salary was not meeting their needs, especially with Danny's tuition, so he'd signed on to edit personal ads for the *Bay Guardian*. He was ashamed to tell Deb. Now Donald and Deb are running their own successful public relations firm, Hot-Tub.com. A testament, Sabrina thinks, to Donald's skill at turning a dark tale into a feminist victory of sorts.

That was the approach Donald took in his *Time* interview, excerpts of which appeared in major newspapers around the globe.

These four women, women of a certain age, as the French say, went off to be together, to have a well-earned respite from their busy and demanding lives as wives and mothers and helping professionals. They

went off to be in nature. To rest and refresh themselves. To have a bit of fun. To feel young again. Because in the heart of each of them, indeed, in the
heart and soul of every woman, whatever her age,
there lives a girl, and that girl is her truest, strongest,
most resilient part. Yes, there are risks in accessing
that "girl," but far greater risks if one forever loses
touch.

The article ended with Sabrina's pithy quote: "Over-
forties: once invisible, now invincible."

The organ is just sounding as Ann walks into the
chapel. To Sabrina's eye, Ann is thinner than ever in her
short black silk dress, but her skin and hair are shining with
health. Ann spots Sabrina and smiles shyly. That is a new
expression for Ann, Sabrina thinks, this soft hesitancy. She
feels her own face mirror that same openness as she gestures to the empty seat on the wooden pew next to her.
Ann slips in beside her.

The two women sit in tearful silence listening to the
somber music. It was a death that separated them, Sabrina
thinks sadly, and another death that is bringing them back
together. Their friendship was sorely tested and badly
shaken. That carefree innocence is gone. But perhaps
they've come out of adversity better equipped for the
challenges and rewards of a true friendship.

There are so few people in this world whom we love
and who love us, Sabrina thinks. Today she has lost one.
She will not lose another. Feeling the familiar warmth of
Ann's presence, she reaches out her hand to her old friend.

Ann takes the proffered palm and closes her fingers tightly around it.

"Missed you," Ann whispers.

"Me, too," Sabrina says. "Like crazy."

They sit there, hands entwined, as the service begins. There are prayers in Spanish and English and sweet rousing hymns by a children's choir in bright red robes, and then Maria's sister stands. She is a younger, rounder version of Maria.

"I am Consuela," she begins softly, "Maria's baby sister. I am here to say goodbye to the bravest woman in my life. If not for Maria I would not be here today. I owe her everything. She put me first. She gave me pride. I love you, Maria. You were an angel in my life. I will never forget what you did." Consuela kneels, tears streaming, and embraces the coffin.

Sabrina turns to Ann questioningly, "Do you know what she means?"

"I'm not sure," Ann says. "Maybe that Maria was always there...for all of us."

"Somehow sounds bigger," Sabrina muses. In turn, many of the congregation stand to speak, remembering Maria's generosity, her humor, her dynamite sangria. Deb has brought bunches of blue daisies, which she hands to Ann and Sabrina. They each lay them on the coffin in memory of the Blue House and their dear friend.

As they make their way back to their seats, Ann whispers to Sabrina and Deb. "Come to my place afterward, okay?" She gives the address. "The apartment is tiny, but it's on the water. Very peaceful."

They nod their acceptance, glad to be asked, eager for the chance for private reminiscences, for closure.

Tamar and Kim arrive just as Maria's parish priest begins his heartfelt eulogy. The girls slip into a back pew. When the ceremony ends, they watch their mothers leaving the church, arm in arm, heads bent close, deep in conversation. Charlie notices the girls and gives them a smile and a full salute.

"The ladies are heading to Ann's for a final goodbye," he tells them. "I'm going home. When you're ready, why don't you two join me for a pizza?"

As Charlie leaves, Kim says to Tamar, "You are so lucky to have such a great dad."

Tamar turns to her friend. Kim's black mascara is streaked across her cheeks, her smudged eyes like black coals. Tamar takes a Kleenex out of her pocket and gently wipes the black marks off Kim's tear-stained cheeks.

"Wanna smoke?" Tamar asks.

"Sure, let's go. Is it okay to do it near a church?'

"God loves sinners," Tamar says, laughing, once again quoting her mother. "It gives him a challenge."

They find a concrete porch at the rear of the church and sit on the top step. Kim fumbles in her purse and digs up a crumpled pack. They each light up and take a long puff.

"I loved Maria," sniffs Kim. "Those days at the Blue House were the happiest times of my life."

"Maria was cool," Tamar agrees. "But some of those boys were trouble. Remember Ben the biter?"

Kim laughs through her tears. "Yeah, my mom wanted to give me a rabies shot. I really did hate boys then."

"What about now?" Tamar asks. "Are you seeing anyone?"

Kim studies the long ash of her cigarette. "No, I've given up on guys, at least for now. I've got to get my act together. You know I missed a lot of school last year, just goofing off, and then there was the trial and all. I need to catch up so I can go to college next year."

"College! That's great," Tamar says. "Have you decided where?"

"I'm going to stay close to home. At least for the first year or so. We haven't got much extra cash right now."

Tamar looks at her own cigarette for a long moment. Then, she asks, her voice deliberately casual, "Hear anything from Jerry?"

Kim turns to face her. "Jerry? He was supposed to disappear. Never to be heard from again. Isn't that what Curt said?"

Tamar blushes. "Well, I guess he's allowed to write, as long as he doesn't give away his address and all." She hesitates. "I got a few letters from him."

"No shit!" Kim exclaims. "What's he doing? Where is he at?"

"He's not allowed to say." Tamar looks down at her cigarette again; the ash has fallen to the bottom step where it unfolds in a fluffy gray circle. "He wants me to meet him someplace where no one knows us, like maybe Las Vegas." Tamar waits for a response. When there isn't one, she continues. "Is it okay with you if I meet him? It won't be until I graduate."

"I guess so," Kim says. "I'm just, like, surprised."

"You don't still love him, do you?" Tamar asks.

"No, no, I don't, not anymore," Kim says thoughtfully. "But I still think he's the coolest guy I ever dated."

They sit quietly finishing their cigarettes.

"You, won't, like, tell your mom about Jerry, will you?" Kim asks. "Remember, Gloria made us promise."

Tamar snorts. "Telling my mom anything is like posting it on the internet. No, she'll never know about the deal. She still thinks it was all on the up-and-up. Like Curt was going to reveal Hughie's little health problem gratis. Honestly, I don't know how she can be so clueless."

"Sometimes I'm tempted to tell my mom," Kim confides. "I think she'd be impressed. She used to think I was a fuckup, but she's coming around."

"Our moms don't know the half of it. At least when it comes to us. If my mom only knew about Jerry." Tamar laughs and rises to her feet, pulling Kim up with her. She pulls her cell phone out of her pocket. "I'm going to call my dad. You still get off on pepperoni?"

CHAPTER
SIXTEEN

As Sabrina pulls up at Ann's apartment house, she recognizes Deb's orange Volvo and is pleased to see the sleek
green Jaguar of Gloria Okimoto parked next to it. The
building is a low-rise white stucco affair with decorative
molding and wrought-iron balconies. A popular Mediter-
ranean style bolstered by the stretch of bay it fronts. The
front door is a heavy, intricately paneled oak. Ann buzzes
her in, and meets her at the second-floor landing holding a bottle of French champagne. "I only took a few
things in the divorce settlement," Ann says, pouring the
wine into a delicate crystal flute. "And they had to be both
practical and beautiful."

"Well, this is both," Sabrina murmurs. "I love Lalique."
She runs a long red fingernail along the rim of the gob-
let. The crystal rings out in a clear true note.

Ann leads her inside to where the other two are
waiting.

"To Maria," Ann says, lifting her glass.

"A class act," Gloria says.

"With a heart as big as Baja," Deb toasts.

"L'chaim," Sabrina adds. "To life."

The women take a long swallow of the excellent champagne.

Ann passes a platter of cheese puffs and then offers an apartment tour. IKEA modern, she proclaims, all clean lines and easy maintenance. Nothing fussy, no more antiques. She's through with the past, including Richard, who is spending the next five years in a white-collar prison complete with golf course. Ann has retained Nirvana, she tells them, and has rechristened it the Crow's Nest. She rents it out now for women's retreats. A place of healing.

Many weekends, though, she spends there with Kim. "Can you believe Kimmie likes to fish? She's good at it, too. Damned if I know how she does it with all those rocks. I lose my bait every time."

Kimmie, Sabrina thinks. Ann hasn't called her daughter that in years.

"And what are you doing now?" Sabrina asks, eager to catch up, missing the times of daily phone calls when every small event was shared. "Still practicing law?"

"Yes, turns out I really like it. But not the corporate kind. That's just making the rich richer. I went back to my roots."

"You stopped coloring your hair?" Sabrina feigns horror.

"The day you stop coloring yours," Ann says, smiling.

"I'm in the theater, darling, I have no choice," Sabrina counters. "So what are you doing for a living?"

"It's not much of a living, at least not compared to what I used to earn. But it's a good life. I'm back at legal aid, helping people who really need it, who won't get a fair shake without me."

"That's great," Gloria says. "I really admire that."

"You did it for us," Ann says. "You took our case pro bono. You could have charged a bundle."

"I did that for Maria," Gloria says, holding out her glass for Ann to refill. "It wasn't just that. I owed her. I owed her big. She saved my life."

"How?" Deb asks.

Gloria hesitates.

"Part of the initiation," Sabrina prods. "Confess your darkest sins if you want to join the Coven."

"Is that what you all did?" Gloria asks.

"Hell, no." Ann laughs. "We committed them together."

"Well, then." Gloria settles deeply into the cushions of the couch, slips off her Manolo Blahnik lizard mules. "I guess that's what women's bonding is all about, sharing our stories. It's different in a man's world. They compete, hide their weaknesses, one-up each other. It's alpha male all the way. With us we connect by voicing our insecurities, sharing our mistakes. Knowing we are not alone.

"Ah, the pleasure of girlfriends." She sighs and begins her story. As she speaks, the mask of the accomplished attorney slips off and a young and vulnerable woman appears. Even her speech changes, reverting to a breathy Valley Girl drawl.

"I guess you'd call it date rape," Gloria says. "Although back then, the term didn't even exist. I was finishing up my first year at Harvard Law, one of the youngest students admitted. It was affirmative action, but I deserved it, dammit. I was good. I just didn't know it then. I met the editor of the *Law Review*. He offered to help me revise the paper I was submitting to the *Journal*. He asked me to come up to his apartment. We worked on my paper. Listened to some music. Drank some beer. Kissed a few times. The usual student thing. It was getting late. I said I had to go. He blocked the door. He grabbed my arms, pinned me against the wall. I can still see his face. 'You know you want it, bitch.'"

Gloria springs to her feet as the memory returns. She is pacing rapidly, a pillow clutched against her chest. "He threw me on the floor, tore off my skirt and shoved himself into me." Her voice breaks. "I was still a virgin. There was so much pain. So much blood. Afterward, he didn't even drive me home."

"So what happened?" Deb asks, her voice heavy with sympathy.

"I dropped out of Harvard. I lost my scholarship. Finished at night school years later."

"Why didn't you report the bastard?" Sabrina asks.

"I was afraid. After all, I went to his apartment willingly. I drank his beer. I kissed him. I didn't know I had a right to say no."

"You always have a right to say no," Ann says fiercely, "every step of the way."

"I thought it was my fault," Gloria says quietly.

"I know," Deb says fervently. "We all do."

"So how does Maria come into all of this?" Sabrina, the weaver of stories, asks.

"I went back to San Francisco, back home to Japantown. There was a sign in my corner grocery store. Right above the buckwheat noodles. In Japanese. Rape Counseling Center. I went. I thought everyone would be Japanese. It turned out Maria had posted signs in Tagalog, Cantonese, Hindi, you name it. We were a mini United Nations with one great common wound. And when Maria was through with us, we had cried, raged, learned karate and vowed that no man would ever do that to any one of us again." Gloria asks for a glass of water and sips it slowly.

"I didn't know that Maria was ever a rape counselor," Ann muses.

"The best," Gloria attests. "She'd been through it herself. In spades."

"Maria was raped?" Sabrina says.

"From the age of four," Gloria says. "By her father." Gloria stares into her empty glass. "She tried to tell her mother, but her mother refused to hear it. Accused Maria of being jealous, of being a troublemaker. Then when Maria was twelve, her father went after Consuela. Maria turned him in to the police. He fled to Mexico. Maria's mother left both her daughters and went with him."

"Maria always said some women never learn," Deb sighs.

Ann turns to Deb. "You knew about that?"

"Maria told me. After Hughie. How else do you think she would have had the courage to do it?"

"But she didn't do it alone," Sabrina protests. "We all did. Didn't we?"

"We haven't talked about it since that night," Ann says. "I guess it's safe now. We can't be tried for the same crime twice." She turns to Gloria. "Do you want to know what really happened that night?"

Gloria stretches her tiny pink cashmere frame against the sofa. "Sure, but tell me one thing first. Was the sex worth it?"

"I hate to disappoint you, Gloria, but there was no sex with Hughie," Ann says.

"What! I don't believe it. Why did you bring him back if it wasn't for some fooling around?"

"We really intended to drop him off at the campsite," Ann says. "It was just, when we got there the weather was so awful…"

"And we figured what the hell," Sabrina adds. "There were four of us and only one of him. What could happen?"

Ann gets up and opens another bottle of champagne. She fills everyone's glass to keep the story flowing.

"So what did happen?" Gloria asks.

"Just what we told you." Ann sips her wine, closes her eyes in pleasure. "Champagne is best when it's just been poured."

"Just what you told me…how," Gloria prods.

"He was a good dancer," Deb says. "And he danced with each one of us differently. Chose different music. He held us differently. Touched us differently."

"He chose Garth Brooks for me," Deb says. "'Standing Outside the Fire.'" She hums a few bars.

"Mine was 'I Only Have Eyes For You,'" Ann adds.

Sabrina remembers slow dancing to "The Rose," held tightly in Hughie's arms, his strong and supple lead; the bulge of his groin warm against her thighs. Whoever said dancing is sex set to music got it right.

"Then he offered to give us each a massage," Ann says. "We agreed."

"And then what?" Gloria asks.

"We went to sleep," Sabrina says.

"All of you? At the same time?" Gloria's tone is skeptical. She is in her courtroom mode. Thank goodness she was on our side, Sabrina thinks, or we'd be in some Glamour Slammer right now.

"I went to bed first." Ann says. "Then Sabrina."

"Then Maria," Deb says, and taking a deep breath, "then me. I was last."

"And why was that?" Gloria probes.

"Mine was the last massage," Deb says. "And then...he was my present."

"Your present?" Gloria is puzzled.

"The Coven decided to give Hughie to me for the night. If I wanted him. You see, Donald had been having an affair. At least I thought he had. I was afraid he was going to leave me. My self-esteem was in the gutter. I felt ugly, boring, mega-depressed. And Hughie had been flirting with me at the Last Roundup, so they figured, why not? A little male attention would be good for me. And after all, like Sabrina said, what could happen? There were four of us."

Sabrina gives an ironic chuckle. "There was safety in numbers, all right. And unexpected danger."

"You mean none of this would have happened if you were alone?" Gloria asks.

"Now you're getting deep. This needs chocolate." Ann hurries to the refrigerator and returns with a basket of chocolate-covered strawberries. The women attack them with a vengeance; the bittersweet chocolate and the ripe juicy strawberries are irresistible. Particularly at this moment. Only Deb refuses. She is back into the event, reliving it.

"At first it was real nice. We smoked some of Richard's pot. Hughie showed me how. I couldn't hold the smoke down for long. Not like he could. But I got a little high anyway. I was feeling relaxed and happy. I remember his moving closer to me, putting his arm around me. Telling me how pretty I was. How he loved the way my hair curled in the steam. I was a Kewpie doll, he said. Like Bernadette Peters. Did I like Bernadette Peters? he asked. And just as I was trying to remember what show I'd seen her in, he leaned down and kissed...my breast."

"And?" Sabrina asks. They're all hearing this for the first time.

"It felt good. Donald was never a breast man, although," she says, smiling a little, "he doesn't neglect them now." She goes on, "Then he kissed my other one." She blushes. "Do I have to go into the details?"

"Yes," they say in unison.

Deb concentrates and replays the scene. "He kissed me, all over, lots of tongue, especially here." She indicates the space between her upper lip and teeth. "I've always liked that. Then he licked my toes. All ten...and in the spaces.

He licked everything...even my armpits." She pauses to remember. "He was very thorough. So I was pretty ready when he slipped his hands between my legs and found my, you know..."

"Clitoris," Ann says.

"My love button," Deb says. "And I put my hand on his..."

"Penis," Sabrina provides.

."Donald calls it his roger."

"Was his roger jolly?" Gloria asks, licking the chocolate off her fingers.

"Very jolly. And quite large, too. And it was flying full mast." Deb grows silent as she remembers, her hand inadvertently curling.

Sabrina feels a moment's pang of envy. Traumatic though it was, Deb sure got her little thrill.

"So there you are making waves, feeling no pain," Gloria says. "So what went wrong?"

"He wanted sex."

"And you didn't?"

Deb looks down at the floor, then at each woman's face. Sabrina can see this is hard for her. But she owes it to the rest of the Coven to make that moment clear and simple. And it was neither. "At first I thought I did." She pauses, in tears now. "But then I couldn't. I still loved Donald."

"So then what happened?" Gloria asks.

Deb is reliving the night. Her face is dead white, her forehead beaded in sweat. "His hands were digging into my thighs. Tearing my legs apart. 'Come on, you fucking cock-teaser.' I was crying, begging him to stop. He clamped his hand over my mouth. I couldn't breathe. He was forcing himself inside me. I bit his hand hard. He pulled his hand away and I screamed."

"I heard you scream," Sabrina says. "I was fast asleep. I thought I was dreaming. Then I heard footsteps running down the hall."

"It was Maria," Deb says. "She always slept with her door open. She jumped into the hot tub, leaped onto his back."

"When I got there the three of you were thrashing around in the tub," Sabrina remembers. "Grappling. Flailing. Sending up great sheets of water. I didn't understand what was going on, but I knew it was bad."

"I arrived at the same moment," Ann says. "I grabbed his hands."

"I grabbed his legs." Sabrina adds.

"Maria's arms were around his throat," Deb remembers. "She roared, 'Let her go.' And he did. He released me. I climbed out of the tub."

"We thought it was over," Ann says. "So we let go of him. But the second we did..."

"He went for me again," Deb says.

"We couldn't hold him. He was in a rage. He slapped and punched, butted us with his head. He reared up...and then suddenly...he stopped, gasped and fell facedown into the water.

"Maria must have hit him on the back of the head," Sabrina says. "We never found out with what, though."

Deb's eyes are closed, her body shaking as the memory comes flooding back. "The tray. The silver tray," she says.

"But it wasn't Maria, it was me. And then I got back into the tub and pushed his head down...down to the bottom. And held it there."

"And we held him down until he stopped struggling," Ann says.

"And we held him down until his breath stopped. Until everything stopped," Sabrina says.

"Until he couldn't hurt any of us," Deb adds in a long, shuddering whisper. "Ever again."

"You did it?" Ann says in amazement to Deb. "I always thought it was Maria."

"She didn't have enough strength left," Deb explains. "But somehow I did. When I needed it, I found it."

"And you still have it," says Sabrina.

"You always did," Ann adds.

"Talk about a transforming experience!" Gloria says. She opens her purse and extracts a long filtered cigarette.

"You smoke?" Ann asks.

"I quit, but I still carry them. For moments like this," Gloria says as she lights up and takes a long drag. "So you killed him."

The three women consider the fact, as for the first time.

"I guess we did," Deb says.

Ann and Sabrina nod agreement.

"We didn't know he was a narc," Ann says.

"And if you had?" Gloria asks.

Ann thinks for a long moment. "It wouldn't have made any difference," she says. "Not then."

"What about now?" Gloria asks.

The women look at each other. "I feel terrible," Deb says. "We took a human life."

"It was awful," Sabrina agrees. "But there was no other way to stop him."

"It was all my fault," Deb sighs. "If I hadn't led him on—"

"Don't be so hard on yourself," Gloria interrupts. "I know things you don't. Former Agent Curran was not squeaky clean. There were complaints of sexual harassment and a case of assault was pending. That's why he was suspended."

They are all silent for a moment, considering this new information.

"Well," Sabrina says, "you could always say we weren't in our right minds."

"What state of mind were you in?" Gloria asks.

"An altered one," Sabrina says, smiling.

"Meaning?" Gloria persists.

"You'll just have to see the play," Deb says.

"And what play is that?" Gloria asks.

"Sabrina's play," Deb says.

"I didn't write it," Sabrina demurs. "Euripides did. More than two thousand years ago. But it's as true today as it ever was."

"Hold that thought. We need reinforcements," Gloria says, rising and offering her gift, a box of elegant petits fours and a fine bottle of cognac. She waits until the women have each selected their favorite pastry and have a cognac snifter in hand, then asks, "Now, lay it on me."

"It's opening off-Broadway next month," Sabrina says. "You can see it for yourself."

"But I want to hear about it now." Gloria settles into the couch. "Sounds like heavy women's mojo."

Sabrina takes a long slug of brandy and begins an abbreviated summary of *The Bacchae*. "Once there was a king called Aegisthus, who was very arrogant."

"Is there any other kind?" Ann asks.

"He became jealous of the attention the women in his kingdom were paying to the god Dionysus," Sabrina says.

"The fruit of the vine," Deb says. "Dangerous."

"The king grew insatiably curious about the women's rituals that he was forbidden to watch."

"Men," Ann exclaims. "They all want to know what we can find to talk about for hours."

"So one day he dressed in women's robes, hid in a tree and spied upon their secret ceremonies," Sabrina continues. "He watched as all the women of the kingdom, maidens, wives and crones, including his own mother, imbibed of the god's mind-altering drink and tore off their clothes to dance naked on the mountain."

"Shades of the Last Roundup," Deb says.

"And in his excitement, Aegisthus fell from the tree and into their midst," Sabrina says. "And in their frenzy, the women tore him apart, limb from limb, for he had violated their sacred space,"

"Shades of Nirvana," Ann adds.

Sabrina rises and intones the ending of the play, the coda she has specially written. "For there is a wild side to every woman that must be respected and preserved. There is danger when we touch that passion in ourselves. And even greater danger if we do not. For that negation is death-in-life."

The women raise their glasses and down their brandy.

Onstage the actresses will smash their glasses, Sabrina explains, but here in Ann's urban living room, they place them neatly on the kitchen drain board.

Ann refuses their help in cleaning up and instead suggests a nightcap. "Final libation? Margaritas grandes at La Bamba, Maria's favorite salsa bar?"

Sabrina and Deb readily agree. Only Gloria demurs.

"I'd love to," she says, "but another time. My date's picking me up." As if on cue, the downstairs bell announces his arrival.

"Can't wait to see him," Deb says.

"He must be some guy to handle the likes of you," Sabrina offers.

Ann buzzes the intercom. And a moment later the door opens on Rod Curt, looking sleekly handsome in a black silk shirt and jeans.

He registers their surprise with his usual cool. "Ladies, we meet again. My condolences about your friend Maria, but I'm pleased to see you all looking so well. Including your brilliant attorney." He slips his muscular arm around Gloria's tiny waist. "Shall we?"

As the door closes on them, Sabrina muses, "I don't feel so bad about that pro bono work now. She got her bonus."

The women retrieve their shoes and purses and, wrapping their coats tightly against the San Francisco fog, hail a cab to the corner of Sixteenth Street and Mission. As

Ann pays the driver, they can hear the music blasting down the street. Their hips are already moving to the beat. Shoulders swaying. Fingers snapping.

"This one's for Maria," Ann says as they walk toward the brightly lit neon sign. The women link arms and Deb leads them through their beloved friend's mantra.

"Have you danced today? Have you sung today? Have you let your wild child play?"

As the women enter the bar, Sabrina adds in a full-bodied stage whisper, "Latin cowboys, beware!"